M000206796

THE EXISTENTIAL WORRIES OF MAGS MUNROE

THE MAGS MUNROE SERIES

JEAN GRAINGER

Copyright © 2022 Gold Harp Media

All rights reserved.

No part of this book may be reproduced in any form or by any electronic or mechanical means, including information storage and retrieval systems, without written permission from the author, except for the use of brief quotations in a book review.

For Nora, who helped me to find my voice.

CHAPTER 1

*I*t's 2:50 a.m., and I'm lying here tossing and turning. The kids will be in on top of me in a few hours, and I'll be kicking myself for wasting so much precious sleep obsessing about Detective Sergeant Donal Cassidy. I try to focus on what I've learned at the meditation class in the community hall: breathe in for four, hold for four, breathe out for four.

Nope, not relaxing. It's easy when Paminandra (real name Maura) does it and we're all half asleep on the community hall carpet tiles, but implementing it in my own life seems to be beyond me.

Maybe I should get some incense, I haven't any, of course. I have a scented candle that Kieran's mother bought me for Christmas but that smells like someone burned down a sweetshop.

Beside me, Kieran is peaceful. I glance over. He's fifty-three and grey at the temples now, but I think he's still handsome. Kieran doesn't have trouble sleeping; he falls asleep in one position and stays that way till he wakes. You could draw around his body in chalk like he was a corpse – you know the way they do on TV? – and there he'd be in the morning in exactly the same position. He wouldn't shift if the house fell down around his ears. I remember once him telling his sister Orla that when our girls were babies, neither of them ever woke in the night. Orla threw me that conspiratorial look of mothers. What he meant is *he* never woke.

Not that I'm complaining about him. He's a lovely husband and a great dad. Kieran works hard. He's a roofer and has his own company based here in Ballycarrick, started from nothing, fair play to him. He is exhausted when he comes home every night. It's a very physical job, so he never has trouble sleeping. Still, I work hard too. But I'm not pulling heavy roof slates around, I suppose. And now I'm looking at the ceiling for the sixth night in a row.

My name is Mags, by the way, short for Margaret. And now I suppose you'd want a look at me. If I were going to waste my time listening to someone's ramblings, I'd want to know what they look like, so here goes. Well, I won't say what I look like right now, at three in the morning, that would frighten the dogs, but normally I'm, well, normal looking.

I'm forty-eight. I have blueish eyes, kind of bluey-grey, I suppose, and I'm five foot seven. If I were in crime watch reconstruction, they'd find a middle-aged woman of average height and build with brown hair in a bob and blue eyes. So that's me, Mrs Ordinary.

Oh, and I'm a guard, which is what they call police officers in Ireland. Now, before you start visualising those gritty Netflix cops, fighting crime and gunning down drug barons or finding serial killers. I'm nothing like that. I'm a uniformed sergeant and run the tiny local Garda station in Ballycarrick, and my area of law enforcement involves, on the downside, mostly dog licences, drunk and disorderly conduct, domestics and petty theft, and, on the upside, community policing, helping the people where we live to feel safe and secure, and encouraging young people to become responsible citizens. I love it. Well, not the drunk and disorderly stuff, but I like being the person who makes people relax when things go wrong. People in Ballycarrick trust me, and they know that I'll do my best for them, even the ones who flout the law a bit. We have the community awards coming up on Friday night, and it's always a great night. The people of

Ballycarrick nominate those who have given great service to the community, and the Gardai run it and provide the funding. This year, the Transition Year class in the secondary school are getting an award for teaching the active retirement group how to use social media, Eileen Desmond is being recognised for fifty years running Meals on Wheels, and one of the McGoverns is getting a special award for a project on Traveller life she and her cousins did that is being displayed in the library. They never make Netflix shows about that, and who could blame them, but that's what being a guard means to me.

That's what keeps me going while I lie awake at night worrying about what happened last week when I applied for the job of detective sergeant.

There I am, standing at reception in the brand-new steel and plate-glass Garda station in Galway, waiting for the young woman behind the counter to check where I need to go for my interview, when Sergeant Donal Cassidy – or Duckie, as the lads call him behind his back – appears beside me. Now generally guards, and detectives even, are decent people, but this one is a charmless misogynist of the highest order.

'Good morning, Sergeant Cassidy,' I say.

He looks me up and down – I'm in a suit and he's used to seeing me in uniform – and grunts a greeting, then he starts chatting up the young female guard on the public desk with as much finesse as a bull in a china shop. I sigh inwardly. The deluded eejit is fifty years old, paunchy, with halitosis and dodgy hair, and the young guard is half his age, blonde and very pretty. Do men like him really think they have a shot? I decide they must.

The young woman smiles politely at Duckie, then tells both of us that the interview will take place on the first floor and we can take a seat in the corridor upstairs. It is the first time I even realise Duckie has applied for the same job, but I'm not surprised. He is a sergeant down the road in Dromanane, population eight hundred, which is about one tenth the size of Ballycarrick, but he has always fancied himself as a master sleuth and a man of influence. In real life, he is as thick as a ditch and he's only in the force because his father was a guard before him and his grandfather before that. Also, it helped that his uncle was Minister for Transport – at least he was until he was discovered to be worthy of the Nobel Prize for fiction when it came to his expense account. I know I sound like a right narky old bat – I promise I'm not; I like most people – but honestly, if you met this fella, you'd feel the same, I guarantee it.

On the first floor, two younger male guards are already waiting; they smile hello and we all sit down on the plastic chairs. I'm feeling sweaty and itchy and nervous. I hope the sweat isn't coming out through my shirt. It's hot, but I'm always hot these days. I'll have to keep my jacket on, just in case. For the first time, I think, *Maybe it's the change.* My friend Sharon is always going on about her hot flushes and mood swings and insomnia and the rest of it, but surely I'm not that old yet.

Duckie's voice booms. He finds himself hilarious, though why is anyone's guess. His overpowering cologne stinks up the corridor, and his suspiciously dark hair is bordering on plum coloured and swept unconvincingly over his bald patch. His small eyes, set a fraction too close together, bulge with mirth almost as much as his belly, which is straining at the buttons of his shirt. A fold of fat rests on his too-tight collar.

'Wait till I tell you this one,' says Duckie. 'A fella applies to go to Templemore Garda College, and in the interview the inspector says, "I need you to shoot six knackers and a rabbit."'

His use of the word 'knacker' annoys me. I will not allow it in my station, and I have a right go at Kieran if he says it in the house, especially in front of the girls. It's a horrible word to describe Irish Travellers, who live in caravans on halting sites, spaces which are provided by the local county council for Travellers to park their vans in a big circle with a communal water supply and rubbish collection.

The lads glance at one another, clearly mortified. But he outranks them and they are about to go in for an interview, so they don't want a scene.

Undeterred by the lack of enthusiasm in his audience, Duckie puffs himself up and his voice booms even more loudly. The new recruit asks, 'Why the rabbit?' A pause for the punchline, then Duckie continues. 'Great attitude! says the inspector. "You're in."

The two young lads grimace awkwardly out of respect for Duckie being a sergeant.

'That's not funny, Sergeant Cassidy,' I hear myself saying very loudly. 'In fact, it's disgusting.'

Duckie turns and looks me up and down. 'Yerra, Mags, it's only a joke. Lighten up,' he says, with such condescension in his voice, I want to punch him. The two younger lads suddenly find the carpet beneath their feet fascinating, and three older plain-clothes guys who are walking by stop and look at me before disappearing through a door into a large office.

It's not until my name is called that I realise the plain-clothes guys are the interview panel.

I'm hoping my getting thick with a fellow sergeant in front of younger guards won't make any difference to my chances. I've studied hard for this interview and don't want to blow it over something stupid.

The next day, I get an email thanking me for applying for the job, telling me how it has been a difficult decision but that Sergeant Cassidy did an excellent interview on the day.

Kieran can't understand at all why I'm so disappointed. I think he thought it was stupid to go for it anyway, not that he'd ever say that. He knows I love my job; it's nine-to-five, the money's good, and it's down the road.

In a way, he's right. Detective sergeant is a plain-clothes job, and an ordinary sergeant wears uniform. And there's no difference in rank or base salary, although the detectives do get an extra allowance. But at the same time, everyone thinks detective sergeants are a cut above uniformed sergeants. So now Duckie is officially smarter than me. And he'll never let me forget it. If I'm honest, that's why I'm so annoyed. If one of the young lads waiting had got it, I wouldn't feel so bad.

Oh, to hell with Duckie.

I try again to go to sleep. Kieran throws his heavy arm over me, and instead of rolling away like I usually do because I'm afraid his hand will land on my flabby tummy, I snuggle into him.

CHAPTER 2

The alarm goes off, and it feels like I've been asleep for ten minutes.

'Mam.' Ellie shakes me awake. 'I need twenty-five shells.'

'Wha...?' I am struggling to wake up. It's seven in the morning, and Kieran is no longer in the bed. Ellie is in her Harry Potter pyjamas, and her curly brown hair is like a bird's nest. Brushing Ellie's hair is the bane of her life and mine. Often we just bunch it in a ponytail and hope for the best.

'What kind of shells?' I ask.

My twelve-year-old daughter exhales impatiently. 'The ones off the *beach?*' She's doing that Australian upward inflection. All the kids do it now. Fine for Australians, it's their accent, but it grates on my nerves coming out of a child from Galway.

'Ellie, that accent is like *totes annoying?*' I reply, mimicking her.

'Urgh...you're so embarrassing,' she complains in her normal voice, and I chuckle.

'Totes morto,' I riposte.

She giggles and pulls the duvet off me. 'Come on, Mam! I have to get them, and they have to be pearlescent Miss Cullinane said.'

'What?' I sit on the side of the bed.

'Y'know, kind of shiny?' Ellie is losing patience now.

'But the house is already full of shells,' I say. Of course it is – we live fifteen minutes from the beach and we have two children. The windowsills are falling down with shells, and also stones that looked great when they were shiny and wet but are now a dull dry grey. Surely we have some pearlescent ones?

'No, it's for an *art* project. They have to be white or yellow shells, and shiny, and I need them, and I told Miss Cullinane I got them at the weekend so I can't say I forgot. I need to go down to the beach now and get shells, so come on, get up.'

My sergeant's uniform is hanging, ready to be worn, but I'm not going in until nine thirty so I pull on the tracksuit pants I wore out walking last night and Kieran's GAA hoodie.

'What about Kate?' I ask. 'Have you got her up yet?'

'I tried but she's refusing to wake. It's grand for her – she has Miss O'Driscoll, who gives them sweets and sends them cards on their birthday, not fire-breathing Cullinane who is petrifying!' Ellie wails as she storms off.

The next thing I hear is Kate begging her older sister to leave her alone. I try to find a pair of matching socks and fail; I pull on one grey one and one black as I hunt under the bed for my runners.

My youngest appears in unicorn pyjamas, her blonde silky hair flopping over her forehead. She is the cutest thing, honestly. Small for nine years old but not worryingly so.

'Ellie dragged me out of bed and took my duvet,' she moans, rubbing sleep from her eyes.

'I know, pet, she's a demon,' I whisper to her, kissing the top of her head. 'But we have to get white and yellow shells or Miss Cullinane will have a hairy canary.' She giggles; I love that I can always make her laugh. 'We'll have Coco Pops when we get back, but run and get dressed now.'

'Is Dad gone already?' she asks, seeing the dent in the bed after Kieran.

'He is. He has to get that place out on the Castletown road roofed before the rain that's forecast, so he was gone at the dawn.' I give her a quick squeeze. Ellie and Kate love their dad.

'I thought he came in to give me a kiss, but I didn't know if it was a dream.'

* * *

SO HERE I AM, twenty-five minutes later, standing on the edge of a glittering sea as my girls rummage around in the sand for the right coloured shells. Do primary-school teachers do it on purpose? Like, do they lie in their primary-coloured beds, with their colour-coordinated thoughts, and dream up inconvenient things for parents to find urgently? I smile at the thought. Maybe it's what keeps them sane with all the wheels on the bus and finger painting. Whatever gets you through the day.

'Have you enough?' I ask hopefully as Ellie approaches.

'I've only twenty-two and I need twenty-five,' she replies, clearly beginning to panic.

Ellie feels about Miss Cullinane the way I felt about my fifth class teacher, Sister Patrick – sheer terror. The whole town can't wait for her to retire. I don't blame the child; I met the famous Miss Cullinane at the parent-teacher meeting, and she scared me. And I'm a guard for God's sake. She's what you'd call forbidding. If it were any one of the other teachers, I'd write Ellie a note, but not her.

Suddenly I'm eleven years old and in Sister Patrick's class. I got eight out of ten on the spelling test. I was always good enough at spelling. Reading does that – you kind of learn it subliminally, and my nose was always stuck in a book. But she pulls me up to the top of the class to spell the two words I got wrong. Even at the time, I thought it was ridiculous. If I could spell them right 'Wednesday' and 'sincerely' – I still remember them all these years later, I would have done it right on the test, wouldn't I? So the purpose of the exercise was humiliation. It worked too, of course it did. Even now I hate writing either of those words.

'Don't worry, pet, I'll help you.' I dig around in the cold, damp sand

and eventually find three more pearlescent shells. Thank God. We can go home and get some breakfast.

It's warmish and the sun is up, but there are rain clouds already drifting this way. I spare a thought for poor Kieran trying to get the roof on before the weather changes. He always says being a roofer in Ireland is the triumph of hope over experience, like second marriages. Luckily, he has three Polish guys with him, Wojtec, Jacek, and Marius, and they are great workers altogether, very fast. He's lucky to have them. He gets a bit of stick from local fellas about only employing Poles, but he always says he employs men who'll turn up on a Monday morning, work all day and leave the job neat and tidy at the end of the day. And the chances of getting that in a Polish worker are higher than in an Irish one unfortunately.

Back home, I shovel Coco Pops and toast into my girls and make packed lunches of roast chicken sandwiches, yoghurts, grapes and rice cakes. I drop them off to school at one minute to the bell.

I watch them as they walk in together, the school bags as big as themselves, happy, healthy and full of potential, and the job rejection seems insignificant. I'm so proud of them.

I go home and get myself ready for work. Up in the bedroom, fresh out of the shower, I see myself in the mirror – all soft belly and full breasts. I'm a bit overweight. Not massive or anything but definitely not skinny. Every so often I go to the slimming club in the hotel to get myself in order, but to be honest with you, the one who runs it, Elaine, wrecks my head, or maybe I'm just jealous of her skinny thighs. So I endure it for the few weeks, after Christmas, for instance, or before Ellie's Communion to fit into the dress, but I can't stick it for long.

You see, the trouble is I don't love green juice or steamed fish and I do love Cadbury Fruit & Nut and red wine and chips. As I said, a few weeks is the best I can do. Then Elaine and her scales and her sympathetic face and I have to part company.

Sharon is forever warning me not to 'let myself go' and not to take Kieran for granted. Her husband, Danny, has gone off with Chloe Desmond from the chipper, and she's young enough to be his daughter, so Sharon's ultra-sensitive on the topic of husbands. She's always saying what a fine man Kieran is and I'd want to watch him, that there are plenty of women willing to snap him up, but she doesn't know Kieran. He'd never do that. Not to me, and not to the girls. He's a straighty one-eighty.

I sit into the car and pick up the phone. After pausing for a second, I write a text.

Hope day going OK and you get roof done before rain. Will get lamb chops in Mahony's for tea. See you later. x

Hardly a great love letter of our age, but it's the best I can come up with on the spur of the moment. The bit about the lamb chops is a sign of love. I complain a bit about Kieran taking *me* for granted, letting me do all the shopping and cooking even though I work as hard as he does. Mind you, I suppose Sharon is right – I do take him for granted as well. I haven't taken out a bin in fifteen years.

As I reverse out of the driveway, my phone pings. I glance at it.

Great, can't wait. See you tonight. Love you. x

I'll text him back when I get to the station. The local sergeant texting and driving is not exactly the message we're trying to send.

CHAPTER 3

*I*t's only a five-minute drive from where we live just outside Ballycarrick to the Garda station on Market Street. As I pull into my spot, my heart sinks into my police shoes. That black Audi A6 belongs to Duckie. My phone pings again.

Mags, Duckie's inside and he's bulling over something, forewarned.

The text from Nicola, the youngest new recruit and only other woman in the station, lights up the screen on my phone.

Sighing inwardly, I get out of the car and walk reluctantly into the station. I need him like a hole in the head. Nicola, who is on the public counter this morning, gives me the eye so theatrically she could be in a pantomime, and I grin back. Then I hear it, his big boomy voice from right behind me as the door to the gents slams.

'Ah, Sergeant Mags Munroe, you finally grace us with your presence.' It's my station, and even though he's now a detective sergeant, he's officially the same rank as I am, but here he is acting like he's now my boss.

'How can I help you, Donal?' I ask, keeping my voice as neutral as possible.

'A word, in your office.'

'Certainly. Just a minute,' I say calmly. So I go to the counter and ask Nicola if there's anything to follow up on urgently, any complaints or reports, and she says no. Then I read through the incident book for the last few days, not because it's urgent but because I will not be summoned like a bold child by that plonker Duckie.

He lingers behind me and glances up and down at Nicola. Despite the threat of rain, it's a warm day, and she's on the desk so she's only wearing her uniform shirt and trousers, no jacket.

'Make me a coffee like a good girl, would you?' He gives her what he thinks is a charming smile when in fact it's a creepy leer. 'Milk, three sugars and something sweet if you can find it.' I wait for him to add, 'Though you're sweet enough,' but he doesn't, which is something to be thankful for, I suppose.

In my office, Duckie stays standing as I sit, another not-too-subtle way of putting me in my place. '*Sergeant* Munroe...' He emphasises the word 'sergeant' to remind me it's not 'detective sergeant', like him. He always calls me Mags and I call him Donal, so this new formality is all point-scoring.

'Sergeant Munroe, what *are* we going to do about the members of the *Travelling community*' – he grins – 'in your backyard?'

He's trying to wind me up, I know he is, using the correct term for the Travellers when I know he always refers to them by that horrible word I heard him use the other day. But I refuse to rise to his bait.

'What about them?' I ask with an innocent smile. There's a halting site in Ballycarrick, out the Dublin road near the waterworks, over twenty caravans; it's one huge family. They're no trouble because there's an elderly woman who runs the whole thing with a rod of iron. Halting sites are often fairly soulless places but the McGoverns have planted flowers and trees, and actually it looks quite nice.

Other traveller families fall out with each other all the time but not the McGoverns. They're tight, and if they have feuds with other families like the Carmodys nobody ever hears of it. Mainly because Dacie runs the whole show and from the biggest down to the smallest, they know her word is law. The McGoverns always send the kids to school and many of them have jobs, and unlike the squalor of where the

Carmodys live out the Tuam Road, much nearer Galway, Drumlish is spotlessly clean.

The halting site is operated by the county council, and the officer in charge often remarks to me that he can hold Drumlish up as an example of a perfect site.

'Well, for a start, you need to arrest Natasha McGovern for shoplifting.'

I raise my eyebrows quizzically. Natasha is a bit wild, but I've never known her to be anything but honest. 'Really? Why? I wasn't aware of any complaint against her.'

He puffs up, acting all superior. 'Well, now you are aware of it, Sergeant, because I'm going to the trouble of informing you of what's happening right here in Ballycarrick, under your very nose. Natasha McGovern tried to shoplift a very expensive jacket from Dillon's this morning while a gang of her delinquent cousins distracted Joe, and if I hadn't been there to stop her at the door, she'd have got away with it.'

Now I'm off balance. Nicola told me there'd been no complaints or reports. But maybe Duckie was in the shop at the time, buying one of his too-small shirts, no doubt, and Joe Dillon, who owns the clothes shop, thought it would be enough to tell him and then Duckie could tell me. I say, 'I appreciate the information, Donal. I'll call on Joe later this morning to see what happened.'

'See what happened...?' Duckie splutters, his face going puce. 'I've just told you what happened! Natasha McGovern was in there with her gang of tinker young ones – they go around in a pack, as you know. They were obviously up to something, and I stopped it before they got out of the shop. There's no point in talking to Joe – he didn't even see what was about to go down.'

About to go down. Where and who does he think he is? Starring in an episode of *Hill Street Blues*? Plonker. I fight the urge to giggle; I don't want to rile him up because it looks like I may have underestimated his connections and influence, and maybe he isn't above arranging to have someone higher up transfer me to some random back of beyond, which would be a disaster for the kids and Kieran because their whole lives are here.

'We'll look into it.' I speak slowly but not so slow as to seem rude.

Nicola knocks on the door at that point, bearing the only coffee cup in the station without a chip and with a handle and a small pink plate bearing two chocolate club milks; instantly Duckie leers his thanks. Nicola and I share a conspiratorial glance as he stirs sugar in and she withdraws.

'Well, make sure you do, and remember, I'm your witness, not Joe Dillon. He didn't see anything, so there's no need to bother him. Best just go out to that kip they live in and arrest her.'

Again with the instructions. I'm going to try to use this as an opportunity to practice my mindfulness and resist the urge to nudge his elbow and make him spill his coffee all over himself, which would be very unprofessional. Satisfying definitely, but unprofessional.

Thankfully, we're relieved of his company soon after. He has to 'lean in' with some 'top brass'. He watches too much television, clearly.

The next hour passes in a busy flurry of dealing with correspondence and then an internal meeting. One of the new lads, Darren Carney, is turning out to be a really good community guard. He wants to set up a youth group for vulnerable young people and is looking for advice from the rest of us about who to approach and how. Prevention is always better than enforcement, so I'm all for it, and I suggest he approach the council about an old café that has been unoccupied for ages. Maybe the local employment scheme could be brought in to open it again as a youth café, a place young people would be welcome to hang out. At the same time, it would give a bit of employment to the area. Nicola suggests running courses that would allow teenagers to get part-time jobs, safe pass course for building sites, driving theory test courses. She has a friend who trained as a barista in a weekend and is working in some fancy coffee place in Dublin, so maybe that is something else they could offer. Darren goes off with a sheet of ideas to investigate.

While I'm in the meeting, my friend Sharon texts three times but I don't text back. I'll give her a call after work when I've more time. It will be same old, same old anyway. Danny and his latest exploits. He's bought a new car, he took Chloe to the races, he was half an hour late picking up their six-year-old son, Sean, because Chloe was at the hairdresser.

I feel bad for Sharon, of course I do, but Danny is gone and getting on with his life and so should she. Obsessing over his every move is driving her up the wall. And me too if I'm honest.

Eventually, about noon, I take a walk up Main Street to Joe Dillon's. It's not far from my own mother's clothes shop, but they're not in competition because she does women and girls. I do wonder what Natasha was doing in a menswear shop, but of course she has brothers and probably a fiancé on the horizon now that she's sixteen – Traveller girls get married very young – and maybe she was buying one of them a birthday present.

Joe looks surprised to see me. 'How can I help you, Mags?'

We've known each other for years, partly because he and Mam are in the same business and are great friends. I sometimes wonder why they don't get together now that they're both widowed, but as far as I can tell, they seem content with keeping it to a weekly lunch in the Samovar, previously McLoughlin's, where they chat about the clothing trade over Tatiana's delicious beef and Guinness stew.

'I heard you had a bit of bother in the shop this morning, Joe,' I say.

He gives me a look of surprise, then recollection, and he starts to laugh, his warm eyes creasing up. 'Can't do a thing in this town without everyone knowing about it by lunchtime.'

Now I'm the one who's surprised. An attempt at shoplifting by a gang of Traveller girls doesn't seem like a laughing matter to me. I take a breath. 'Didn't *Detective* Sergeant Cassidy…'

Joe stops laughing and looks at me softly, and in that moment, I realise he knows all about the job, because of course Mam has told him.

I battle on regardless. 'Did Detective Sergeant Cassidy not stop Natasha McGovern from walking out of here with an expensive jacket this morning?'

His soft eyes harden. 'Is that what Duckie Cassidy told you? I did try to tell him. Ten euro a week she was paying me for the last six months, and there was nothing left owing on it, so nothing to pay. She called in earlier and said she'd collect it when she was going home, not to be carrying it all day.

'It's a present for someone. I was out the back when she came in, so she just took it, but that didn't stop him going off bald-headed on her when she went to walk out with it. He grabbed her, and of course then she goes mad at him for touching her and says her boyfriend and her brothers will sort him out if he doesn't take his hands off her and how disgusting he is and calling him a pervert and all the rest. She and her cousins who were with her, they made a right eejit of him, laughing.'

'Ah.' This makes a whole lot more sense than Natasha shoplifting the jacket. But it has its own complications, not least because Duckie will now be trying everything to get back at Natasha and her cousins for laughing at him. It reminds me of that quote from Margaret Atwood, who wrote *The Handmaid's Tale*: 'Men are afraid that women will laugh at them. Women are afraid that men will kill them.' Obviously I don't think Duckie will kill Natasha or anyone, but he can certainly make her life a misery. I make a mental note to add a visit to Drumlish halting site to my schedule. I'll drop in on Dacie McGovern for a cup of tea, get her to warn Natasha to keep her head down until the whole thing has blown over.

Dacie is the matriarch of the McGovern clan. She wouldn't thank any one of her family for bringing the guards in on top of them for whatever reason, but she and I have an understanding. I leave them alone, make sure they aren't harassed about tax on their cars or bald tyres or racing sulkies on the Galway road on Sundays, and in return, she keeps her huge family in line. Dacie is a good woman, looking out for her brood, and it is an arrangement that works.

I am confident she will be able to sort things out with her granddaughter. I'll call tomorrow. I know the men will be gone to the horse fair out towards Castlebar all day, and it's easier for me to go to the halting site when the men are gone.

While I've been talking to Joe, the rain has started again, and after promising him I'll sort this all out, I hurry back up the street to the station before it gets too heavy. As I pass Mahony's, the butcher shop,

I remember I've promised Kieran I'll buy lamb chops, so I duck inside. All the time Bertie Mahony is serving me, he carefully avoids my eye like he has done ever since... Sorry, that's confidential.

At 6 p.m., and with a million things to do going around in my head, I climb into the car for the quick drive home. The wipers have to struggle against the incessant rain, the blower is on the screen to stop it fogging up, and the car is getting very hot...or at least I hope that's what's happening and it's not a hot flush.

As I wait for the traffic to let me out of the Garda car park, my phone lights up with a text.

Hey, Mags – can't believe what he's done now. Selfish pig only booked two weeks in Lanzarote for him, Sean and her. Denise in the travel agent told Eddie, who told me. Can you believe him?

Yes, Sharon I can believe him, I think, with a pang of sympathy for my friend. *He's bringing his young sexy girlfriend to a hot country where she can wear a bikini and he can show her off and feel like a right stud in front of everyone.*

I can't write that, of course, but honestly I wish she could do an Elsa from *Frozen* and 'let it go', for her own sake. This is driving her nuts. Danny Boylan was an eejit when we were kids, thought he was God's gift, and Sharon used to take the mick out of him more than anyone else. But next thing she's going to the debs dance with him, and he took her to his grads in return, and before we knew it, they were going out. I should have told her at the time how he tried it on with me on their wedding day, but it felt wrong. It *was* wrong, but wrong by him, not me. Hitting on the bridesmaid on your wedding day – not exactly classy. But then as I said, Danny Boylan was always and ever an utter eejit.

And then there were the other women all the time she was married to him. Danny would get up on a gust of wind, as they say here, and everyone knew it. I doubt there was a woman with her own teeth in Ballycarrick he didn't have a crack off at one time or another. I told Sharon the whole thing one night – it felt wrong to have my best friend made such a fool of – but she's never really believed it. She thinks it's all small-town gossip and just wants to blame Chloe.

She's much better off without Danny, of course, but I suppose that's no consolation at this stage. Chloe Desmond is only nineteen, and a saucy pup with it. She's been giving guards backchat ever since she started drinking down in the castle grounds when she was twelve. Danny will have his work cut out for him dealing with her, no harm too. He needs a bit of tough love. I feel bad for Sharon, I really do, but she was way too soft on him.

I text quickly. *Sharon, forget about him. Why don't you book something lovely for you and Sean, maybe ask your sister to go with you? You always said you'd love to go to Italy.*

As I press 'send', I remember I never answered Kieran's text from this morning. I should really text 'love you' back to him. But there's a gap in the traffic, letting me out, and I'll be home in five minutes with the lamb chops. Anyway, he knows I love him.

CHAPTER 4

S ix pairs of dark suspicious eyes are trained on me as I get out of the squad car. I leave my hat on the back seat, and I've thrown a navy hoodie over my uniform. They know exactly what I am, but it seems to help a bit if I don't look like one.

The children watching me have stopped playing with the pups they have in a cardboard box, and they are unashamedly staring as I make my way to Dacie's, the main caravan in the concrete compound. The doors of the other caravans are open, but there doesn't seem to be anyone about. The women are probably inside, and the men are gone to the horse fair.

'Morning, Mrs McGovern,' I call as I knock on the open caravan door.

Most of the vans in the halting site are brand new and top of the range. Satellite dishes, flat-screen TVs – you name it, they have it. Bought for cash. One of the many big misconceptions about Travellers is that because they live in caravans, they're poor. They'd buy and sell your average worker, money is never an issue for them, they seem to have loads of it. Most of it legitimately earned through buying and selling things and breeding horses, and some of it a bit shadier, but mostly they are OK.

Dacie's caravan is the old type, but that's her choice. She is old school in every way.

'Ah, 'tis yourself, Mags, come in.' She is standing at her threshold, and the eighteen-foot caravan might as well be Downton Abbey and she Lady Grantham the way she exudes authority. She is tiny and wizened, her face like one of those crinkled, yellowing old maps you'd see in the kids' TV shows about pirates, and her snow-white hair is pulled back into a bun. Traveller women never cut their hair, even into old age. She can't weigh more than six or seven stone – no need for her to go to annoying Elaine's slimming club – and she is dressed in the old style: a tartan skirt to the knee, a modest blouse and cardigan, a gold chain around her neck with a crucifix on it. She got the necklace in Medjugorje, she told me; she and her daughters go to the Bosnian town every two years without fail to see the place where many people believe the Virgin Mary appears, even now, I think, or at least in recent times.

To the frustration of the airlines, Dacie always insists on bringing home huge ten-gallon drums of holy water in her luggage. They used to fight her on it years ago, but they've learned not to bother. She's that kind of woman; she just gets her way. She doesn't threaten or behave in any way that is unladylike, but she gets what she wants all the same. It's an art form. I sometimes think it would be more useful to send the new Garda recruits to Dacie for a week or two to learn the powers of persuasion rather than the Garda College above in Templemore. People think the police have all kinds of powers, and we do have some, but honestly, ninety percent of the job is persuading and cajoling and trying to bring people with you rather than using the authority we have.

'Thanks.' I step in, and the van is exactly as I remember. I had to come here a few months ago because one of her grandsons had beaten his wife so badly, the poor girl had to be hospitalised. The girl would never press charges – there was no question of that – but I told Dacie and she made sure the young fella got a right hiding himself, from his uncles and his father, and was told to never hurt a hair on her head again. It was rough justice, but justice all the same.

The Traveller culture looks lawless from the point of view of settled people, and while domestic violence isn't exactly condoned, it certainly happens, but I'd have to say at more or less the same rate as in the settled community. You'd be astounded at the houses of the great and the good of the place where we're called with women half out of their minds with terror from a violent brute of a man.

In the Traveller community, girls are married off at fifteen or sixteen, usually a made match, agreed by the families concerned, and the young couple know from a young age who and what is intended for them. Amazingly, they seem to accept it, and from what I can see, the marriages are happy.

Traveller girls have to be virgins until they are married, and though a lot of them dress very provocatively, all short skirts and fake tan and big hair, they really are very innocent. Family is everything to them, and they are loyal to each other, to a fault.

Looking at Dacie now, you can tell she has all the signs of a hard life. She would have grown up when Travellers lived on the side of the road, not on a halting site, and they stayed outside all year long. I recall seeing them when I was a small girl, the McGoverns, eating their dinner under a tarpaulin slung across the bars of a pony trap in the pelting rain. It was a hard life, no doubt about it. I know they have all the flat-screen tellies and that nowadays – the Travellers like to be flash with the cash when they have it – but it isn't a life anyone I know would choose. However, I also know the McGoverns or the Carmodys or any of the other Traveller families are proud of their heritage and wouldn't have it any other way. Horses for courses, as my mam always says.

'How are you, Mrs McGovern?' I ask, taking a seat on the brown velvet–covered U-shaped sofa that makes up one end of the caravan. All over the walls are holy pictures and statues as well as a staggering array of family photos in gold, glass and silver frames. Weddings, Communions, confirmations, new babies – every event of the McGovern family life, usually associated with a church ceremony, is celebrated and recorded on the walls of Dacie's caravan. On her bed is a really beautiful patchwork quilt, every colour you can imagine. She's mentioned to me before that she made it for her husband for their wedding bed as a present. She said it kept them warm on cold wet nights and that Paddy always used to say that no matter what happened during the day, once he got under that at night with her, he felt happy.

The Travellers are extremely devout Catholics and often birth control isn't used, so the women often have a baby a year from marriage till they can't any longer. To them each child is a blessing and they are all dearly loved. Dacie told me she married at fourteen, and her husband was sixteen. They had twenty children over the course of their marriage but four died, and she has sixteen left, six girls and ten boys and each one of them has their own caravan for their family out at Drumlish. Several grandchildren too have married by now and they have joined the family in their own vans.

'I'm grand, thanks, Mags. And yourself?' she says. 'How's your husband and your little girls? I suppose they're getting big now, God bless them.'

'They are indeed.' I smile and take out my phone to show her a picture of Kate and Ellie.

'Ah, aren't they lovely, God be good to them.' She stands, and I notice she's less agile than she was last time I saw her. She's only in her sixties, but she looks eighty. Her husband died years ago. She has a Mass said for him every year on his anniversary, and he is buried in the enormous family plot in the old cemetery out the Headford road. The headstone is a giant thing covered in sparkly stone that over-shadows everyone else, but that's just the Traveller way. I smile, thinking of it. Kate always says it's like a fairy castle, the McGovern family plot, with stone angels and marble hearts and all manner of adornments. We pass it on the way to my father's grave with its plain granite headstone. Settled people tend to be a lot more sedate with their memorials to the dead.

'You'll have a cup of tea?' she asks.

'Lovely.' I smile. 'So how are all the family? I saw Eileen in town the other day – the baby must be due soon?' Eileen is Dacie's youngest daughter. I make it my business to keep track of the goings-on in the Traveller families, weddings, funerals, babies.

'Sometime next week, I think. Sure, 'twill be her sixth, so she's grand.' Dacie seems wary, and I know I am the cause of it.

She makes tea and brings it over in a china cup with a saucer. On a matching side plate, she has cut a slice of cake. She doesn't have anything herself. After setting the tea things down on a polished side table, she closes the door of the van and sits opposite me again, waiting for me to tell her the reason for the visit.

'I wanted to have a word about something, Mrs McGovern, that maybe you can help me with,' I say.

'Go on. You know you never got any trouble from us, Mags.'

'I know that, and I don't want to bring any trouble to your door either.'

Her wrinkled old face is wise. She reminds me of a tree in one of the girls' storybooks, maybe *Pocahontas*, this wizened, wise old tree that's seen it all.

I tell her as straight as I can the situation with Duckie (Detective Sergeant Cassidy, I call him) and suggest she tell Natasha and the Traveller girls who were with her to keep their heads down for a while until he's got over his hump. I don't put it like that exactly, but she knows what I mean.

'And you're a hundred percent sure that 'twas Natasha bought the jacket?' Dacie's dark intelligent eyes lock with mine. I realise that something other than Duckie is bothering her about all this.

'I am,' I say with conviction. 'Joe said she paid ten euro a week for it for the last six months.' I've just realised maybe this is a secret Natasha was keeping to herself, but I can't lie to Dacie; the trust I've built up over twenty years would be gone in a flash.

'I'll take care of it. Tell Mr Dillon I'm very sorry there was a difficulty in his shop, and I'll say a prayer for him and his family. And tell him that Natasha won't cause him any more trouble and she won't be seen around town for a while. I'll see to that. It's time she calmed down and got ready for married life.' There's a snap to her voice, and I realise Dacie is worried her wild young granddaughter might be a hard one to herd to the altar. I hope the jacket Natasha was buying was for her fiancé, or a brother. But I can't help feeling something is odd about her buying it at all.

I finish the cake and the tea and stand to go. There is nothing more to be said. I know Dacie is true to her word. 'Thanks, Mrs McGovern. Is there anything else I can do for you? Are you OK for everything?'

She hesitates. I can tell she's deliberating; there's a faint pink flush on her cheeks among the lines.

'Well, Mags, if you've a minute, there was something. Delia, Natasha's cousin – she wouldn't have been with her yesterday morning – she was very good, they tell me, up at the school, with the books and everything. She's a bit different from the rest – quiet, like, and doesn't go out much. Her parents are worried there's something a bit wrong with her actually, but I'm very fond of her. She's unusual.'

I sit down again while Dacie thinks about what she's going to say next, like this is difficult for her.

Finally she clears her throat with a reedy noise. 'Well, Delia came home to me a few weeks back saying she wanted to be some sort of volunteer guard. Don't ask me what that means, but she knew all about it.'

I try not to look astonished. No wonder Dacie is finding this hard to say. The Garda Reserve isn't part of the real police force – it's an unpaid volunteer organisation – but it helps out the guards and is supposed to form a link between them and the local community.

The old lady continues. 'She's a bright girl, taught herself to drive and everything. Her father nearly had a heart attack when she showed him, but she's well able. She should by rights be finished with the books now as she's just turned eighteen, but she persuaded her daddy to leave her there to do the exams or whatever they have. Her father is dead against the idea of the guards of course – he has her in mind for one of the Reilly boys in Longford – and her mother isn't keen either, but she came to me because she said there's some kind of way that she could be this kind of a volunteer without being in the actual guards or anything.'

'She's talking about the Garda Reserve,' I say. 'It's a volunteer force, and often people who'd like to be a guard, they train to be a volunteer first – it looks good on the application. But it's not a paid job.'

'Oh sure, she has no need of a paid job, her father is providing for her, but she's heart set on it, and sure, it probably wouldn't do any harm for a small bit anyway before the engagement is announced. I probably shouldn't be encouraging it – Her father is dead set against it, I told you that – but she came to me and begged to be allowed to have a bit of a life anyway, as she calls it, before she settles down to have the babies. And sure I'm gone soft in my old age, so I said I'd talk to you and see. She won't ever be a proper guard like yourself, Mags – that's not for us. Don't get me wrong, 'tis fine for the likes of you, and I'm sure your man could take care of you and the girls fine if you wanted that. But that's your way, not for one of ours.'

No offence is meant and I take none. The sad truth is there is no way Delia McGovern will get into the Garda College in Templemore anyway. I mean, not properly. It's where she would do her training for the Reserve, and I am sure they'll take her for that. The Gardai are always trying to be 'diverse', even though I doubt if anyone from the Garda Síochána HQ in the Phoenix Park in Dublin has ever actually been on a halting site. But to be a proper guard, she will need a degree, and I very much doubt that is going to happen. And even if it could, I doubt Delia's father or Garda HQ would allow it.

'And would you take her, just for a while?' Dacie asks me, and I know what a huge leap this is for her. Police, governments, schools, hospitals – they are all institutions to be avoided if you are a Traveller; they don't trust them. So sending her favourite grandchild into the lion's den is a very big thing for Dacie McGovern.

'Well, it wouldn't be up to me, but I'd be happy to meet her and help her with the application and put a word in for her if that would help?'

'Would she have to go in and talk to them, other real guards, not just you, like?' Dacie suddenly seems less sure of the idea, obviously thinking about Duckie.

'She would. She'd have to do an interview. But I will tell you this, Mrs McGovern, we are very interested in people from all walks of life in Ireland becoming part of the Garda Reserve. So any member of the Travelling community would get a good hearing. I'm not saying she'll get in or anything, but why don't I meet her and we can talk about it?'

She deliberates but then decides and stands up, opens her door and calls something to the gathered children. Travellers have their own language called Gammon, and while it is sometimes interspersed with English words, they speak quickly and with lots of their own words and phrases so it is close to impossible to understand them if they don't want you to. And they never want you to. Even so, I've made it my policy to pick up a few words over the last twenty years, and I know she's telling the children to go and fetch Delia right away.

Within two minutes a girl appears. She looks to be in her late teens, poker-straight natural blonde hair all the way to her waist and a slim, curvy figure, and she looks just like all of her cousins, except for what she's wearing. The rest of the girls, including Natasha, dress in black Juicy Couture leggings and hot-pink velour hoodies, their midriffs bare despite the cold, diamond studs glittering in their navels and each with a full face of make-up. And when I say full face, think drag queen meets Bozo the Clown. Lips filled so they look like they've been stung by a bee several times, and eyelashes so long and dark, I wonder how they manage to keep their eyes open. Long talon-like fingernails with sparkles on them. And they have a great love of very high heels, which make most of them walk like newborn deer.

They love the style and use whatever spare money they have to create the look. It's harmless, and I see settled girls going for the same overdone look all the time nowadays. I thank my lucky stars that when I was their age, it was all baggy jeans and oversized jumpers. I don't think I ever had the body for that fashion.

Delia, on the other hand, is wearing jeans, runners, a plain white t-shirt and no make-up at all.

'This is Delia. She's Jerome and Dora's girl. This is Sergeant Munroe, Delia. Now tell her what you told me.'

'Hi, Delia.' I look at the unusual girl and wait for her to speak.

'I want to be a guard.' She says it like she's angry, her jaw at a confrontational angle. I know the aggressive tone is masking fear and worry, although she'll need to lose that edge before the interview. Travellers are so used to rejection, they try to shield themselves before the fact. 'I know I can't be a proper guard, like, but a volunteer.'

'And what makes you want to join the Reserve, Delia?'

She doesn't answer my question, instead posing one of her own. 'Will they take me?' She holds my gaze intently.

Delia has no advantage in life, being a girl, being a Traveller; everything is stacked against her. She must have real strength as well as being a favourite of her grandmother's to have withstood the pressure to have her own caravan, a few babies and a husband by now.

'Well, as I told your nana, it's not up to me, but I can help you to apply and we can take it from there. How would that suit you?'

'But will you tell them that I'm a Traveller, like?'

I understand the wariness. From both sides actually. Travellers are often in trouble, and there are more of them in jail than should be, given their percentage of the population, so settled people are suspicious of them. They don't want them around. If a Traveller family arrives in town, or some Traveller fella is going around selling stuff out of the back of his van, the phones in the station are hopping within minutes. I've heard of whole towns where all the pubs and shops shut up in the middle of the day rather than allow the Travellers in. I know that sounds awful, and it is, but it's complicated.

Still, none of that is young Delia's fault, and the 'inclusion and integration' heads in Garda headquarters will be thrilled to bits with themselves to say they have a female Traveller as a new recruit so they'll probably snap her up just for the photo opportunity alone. The other thing is – and I hate saying this or even thinking it, but I can see now the way she looks and dresses isn't like a Traveller at all – she could 'pass' as a settled girl, if she wanted to.

'You can tell them about your heritage yourself.' I smile. 'I was telling your nana that the guards nowadays are very anxious to have all parts of Irish society represented in the Gardai. We should be as diverse as the population is, so I'm sure they'd be glad to give you a hearing.'

'So what do I have to do?'

'Well, how about you drop into the station some day and I'll print off a form for you, and we can fill it in together and take it from there?'

'All right.' She agrees like she's doing me a gigantic favour. I stand and so does Dacie.

'God bless you, Mags. I'll light a candle for you. Isn't your little girl for Communion this year?' Dacie McGovern sees Communions and confirmations as huge events.

'She is, Mrs McGovern. She's all excited.'

'Ah, God bless her.' She goes to the cupboard in the kitchen part of the van and takes out a little bottle. It's one of those plastic ones in the shape of Our Lady, and the top is her blue crown that twists off.

'This is from the holy well. I got it on St Brigid's Day. 'Twill keep her safe and sound.'

She presses the bottle of holy water into my hand, and I accept it. The nearest holy well is on Terence O'Connor's farm, and the Travellers going there to leave offerings and take holy water is a constant source of consternation to him. He has me driven distracted with complaints. But now is not the time to raise that.

'Thanks, Mrs McGovern.'

I can feel the eyes of the whole clan boring into my back as I walk to the car.

CHAPTER 5

On the way into work, I want to listen to a podcast, but the Bluetooth thing is playing up. I'll ask Kieran to take it to the garage one of these days, but the problem is, I need my car every day, either to get to work or drop the girls somewhere. People who do business with the main dealer in Galway get a courtesy car, but no such luxury is supplied for the customers of Phillip O'Flaherty's greasy garage in Ballycarrick. Still, he doesn't charge main dealer prices either.

So I try the radio instead and find myself listening to some guy with a plummy English accent who has written a book about reasons to be optimistic. Delighted, I turn it up. He's talking to Sean O'Keeffe, the longest-serving presenter on Irish radio.

According to Mr Plummy, the world is safer now. Cars are safer, crime is detected more often, you have a better chance of making it past three score and ten than at any time in human history. All good. And he's right about crime. DNA is the best thing, and mobile phones. Those two have solved more crime in the last few years than anything else. It's close to impossible to get away with things now. There's always either a physical or digital trace.

I have a theory, by the way, on crime and punishment. Since I'm a guard, it's kind of my bread and butter, but you'd be stunned at the number of people who spend their whole lives in policing and have no theories whatsoever on the subject. So here's mine.

Each person should have a log of their actions, but instead of it just being a list of crimes, there should be a statute book of good deeds too, from minor to major, just like crime.

Take Bernard Carmody, for instance. Blades, as he would like to be called – I make sure to call him by his real name, Bernard; it drives him mad – will be released in May after a six-month stretch for burglary. As soon as he resurfaces, the rest of the pond life he associates with will too. The Carmodys are a Traveller family, some of whom see themselves as criminal masterminds when in fact they are a small gang of petty thieves. Anyway, when Bernard is up in front of the judge again in June, for a case pending, breaking and entering a scrap yard, the judge should be able to look at his previous good deeds and, if there are any, use them in mitigation. It might sound like a mad thing, but it's how other social interaction works, isn't it? When you think about it? Like, Kieran always leaves the toilet seat up, and it drives me nuts. Me and the girls have to put it down every single time, and no matter how many times we give out about it, he either can't or won't change. But on the other hand, he always mows the lawn. So that's why I don't smother him in his sleep about the toilet seat.

I'm turning into the station, so I switch off the radio in the middle of Mr Plummy explaining how Elon Musk and his inventions are another reason for delight. I park in my allotted space, but instead of going into the station, I decide to stroll down Main Street first, check in on Joe and maybe drop by Mam's shop because I haven't seen her for a few days. It's threatening rain again, but the fresh air will wake me up, and I can grab a cup of tea and a scone from Teresa's Bakery because I had to run out of the house this morning without breakfast.

The strange thing is, I find that I'm in great form. Mr Plummy has obviously penetrated through to my subconscious. *OK*, I think, *everyone says if we don't act yesterday about climate change, the temperature will rise.* Well, I live in the west of Ireland where people rust more than tan, so that's hardly a crisis if we warm up a bit? It's awful for Africa and those flat sandy islands in the Indian Ocean where people go on honeymoon, but for us, it might be grand.

I know. I realise thinking the west of Ireland could do with getting warmer is selfish, but I can't help my thoughts and this one cheers me up.

Old Frank Mooney is sitting on the red wooden bench outside the Samovar waiting patiently for the doors to open at ten. He's a martyr to the drink, as Mam would say, poor old divil. He's harmless, though he's always battered looking because he falls a lot when he's drunk. Sometimes I think he believes the squad car is a taxi, the number of nights we take him home, but it's either that or have him staggering all over the road being a danger to himself and everyone else. That's another reason to be cheerful – not about poor old Frank, but about the pub he is sitting outside of. It used to be an awful dive called McLoughlin's Bar. Benny McLoughlin, the owner, was a sweating forty-stone mountain of a man who would incinerate you a full fry for five euro, and if he had his hands full of plates, he'd helpfully pop the blackened toast under his sweaty armpits and bring it to you that way rather than go to the trouble of making two trips.

Two years ago Benny had the bright idea of subscribing to RussianBrides.com, and Tatiana, a native of Vladivostok, agreed to come to Ireland and hook up with the slightly creepy Benny. But when he tried to make her do his bidding in every area – bar, house, bedroom – she refused in the strongest possible terms. Tatiana is not the innocent flower she presents herself as. Nobody really knows what happened, but one night there were raised voices, and the next Benny was gone. And now Tatiana is running the bar, which has become a spotless establishment where the bacon is done to perfection and the toast is brought to you in a rack, with a curl of butter and little pot of marmalade.

Tatiana never reported Benny missing, just told everyone who was interested that he'd left her, so I made a few enquiries. Or in other words, I rang his mobile and he picked up and said he was in London, doing some business. He bluntly told me to mind my own, and I was happy to leave it at that.

And here's Teresa's Bakery, another good thing, and I pop in and buy two scones and two cups of tea in case Mam feels like a late breakfast as well. Teresa Donnelly, who serves me herself, is as thin as a rake despite spending her life surrounded by the best cream cakes in Ireland, but even that doesn't fill me with the usual despair about my own weight. She's probably sick of the sight of cream doughnuts and custard slices by the time she gets home and longs to sit on the couch bingeing on carrot sticks and hummus.

The chemist has new window display, dedicated to beauty. Julie Dullea who owns it has access to all the free samples of expensive creams and still looks as fresh as a daisy. Maybe I should be spending a hundred euro on her creams, maybe that's the key to eternal youth. She asked me the other day when I was in collecting Mam's prescription for her blood pressure tablets which skincare regime I used. I told her I just washed my face in the shower and threw on a bit of moisturiser when I remembered it. Her pencilled eyebrows are raised in permanent amazement all the time – well, amazement or Botox, I'm not sure which, but she looked even more startled at this revelation. I can't decide if she thinks I look young or absolutely ancient. The latter most likely. I try not to chuckle at her reaction.

Kieran is so good. He always says I look beautiful and whistles appreciatively if I get dressed up, but I think it's just a habit rather than him really thinking it. I imagine he knows I'd be disappointed if he said something a bit more honest, like 'not too bad'. But that's probably closer to the truth.

I know my limits. I'm not awful looking, but not gorgeous either.

Gerry waves to me from the hairdressers, he's putting out a sign encouraging people to book early for the upcoming Communions, and again my heart lifts. Truth be told, I'd have grey hair if I left it to its own devices, and not that sexy silvery grey, Judi Dench or Helen Mirren hair, no such luck. I have the kind of mousy salt and pepper grey that doesn't know what it wants to be, so I get Gerry to touch up the roots every six weeks. The posher members of Ballycarrick society drive an hour to Galway City for their haircuts but for most of us, Gerry is grand. No Vidal Sassoon and not charmingly chatty and gay like the male hairdressers you see on TV, but fine. His kids go to school with mine, and he's married to one of the Heffernans – Louise, I think, – who never did a day's work in their lives. She spends her time playing golf. It's hard to imagine a person with two small kids having time for a sport that takes six hours, but she does. They have an *au pair* from Germany and apparently it's the best thing ever. I don't know if I'd like an *au pair* even if we could afford it. A gorgeous young one wandering around in a towel? Best not. Kieran is a good man but he's only human, so why drive him mad?

I spot Nell McNamara heading towards me, so rather than sticking my head into Dillon's for a quick chat, I whizz around the corner towards Mam's. I feel mean doing it, but I really want to see Mam and time is limited, and if Nell catches me, I'll be there for a half an hour on the same topic she always has. Nell McNamara lives next door to Trevor Lynch, the drummer for Tequila Mockingbird, Bally-carrick's answer to U2, and she is never done complaining about the noise. It went to court last year, and the judge ruled Trevor could play during certain hours. He sticks to it, but even five minutes drumming is too much for Nell. She wants to put 'a Stanley knife to his skin' – a direct quote – though I'm sixty percent confident she means the skin of his drums. I don't blame her; his thumping would drive you daft. But it's totally pointless explaining to her that once a judge has made a ruling, there's nothing we can do. Trevor was going with a girl from Cork there for a while, and Nell was having Father Doyle saying Masses the romance would work out and he and his drums would move south to torment the Corkonians. But the girl confided to Nell one day that he was a nice fella but she couldn't stick the endless drumming either, so back to Cork she went, without Trevor, much to Nell's disappointment.

Mam's shop, Marie's Boutique, is opposite the music shop and beside the barber's. My dad died when I was seven, and Mam had to raise me and my sisters on her own. Even when he was alive, Dad was never well, so the shop was our livelihood. Mam worked so hard; she was in the shop six days a week, from eight in the morning to six in the evening. She had to do it of course, but we missed her. And I swore when I had kids, I'd be there for them, so I suppose I should be glad I'm not a detective sergeant now, poking around looking for bodies in the bogs of rural Ireland.

I really am on a roll with all this Mr Plummy positive thinking stuff. The top brass, as Duckie calls them, in Galway did me a favour in not offering me the job. If they had, I might have considered it and even taken it, and then the promise I made to myself to be there for my kids in a way my mother couldn't be for us would be broken.

The words of that American country singer Garth Brooks enter my head, about thanking God for not answering every prayer. Sharon's mad about Garth Brooks. When he came to Ireland, the whole place went mental, line dancing and wearing cowboy hats. I don't get it myself, but he seems to be very well-loved.

I chuckle at a memory. At the time of his visit, Sharon was working in the secondary school as a special needs assistant, and she was determined to get tickets to see Garth Brooks. So while the teacher was at a meeting and she was temporarily in charge of the second years, she took the class to the computer room, wrote her credit card details on the board, complete with expiry date and three-digit code, and got all thirty of them to log in to the site selling the tickets. So much for my internet security talks!

I do a course every year on internet safety for kids, and while some of the methods the criminals use to get access to children would make your blood run cold, at least we're able to help parents be aware of it. We do a couple of nights a year in each of the schools, explaining what to look out for, and people are great to attend. I offer to be available for any parents who are concerned, and lots of them take me up on it. One particular group of girls in the convent secondary were in touch with this guy who was claiming to be a teenage girl when in fact it was a German sex offender in his fifties. Through the parents' vigilance and the kids' savvy, we were able to bring it to the attention of the special unit in Dublin that deals with that, and they in turn worked with Interpol, so the guy was caught and convicted.

Sharon got the tickets anyway, so according to her, that was all that mattered.

As I walk, I think about why I was so upset about the job. The rejection hurt, I suppose, and the idea that they picked Duckie Cassidy over me. That stung too. But in the cold light of day, it's for the best. Employers accuse women of not being as committed, of having other things, like their family, take priority ahead of their job, and they're not wrong. The truth is my girls would come before the job every single time. So then it stands to reason, those jobs that need you to be all over the country and working all the hours should go to the men or women without children. Or the men whose wives take the kids to the dentist and the school concerts. It's not fair and it's not feminist to say it, but it's true and it's nobody's fault.

CHAPTER 6

The door to Mam's shop has a tinkly chime, and my mother looks up from where she's unpacking white lacy Communion dresses from boxes, even though it's only March still and the Communions aren't until May. 'Hi, love, how's things?'

'Hi, Mam, everything's great. Tea and a scone?'

'Ooh, one of Teresa's. Fabulous. Listen, I was just about to ring you. I wanted to tell you I got the Communion dresses in today and I want Kate to have first pick. I won't sell hers to anyone else then.'

Mam's shop will be inundated once word gets around she has the Communion dresses. It is the biggest market she has, that and school uniforms, and Kate will be delighted to have the inside track.

'Thanks, Mam. I'm off on Thursday, so I'll bring her in after school.'

'Ah, Mags, they'll have the doors off the hinges by Thursday – they'll have seen the courier van today. No, you better bring her down this evening. I'll leave the heat on in the shop for her so she won't be frozen, the poor pet.'

I smile. I know she's right. There's fierce competition when it comes to the Communions. 'OK, fine, I'll bring her down after dinner, depending on what happens here at the O.K. Corral. Did Joe tell you about...'

Mam makes a gesture with her eyes towards a customer I haven't noticed, who is browsing the sandals. Elsie Flanagan never buys anything but is known as a terrible gossip, so she is no doubt earwigging on our conversation.

'Are you all right there, Elsie? Can I get you a size to try on or anything?' Mam asks pleasantly. 'Those new silver ones are fierce comfortable altogether. Mona Keane got a pair last week, and you know she only had her knee done a short while back, and she said they're the only things she can wear for now.'

Elsie puts the sandal down as if it's radioactive. 'Ah, no thanks, Marie. I only wear the Carvela, and you don't stock them, do you?' she says sweetly.

'No then, Elsie.' Mam suppresses a grin. 'They're a bit rich for our blood, those ones. You'd have to go to Galway for them, or even Dublin.'

'Oh, you do. Brown Thomas have them, but my Noreen gets them for me.'

Mam and I share a silent conversation, noting how Elsie has managed to deftly get the subject around to the multiskilled and wonderous Noreen once again. We could be here until lunchtime now hearing about the latest achievement of Noreen Flanagan. Despite an unremarkable career in the fisheries department, it seems Noreen knows everyone who's anyone, is an expert on most sports and is a champion Irish dancer; she is also an artist and a poet and an expert chef into the bargain. She works in Dublin and knows everyone famous. How she has time to attend to the tedium of the fisheries department nobody knows, because according to her mother anyway, she spends every spare second on her many extracurricular activities and excelling at them all.

'Isn't she marvellous,' my mother says without a hint of sarcasm.

'She is. She has a great eye for quality and craftsmanship, and of course she's right on trend because she knows them all, the ones that would be in *RSVP* magazine. She's always *in vogue*, so I never need worry. Some people might be hoodwinked into buying last year's style for cheap, but not my Noreen.' Elsie lifts and replaces another shoe from the stand; it's clearly not the quality she has come to expect. 'She gets her artistic talent from me, of course. Poor DinJoe, God be good to him, couldn't draw a straight line.'

I look at the floor. I can't get into the topic of Elsie's artistic talents without giggling. She joined the painting class in the community school last year, after the death of the long-suffering DinJoe. We think she talked him to death on the subject of their only child. Anyway, Elsie's was a late vocation to the world of artistic endeavours, it would seem.

'I could drop you in a few of my pictures to sell in the shop if you like, Marie?'

Mam stays neutral without a hint of a smile. I don't know how she does it, I swear.

'Oh, thanks so much, Elsie, that would be lovely, but I wouldn't like to upset Mr Holloway in the antique shop. He's your main stockist, and we try not to tread on each other's toes in the town if we can. If I started stocking your paintings, he might start selling tights and bras, and then where would we be?'

The idea of proper Mr Holloway dealing in ladies' undergarments is also hysterical. The only reason he has Elsie's desperate paintings in his beautiful shop is he hasn't the guts to refuse her. She only paints one scene, the castle on the shore of Carrick Lough three miles from town. She paints it repeatedly, like hundreds and hundreds of times, the same chocolate boxy castle, green fields, blue lake and two swans.

'I did six more on Saturday,' she announces proudly.

'Aren't you incredible?' Mam says.

'Sure, your man above in the school, the art teacher, calls me Speedy Gonzales. It takes some of them in the class weeks to do one picture, imagine that? But I can do five or six in an hour. I don't know what does be keeping them, but I suppose I just have the gift.'

'You really do, God bless you,' Mam agrees, and Elsie finally goes on her way. I'm biting my bottom lip not to laugh.

'Now, now.' Mam waggles her finger. 'Don't be mean. Sure she loves it, and it keeps her off the streets.'

'She called us a few months ago,' I say, 'convinced she'd had a burglary. She didn't, of course, but it's like the twilight zone in her house. A huge picture of the castle in the hall, three or four more going up the stairs, more on the landing, the bathroom, everywhere. There isn't a square inch of wall not adorned by the castle, lake, field painting she loves so much.'

'Don't forget the swans.' Mam grins, then we tuck into the melt-in-the-mouth scones slathered with butter and jam and enjoy our tea.

She asks about Kieran and the girls and gives me a pair of jeans, a new brand that holds everything in apparently. The rep for the company called with a sample, and Mam asks me to give them a try. If they're any good, she'll order some. Mam's clientele are all in the market for a pair of 'hold you in' jeans.

As I leave, Mam calls after me, 'Mind yourself, pet, and don't go near anyone with a gun.'

I have to smile at that. An Irish guard's mammy's advice. Don't go near anyone with a gun.

My poor Mam nearly gave herself an ulcer trying to talk me out of the guards when I was younger, not because I was a girl, but because she was convinced it was dangerous. The reality is that it isn't, not the way I do it anyway, unless you call it dangerous explaining to Mrs Finnegan why her Yorkie Poo doing his business outside the florists every morning is upsetting Violetta. I've had to have my wits about me a few times, fellas throwing punches when they were full of drink, but alcohol and coordination are not friends, so on the few occasions I've been physically inferior to a law breaker I've managed to duck in time.

* * *

ON THE WAY back to the station, I check in with Joe and give him Dacie's message. 'She said to tell you she's very sorry there was a difficulty in your shop.'

'Sure, it wasn't the poor girl's fault. It was that puffed-up eejit Duckie Cassidy who always buys clothes too small for him. I try to tell him but he never listens. Did I tell you, just before he grabbed the young McGovern girl, he burst the seams of a pair of trousers he was fitting on that were miles too small?

'"I'm a thirty-four waist, Joe," says he, and his days of being a thirty-four waist are gone like the snows of last winter. I'd say the girls saw it and were laughing and that's what made him lose the plot. He's a right clown.'

I laugh with Joe, but something is really bothering me about that jacket. Ten euro a week for six months comes to over €250, which is a very expensive present. And her grandmother knowing nothing about it is strange, because normally Dacie knows everything that is going on in her family, down to who had what for breakfast. 'You don't know who Natasha was buying the jacket for, do you?'

Joe grins ruefully. 'I did ask who the lucky man was – it was a North Face jacket, the latest style, any lad would love it – but she gave me that fierce glare of hers and I didn't ask again.'

So I walk away, unable to get the thought of that jacket out of my head, It doesn't sit right with me. It makes me anxious.

THEN I WONDER if all this anxiety is the "change" coming on. Sharon says she is awake too with all kinds of claptrap going on in her head.

Maybe I should go to Doctor Harrison? But Doctor Harrison's receptionist is Mrs Burke and whatever else Sharon is wrong about she's right about this, Joanna Burke is a huge gossip and if Doctor Harrison gives me a prescription for Xanax or something, the whole town will know by lunchtime that their local community guard has gone off her head.

No, I decide. I'll go another route. As soon as I have the time, I'll run into Galway and pop into the Women's Health Clinic.

CHAPTER 7

*I*n the run up to Holy Communion, Ellie seems a bit down in the dumps but says nothing is wrong; she's just got bad growing pains in her legs. Because Ellie is growing, Kate insists she has to put on her Communion dress every day to make sure it still fits, which of course it always does; she's hardly going to bust out of it in two months. Kieran is non-stop with the roofing because the weather has come good, and I helped Delia fill out her application for the Reserve; she's got through the exam and interview and is gone off to Templemore for her few weeks' training.

And now it's the big day, and Kieran is supervising a pink and purple bouncy castle that's inflating before our eyes in the back garden and Kate's making the Communion this morning. The excitement is up to high doh.

The party is all under control, I think. I got Tatiana from the Samovar to do the catering, so at least I don't need to worry about that. A big pot of beef stroganoff and another one of chicken curry with rice and a tray of baked spuds.

The Spanx that Sharon convinced me to buy are cutting off the blood flow to my legs on the bottom and my lungs on the top. They're like something you'd see in one of those medieval torture chambers.

There is no way I'll make it through the day with them on, but it is either that or abandon all hope of fitting into the dress I got two months ago in the March sales in Galway. It's lovely – well, you know, lovely in a way a dress for a middle-aged mother of two can be. It's red – well, kind of wine – and it's a wrap dress so it makes my boobs look very obvious. But the ruching on the tummy hides a multitude of sins, I think. I'm wearing the gold necklace and earrings Kieran got me for my birthday with it, and I had Gerry do my hair first thing when I went down with Kate and Ellie. Kieran gave a wolf whistle after I nearly gave myself a hernia getting the dress on this morning. I'm wearing sandals Mam gave me, which are ingenious. They look all strappy – you know, like the ones that feel like they're made of recycled razor blades after five minutes? – but actually they're really comfortable. And I even got the legs waxed and put on a bit of tan to stop me looking like a milk bottle, so all in all, the effect isn't too bad, I think, even if I can't breathe with the torture knickers.

I'd convinced myself I'd fit into it, that I'd go down to Elaine and do my penance and get down the half stone and the zip would glide effortlessly up the back. But did I do that? Well, the horrible 'flesh-coloured' shapewear is your answer. Flesh-coloured? Maybe flesh that's been lying in the morgue for two weeks, or at the bottom of a lake.

'You look lovely, pet' Mam's voice greets me as I descend the stairs.

'Thanks, Mam. This is a bit tight, but if I can get as far as the end of Mass, at least I can change. I might spill something over myself on purpose.' I laugh and she joins in. We're a team, my mam and me.

She looks genuinely lovely herself in a biscuit-coloured dress and coat, with light make-up and her hair blow-dried. Mam is such a lovely woman and has had a hard life really. I'd love her to meet a nice man to go dancing or to the pictures with, but she's always dismissed the idea. A weekly pub lunch with Joe is as far as she gets on the dating scene.

'That's exactly what you'll do. I'll nudge your arm and we'll get you rightly smudged, and then you can enjoy the day.' She gives me a conspiratorial wink. 'You'll have been seen in the dress, and that'll do them.' She turns to the fridge. 'I got a pavlova in Teresa's and some of those chocolate mini rolls from SuperValu that Ellie loves.' Mam adds the desserts to the already bursting appliance.

There is enough food to feed an army, but then the Munroes are all coming. And they might as well be an army, an army of marauding elephants. Kieran has three sisters and nine nieces and nephews between them. Gearoid, Kieran's only brother has no kids and is single. And of course there are Kieran's parents, Nora and silent Kevin.

'We better tell monster-in-law we made the pavlova.' I say it under my breath in case Kieran walks in. His mother, Nora Munroe, is the bane of my life. She is married to the monosyllabic Kevin, and her favourite and only two topics of conversation are her children and their accomplishments, and the ailments of people in town.

Her children are the five best examples of human perfection to ever grace the earth. And us outlaws, the girls' husbands and me especially, should be forever down on our knees in gratitude to have had the honour of marriage to a Munroe bestowed upon us.

Her other cheery topic is the terminal illnesses of the people of Ballycarrick. Poor Kevin is never allowed to speak. He just stands behind her as she tells us who has cancer, whispering the word, who has multiple sclerosis, who is being 'shifted' to the county home, whose prostate is in trouble – no matter what your ailment in Ballycarrick, if it is serious, or better again, fatal, Nora can fill you in on the gory details.

'She'll know the pavlova's from Teresa – they're famous. Don't let her catch you out in a lie,' Mam says wisely. 'But you could let on you're very busy with a top-secret case, and then she'll be able to tell Willie in the post office how you are leading a very important investigation and she knows the whole story, but if she told Willie, then she'd have to kill him.' Mam chuckles; she knows Nora of old.

'Oh, for the love of all that's holy, I've nothing to do with any important cases thankfully, but if she wants to go around pretending I'm some kind of RoboCop, I suppose I should let her. It might excuse me having pavlova from the bakery.'

'Exactly.' Mam nods.

Mam did enough of a hard road with my Nana Peg, Daddy's mother, to know how to handle a mother-in-law from hell. Nana Peg moved in with us in the end. My mother was a saint to allow it, as Daddy was dead. Nana Peg had a daughter, my auntie Kathleen, who refused point blank to take her, so Daddy's mother ended her days trying to torment my poor mam. Mam was cute enough, though. She gave her a drop of brandy every night, sometimes a lot more than a drop, and it mellowed her out fine.

After the bouncy castle is up, Kieran goes in to shower and change and comes down the stairs looking gorgeous. He's almost always in work pants and a hoodie with big side pockets and all manner of tools clipped to him, so it's lovely to see him dressed up.

I go over and hug him, burying my face in his neck appreciatively. 'Mmm...you smell delicious,' I murmur, but Ellie hears us and pulls us apart, half-jokingly.

'Urgh, Mam, get off him! You two are a disgrace. Kate, don't look.' She covers her sister's eyes theatrically, and Kate giggles. 'You'll be traumatised on your big day.'

'How do you think you two got here?' Kieran resists her and wraps his arms around me, grinning, and the two run screaming in dramatic horror at the mention of it. We laugh and head out to the car.

Mam drives herself to the church, and myself and Kieran follow with the girls. The neighbours come out to see Kate in her finery, and she loves it all. She looks gorgeous in her white, lacy dress – the nicest one out of Mam's shop, in my opinion as well as hers.

I'm kind of against the whole Communion thing if I'm honest. Like, if we saw another culture dressing kids up in ridiculous outfits and showering them with money in some other place in the world we'd think it was mad, but here in Ireland it's what we do.

So my little one, like all the girls in her class, is dressed as a tiny, over the top bride with lace gloves. I mean really, who on earth wears lace gloves in this century? And frilly handbags? Again, what?. And along with all her friends, she got her hair curled with the hot iron thing by Gerry's three teenage nieces roped in for the Communion morning.

When we get to the church, she goes up to the front with the rest of the class, and mad as it all is, they do look so sweet.

And when they are all singing up on the altar, I think to myself, *I'd like to believe in God.* It's not a thing you decide, not for me anyway. I was raised a Catholic, not fervently or anything, just a normal Irish level of devotion, which to other countries might border on fervour but for us was a kind of robotic thing. It was what you did, but I don't ever remember there being any depth to it. Lots of going through the motions of Mass, and sacraments and prayers in school, but no soul-searching or deep thinking.

Kieran and I got married in this church. My father's funeral was here, the girls' baptisms, my own Communion and confirmation, and I love the place for that, but it's based on a personal nostalgia rather than any connection to a crucified man from the Middle-East two thousand years ago.

I glance around at our neighbours. I grew up in Ballycarrick, and Kieran is from Shanafree, a village twelve miles away, and so between us, we know every person in the church almost. They know us too.

There's Gerry the hairdresser and his wife, Louise; their little girl is also making the Communion. And Teresa from the bakery, whose grandson is up there dressed in one of those smart suits the boys wear, like tiny grooms to go with the tiny brides. And the butcher, Bertie Mahony, who goes to Mass four times a week and is a minister of the word and a minister of the Eucharist and chairman of the parish council and leads the diocesan pilgrimage to Lourdes every year.

But do any of our neighbours, even holy Bertie, honestly think the little bit of wafer, made by the nuns in Limerick, that the priest is placing into our little boys' and girls' mouths is actually the body of a man called Jesus Christ? Seriously? I doubt it. But yet here we all are, going through the motions for each other. I wonder what would happen if I just stood up now, this very minute, and interrupted the whole thing? Walked up there and said, 'Sorry to barge in, but actually

I don't believe any of this, that babies are born with sins on their souls and that we are the one true church or any of it. Angels, God, saints – not one word of it rings true to me, so we might actually go away home for ourselves.'

I smile at the thought. Kieran thinks I'm smiling at the loveliness of it all and reaches over and squeezes my hand. I squeeze back. He loves these days, having all the family around, a big lunch, a few beers, feeling part of something. These are the days that make laying roof tiles on a wet February morning worth it. He doesn't find Ballycarrick claustrophobic or suffocating; he is happy just to live his life and not worry too much about anything. As far as he's concerned, he's got a great family, a nice house and enough money. That'll do. The simple things please him. He's so zen and doesn't even know what that is. Kieran practices mindfulness effortlessly, and there I am above in the community hall on a Tuesday night doing a meditation course to try to stop my racing brain, but it's like a runaway train. And all the incense and Tibetan singing bowls in the world won't stop it.

ALMOST ALL THE McGoverns are up the front, their finery surpassing all the settled people. Delia is there, but I don't see Natasha; I'm surprised at her for missing such a big day. Little Julia McGovern is in Kate's class, and the dress they have her in must weigh a ton. It has lights in it, actual fairy lights, and she has a gold tiara with more lights. The child has fake tan on as well, and her curls are piled high under the tiara. She's like one of those kids you see on the telly in those child beauty pageants. The other little girls are all round-eyed with admiration, but some of the neighbours are elbowing each other and looking snooty. They don't get it, though. The McGoverns aren't trying to be flash or show off, but these days for them are so important, nothing is too much.

The Carmody twins, Billy and Julianna, are making Communion too. They've decked Billy out in a very sharp suit; he's sporting Manchester United hair tattoos and a Swarovski diamond earring in his left ear. He's a total rogue, but I like him. He convinced me once to drive a bag of kittens he found on the beach – some evil person had tried to drown them – to the animal shelter in Galway an hour away because his father wouldn't let him keep them. He's cheeky and incorrigible but you'd have to love him. Julianna, his sister, is like the Pears soap child, really beautiful. She's almost lost in a cloud of organza and lace and has had her hair curled and highlighted.

The Carmodys are such an anomaly. That family are up to all sorts of mild skulduggery, from illegal cigarettes to washed diesel, but here they are all praying, like genuinely praying. They are spiritual, God-fearing people, yet they break the law in a heartbeat. They are very sure on things like no sex before marriage, but the women seated around their children are definitely 'sending the wrong signals' in terms of provocative dress. The twins' mother's boob job was the talk of the place last year; she went to Turkey for them apparently and they look well, very impressive. Some settled women roll their eyes, but maybe they're a bit jealous that the Traveller women have such great figures. Who knows? You can bet none of them are in the grip of a pair of life-threatening Spanx. They're great parents in that they love their kids dearly, but they have different values to us. They don't care if the children never go to school, but they are very well disciplined at home; you won't hear a Traveller child talk back to their parents like other kids do.

The twins' two older brothers, Jimmy and Neil, are both in prison, but I hear their Uncle Bernard, Blades, is just out. He's not here, though, which is odd, because normally they all come.

Despite the letter from the school asking that no more than four family members accompany each Communion child because the church is so small, all the rest of the Carmody and McGovern families are in attendance, filling out the place. You see what I mean? That kind of thing drives people mad. Nobody would dare say anything – you wouldn't want to draw them on you – but that kind of behaviour is one of the many reasons the two communities don't get along.

The thing is, though, they aren't doing it to be annoying. Communion is a massive thing for the Travellers, and family is also hugely important to them, so it just would be beyond their comprehension that the entire clan wouldn't come to celebrate the day. And by the entire family, I mean aunts, uncles, cousins, grandaunts, the whole shebang. They keep their extended family very close, so they have a lot of people whenever there's an event on.

You could argue they are the one group in the church who genuinely believe every word out of Father Doyle's mouth. Maybe they have more of a right to be here than most; more than I do anyway, that's for sure.

Bertie Mahony does the reading, and he's doing all the voices of the Pharisees and the tax collector and whatnot; he loves showing off how allegedly holy he is.

The children are up on the altar. Their teacher, Miss O'Driscoll, is a pure dote; they love her. She's not one bit like Ellie's teacher. Miss O'Driscoll is like a Disney princess herself, tiny and pretty and girly, and Kate and her buddies think the sun, moon and stars shine out of her.

She conducts them singing 'This Little Light of Mine' as they each hold a candle. No matter what your feelings on transubstantiation, or the second Vatican council, this would melt you. Their little innocent faces, beaming down at their mammies and daddies, grannies and grandas, delighted to be the centre of attention. Everyone sings now, including Bertie, who is belting it out really loud over the children, which is making me cringe and Kieran chuckle. Bertie's the sort who holds the last note on longer than anybody else, but the whole church is happy and nobody seems to mind about him at all.

Happiness is a special thing, so maybe I'm not being a hypocrite, buying into all the trappings of religion while not believing a word of it. This Communion is making my people happy. Kieran is proud as punch. Kate is loving it all, and Ellie can't wait to have all the cousins round to our house for the afternoon, where they'll make up dances to songs she has downloaded on a Spotify playlist and eat as many sweets as they like. Mam is beside me, and I know she's having a great day and that seeing her granddaughter in the nicest dress in the class gives her a surge of pride. She deserves it; she's dressed every Communion child in the parish for forty years.

And then the church bit is over and there's photographs outside and the less-than-subtle passing of the 'cards'. They make a fortune now out of the Communion. I made £27 myself, but that was back in 1978 so that was good-going. I slip the cards, with the money in them of course, to Kate's besties, and their mammies do the same for Kate. It's all a racket of course, but it's how it is. She'll collect from all the family later, and then I'll let her spend some of it – we'll go to Smyths Toys next weekend maybe – and save the rest. Though I have been known to dip into Ellie's stash from two years ago from time to time, for milk. I don't feel bad about it; kids don't need big wads of cash.

We stand around the churchyard in the sun, and Kieran is taking pictures with his phone of Kate and her friends when I see the van from Wildfire Productions, the local film-makers, setting up outside the church and the Carmodys posing. I smile. They're so over the top. Trust them to hire a film production company to capture the big day. The twins had been delivered to the church in a horse-drawn carriage of the Disney variety. Though the mothers were appalled, every little girl who came in their parents' boring old car was so jealous. Little kids don't get subtle, and the Carmodys are not subtle. They're flash to the max.

Out of the corner of my eye, I see that the McGoverns are leaving the church, and I notice with a pang that Julia McGovern isn't carrying a bundle of cards like all the other kids, and she's surrounded by her family, not the girls in her class.

'Mam, get Kate for me, will you?' I whisper to my mother urgently, and pull out the spare card I keep in the bag. I was caught badly at Ellie's Communion when a child she's not that friendly with gave her a card and we had none to give her in return. It was mortifying. So this time I have two spares, with twenty euro in each, just saying 'wishing you a lovely Communion day, love Kate', in case of such an eventuality.

Mam takes Kate's hand and brings her over, and I bend down to my lovely little daughter. 'I want you to give this card to Julia, and I'll take a picture of you, OK?'

She looks up at me, her blue eyes perplexed. She isn't really friendly with Julia, but she trusts me.

I say, 'She doesn't have any cards, and I don't want her to feel left out, all right?'

'Course.' Kate smiles. She takes the card and walks over. The McGoverns watch her warily, but my daughter has no understanding of that.

'Can my mam get a picture of us, Julia?' Kate asks kindly. 'Your dress is lovely.' The little girl beams brighter than all the mad twinkly lights on her dress.

Suddenly the flashes are going and every one of the McGoverns is beside me taking the picture of Kate and Julia. Julia's father hands Kate fifty euros, way too much, but I don't protest. She grins. 'Thanks, Mr McGovern.'

Then, and I have never loved her more, she turns to Julia and says, 'We have a bouncy castle in our garden, and I know today we are all with our families, but my daddy asked the man if we could keep it tomorrow too, so some of the girls are coming over to our house tomorrow afternoon to eat all the leftover food, if you'd like to come?' And Julia's smile lights up the entire churchyard like she's won the lottery.

I grin apologetically at Julia's mother with that 'kids would hang you' conspiratorial look of mothers. 'It's not all leftovers. I promise we'll make fresh chips,' I say.

Julia's mother is originally a McDonagh, another big Traveller family from down near Athlone. She's not to be trifled with, and I hope she's not going to refuse Kate's kind offer, thinking I'm spying on them or something. I feel a gut-wrenching anxiety for my daughter, who made the offer in good faith.

Before she can say a word, Dacie pipes up. 'Isn't that a lovely idea, Julia? Would you like to go and play with your friends at Mrs Munroe's house tomorrow?'

'I'd love it, Nana,' she says.

'Great.' I sigh, relieved. 'If someone wants to drop her over around two, Kieran or myself will bring her home? We'll be dropping others too, so it's no bother.'

Julia's father, a man whose hands are covered in tattoos and who looks like he'd batter you as quick as look at you, nods. 'I'll drop her over so.' His voice is gruff.

'See you tomorrow, Julia,' Kate calls as she returns to my mam, and the McGoverns begin to disperse.

'You're a good woman, Mags Munroe.' Dacie grips my hand. And for some reason, that compliment means more than I can say.

Kieran makes no bones about the fact that he wouldn't trust some of the Travellers, he sometimes uses the other word, the one I hate and won't allow in the station or the house, as far as he could throw them. But he does admit it's wrong to tar them all with the one brush, and the McGoverns are fine. To be fair, he's had tools and things stolen over the years, and it was Travellers who did it, so he's wary.

But it's only to drop off Julia. She's just a child, and Kate was being so kind. And they won't rob the gates. Probably.

Especially if Bernard Carmody, aka Blades, continues to keep his distance.

CHAPTER 8

The Communion party goes beautifully, and so does the party the day after and nobody stole the gates or Kieran's tools out of the garage so all is well.

Better again, Kieran has taken the car to the garage and the Bluetooth is fixed which is why I'm able to listen to an interesting podcast, while driving to work having dropped the girls to school.

It's about the history of Irish Travellers, which I've decided I need to know more about. The podcast is mainly about the McCarthy family.

The McCarthys used to have twenty-six castles in the southwest of Ireland, including Blarney Castle. But because they were Catholic and Irish, the occupying English treated them badly, and they rose in rebellion. After eleven years, the rebels were murderously crushed by the bloodthirsty English leader Oliver Cromwell, and the McCarthy clan was stripped of their land and property and left homeless to roam the lanes and travel the byways of their ancestral lands. Their descendants are still roving the Irish countryside to this day. Other Traveller families have similar stories, riches to rags, royalty to living by the side of the road. No wonder Dacie McGovern acts like she's Lady Grantham out of *Downton Abbey* – it must be in her blood.

Today is going to be Delia McGovern's first shift. She's managed to pass the training, and her reports are very good. I've specifically asked that she be assigned to my station, as I want to keep an eye on her. But also I know the lads in my station, and Nicola, are decent people. They won't trust Delia right away – they've too much experience of certain Travellers to welcome her with open arms – but I don't think they'll be standoffish with her or rude.

I told Kieran this morning over breakfast that Delia was starting, and he didn't say anything, just finished his breakfast and went to work.

I'm a bit worried about him actually. He's like a cut cat these days, not like himself at all. And I know I should delve into why he's being like this, but I don't. I suppose I just don't want to hear if he's unhappy. I realise that's not a very grown-up approach, communication being key and all the rest of it, but I just haven't the courage. And it's not like things are bad – they're not; they're grand, most of the time.

Yesterday evening, he suggested we get an early night, his less than subtle code, but I said I had to finish the ironing. He looked sad, and a bit hurt, and I wanted to tell him it's not him, it's me, but I didn't.

I don't know why but I think I've just lost my confidence. I suppose I thought he was just being kind, wanting me to think he's still attracted to me, but the fact is I don't believe him because I don't feel attractive to myself anymore. I feel like a woman heading for the menopause... There, I've said it.

I think of Sharon and her warnings about keeping Kieran happy in case he runs off with a young one. I know he would never do such a thing, and this should be a happy thought, but out of the blue, I feel guilty about standing in his way if he did want to go off with some young one. He's so handsome still, and I've seen nice-looking women giving him the eye.

Maybe when I have time, I'll make his favourite dinner, prawn and salmon fettuccini, and put on the mixtape he made for me years ago. I'll wear the green dress he likes so much, and we'll dance to cheesy love songs in the kitchen and maybe end up on the couch like we always used to do before the girls came along. He'd love that. Although the girls would need therapy if they came in and found us dancing with each other let alone anything else.

I indicate to turn into the station and park and walk around the back rather than go through the main public desk where I'll no doubt be caught to talk to someone. I want to snatch a few minutes before the day starts to chat to Delia. The back of the station is where the few smokers left among us go for their smoke break, so the ground is littered with butts. I'm going to send them out to clean that up this morning. Why should poor Mrs Clancy who cleans the station once a week have to brush up their stinky fag butts?

Inside the back door, the men's locker room is on my right and the women's is on the left, a tiny space, once a broom cupboard, no joke, that was converted for me when I joined the station as a lowly guard fifteen years ago, after moving here from a station in Spiddal, and is now used by me and Nicola. We'll have to squeeze up to make room for Delia to leave her coat and handbag or whatever.

We've been promised a new station since God was a child, but I reckon I'll be well and truly retired before that happens. Just watch. I'll retire and they'll build a new station with a proper women's locker room with a shower and everything.

I hear Duckie's voice booming out of the men's locker room, although what he's doing hanging around using the facilities in my station, I've no idea.

'Mind yourself with that young wan now,' he's saying. 'I know Sergeant Munroe is all knacker-friendly, but they're like rats and they look out for their own, so be careful with her. You can't trust them, but you should know that.'

OK. That's it. I have to say something to Duckie right now, even if his connections in the force get me sent to Ballygobackwards. I turn and throw open the door of the locker room and find him lecturing Darren and the two other young guards, Cathal and Michael, who to their credit are looking very uncomfortable.

Duckie swings round to see me, and the look on his stupid face is laughable. He knows he's been caught and that if I were to take it further, he wouldn't have a leg to stand on. Most Gardai nowadays, especially the ones promoted to senior ranks, got there by never speaking as he has just done.

'If by "that young one" you mean Garda Reserve Officer Delia McGovern, and by "them" you mean the Travelling community,' I say loudly, 'I think we've already discussed how blanket assumptions about an entire group of people are unhelpful. There are some criminals within every group of people in society, so we'll treat each on their own merits, thank you.'

'Ah, Mags, you should hear yourself. Will you stop the PC crap now and get real?' Duckie splutters, purple in the face. 'You know as well as I do about the knackers, and don't mind your "we're all God's children" rubbish – you're fooling no one. You're sick you didn't get a promotion instead of me, and I know well you refused to arrest that one's cousin when she deserved it, so I'm just giving the lads here a bit of friendly advice to watch their backs, that's all.'

He stalks past me and up the corridor, followed by a sheepish Darren, Cathal and Michael. Nicola's on the public desk, and Delia hopefully isn't here yet... But then I see her, sitting in the office, on her own, her new Garda Reserve uniform perfect, and realise she must have heard every word.

I catch her eye and say loudly, 'I'd rather you keep that kind of sentiment out of my station, DS Cassidy. It's not helpful and it's not the way we choose to speak in Ballycarrick.'

He is furious. He doesn't know whether to stay and boom at me some more or storm out, but in the end he chooses the latter. He tries to bang the door behind him and fails because it's one of those doors that closes slowly.

After he's gone, there is a deep sigh of relief and everyone goes about their business. I step into the office with Delia and close the door behind me, and explain to her it's a fact of life that people will be prejudiced but it doesn't mean she needs to lie down and take it. Nowadays, the law is on her side. At least in theory.

Delia sits looking at me, her eyes impossible to read. She's a smart girl; she knows she's not going to get anywhere making a complaint against a detective sergeant on her first day. What a start for the poor girl. I make a decision.

'Do you want to come with me for the rest of the morning, ride around in the Garda car, and I'll show you the whole locality we cover from this station?'

With her chin at that jutty, defensive angle, she stands up and takes her jacket from the back of her chair, still saying nothing.

On the way out past the public desk, Nicola stops her. 'Delia, I just want you to know he's not worth your energy and nobody else in here thinks like him.'

At first I think Delia's going to say nothing to Nicola either, but suddenly she smiles and says, 'Thanks.'

Nicola Holland is a great girl. She's the right mixture of confident and humble. She doesn't think she knows it all, she understands there is a lot of learning on the job to do, but she's got enough sense to take the initiative when she should and ask if she doesn't know. She's only been out of Templemore less than a year, but already I'd be lost without her, and I wonder how I've survived so long being the only woman in the station.

And now I have Delia as well, though I don't know how that's going to work out for me.

We get in the car and drive down Main Street, then park for a while at the edge of the big car park between SuperValu and the library. It's market day, and there's a load of traders from out of town selling fruit and veg, cheap jeans and fake Nikes. Just as I'm about to move on, Delia opens her mouth for the first time since she got in the car.

'Uh-oh,' she says. 'There's going to be a fight.'

I look in puzzlement from her to the peaceful scene in front of me, women shopping and children queuing for ice cream from the van. 'What do you mean? I can't see anyone arguing.'

'No, but all the Traveller women have their hair tied up. I knew there was going to be a fight one of the days. My Auntie Eileen has an awful big gob on her and said Mary Seanie's baby was fierce ugly. Mary and her sisters are savage over it, and this must be where it's planned for.'

I switch off the engine and open my door, but Delia grabs my arm. 'No, no, don't get out. You won't be able to do anything. Once they have the hair tied up, there's no going back. We'll just have to wait for the men to arrive and put a stop to it.'

I turn to her firmly. 'Delia, I'm a guard – I can't just sit here and wait for a fight to happen that you've just warned me about and then do nothing to stop it until a bunch of men arrive. No one in this town will ever do anything I want them to ever again.'

She shrugs. 'OK, wait here. I'll sort it.' And before I can stop her, she jumps out of the car and marches over to the women. There's a short exchange, and immediately they start to disperse. She comes back and climbs in again.

I stare at her, open-mouthed. 'What on earth did you...'

She shrugs. 'Easy. I told them the inspector from Galway was coming today with a bunch of raw recruits from Templemore and the whole place is going to be crawling with new guards looking for any reason to show off and arrest someone or accuse them of something. Most of them are my relations, and Nana would slaughter them if they got into trouble like that.'

'Ah...I see.' I smile and start to wonder how I ever managed without her.

And it pops into my head to ask her if she knows why her cousin Natasha bought that jacket. But a few weeks have passed since then, and nothing else has happened, and I don't want to look as if I'm prying into her family affairs.

CHAPTER 9

*U*p ahead, the traffic is slowing, the rain is coming down in a torrent now, the wipers are struggling to keep up and cars are queuing to join the dual carriageway from a slip road on the left. I'm driving back from Galway on the Tuam bypass listening to a podcast about the menopause, and kicking myself for not going to the Women's Health Clinic before. According to the lovely female gynaecologist, who has given me a prescription for HRT, I'm not experiencing the menopause yet but I am in the perimenopause. Insomnia, racing thoughts, low mood, itchiness, irritability, libido on the floor... Apparently, I tick a lot of boxes.

As I change down a gear, I spot an alarming sight – a sulky sneaking down the slip road, leaning at an angle with one wheel on the grass, squeezing past the line of cars.

A sulky is a lightweight two-wheeled cart drawn by a single horse, like a Roman gladiator's chariot and sulky racing is a longstanding tradition in the Traveller community. They have a very horse-based culture, and even children as young as ten years old are known to take part. Most Travellers race safely and take care of the animals properly. There are a few eejits who race them on the main roads, but it's rare enough. If anyone around here is going to do something that stupid and dangerous, I suppose it would be the Carmodys.

I slow down and move into the left-hand lane, keeping pace with the sulky coming down the slip road, wondering how best to head him off. I wish I was in a proper Gardai car instead of my own. I get on my phone and speed-dial Ballycarrick. Nicola is on the desk, and I can hear her calling to Darren and Cathal to get down to Exit 11 straight away. Meanwhile, the sulky is nearing the foot of the slip road where it meets the dual carriageway. The driver keeps glancing back over his shoulder, and then I see there's a girl squeezed in on the seat beside him, clinging to him, her long blonde hair lank in the rain. At the same time, I see what the sulky driver is looking back at: A black Mercedes is slowly following him past the line of traffic, also driving with one wheel on the grass. This is not right, and it's not just a Traveller kid showing off to his girlfriend either.

I get a very bad feeling and call Dromanane as well, even though Duckie's station is further away than Ballycarrick. Luckily, it's Leo who picks up – a nice community guard – and he tells me the squad car is out but he'll call and try and get it to me as soon as possible. Meanwhile, I edge my way across the line of cars coming down the slip road, causing a barrage of blaring horns and shaking fists from red-faced drivers.

The first fella in the queue rolls down his window and shouts, 'Oi! Get out of the way! The place is bad enough without you acting the maggot!'

Now is the moment, from what I've seen on the telly, the American cop would take out his or her badge, which is instantly recognisable even from twenty feet away, and show it for a split second before everyone is cowering and doing what they say.

Not the case in Ireland. I call to him, 'I'm Sergeant Munroe of Ballycarrick Station, and I'm trying to stop an accident!'

But he shouts back, 'Yeah, well, this is ridiculous. I've to get my young fella to training for half six, and I haven't even had my dinner!'

Meanwhile, instead of slowing, the driver of the sulky cracks the whip and forces his horse up on the grass bank at the side of the slip road and down again on the other side of me, nearly overturning the cart. As they pass me, I see the rain-soaked girl is Natasha McGovern and the pale-faced driver is Bernard Carmody, the one who likes to call himself Blades, and he's wearing a North Face jacket. No wonder Dacie hadn't heard about the jacket. She would never sanction Natasha going anywhere near any of the Carmodys, let alone Bernard.

I remain where I am, now determined to at least block the black Mercedes, I can deal with Blades any time, but the car does something crazy. It follows the sulky, roaring up the steep grass bank, wheels slipping and sliding, coming dangerously close to rolling over and down on top of me before it gets past. The windows are the sort you can't see through.

The man in the traffic queue who needs his dinner is open-mouthed.

Furious, I screech in a backwards arc and head up the hard shoulder after the Mercedes and the sulky now flying along in front of it. It's hard to see through the grey sheets of rain. I get back on the phone to Nicola, telling her to get Darren and Cathal to wait at the roundabout ahead, ready to take the registration number of a black Mercedes that is chasing a sulky up the dual carriageway. She says they're fifteen minutes away, so then I know they'll be too late and it's up to me.

The roundabout comes up quickly, but instead of turning around it, Bernard takes the sulky straight over it, wheels bouncing over the concrete surround and the horse's hooves battering down the flower beds that cover the roundabout. The Mercedes forces itself into the roundabout traffic, bringing the cars coming from the right to an angry halt.

I follow the Mercedes around the roundabout, trying to see its plates before it takes the second exit, but now there's a lorry between it and me and I don't see what happens next because I'm blocked. I hear a shot and then another, and then a girl is screaming. I put my hazard lights on, get out and run as fast as I can through the backed-up, beeping traffic in the direction of whatever has happened.

Fifty yards ahead of me, I see the sulky lying on its side, its wheels still spinning slowly. The horse is also down, tangled in its traces, trying in vain to get up. There's no sign of the Mercedes. Several people are getting out of their cars now, but I run through them shouting, 'Garda, let me through, please. Can you all please return to your vehicles. My colleagues will be here shortly to direct traffic.' Amazingly, they do as I say. I hear a siren behind me and think, *Thank God, Darren and Cathal are coming.*

Natasha is the girl screaming. She's crouching over Bernard Carmody, who is lying face down on the tarmac, one leg pinned beneath the capsized sulky.

'Blades! Blades!' Natasha is weeping. She has blood in her hair and all over her clothes, but I don't think it's her blood – I think it's his. I kneel and feel for a pulse in his neck. Dark red oozes from beneath him. The jacket that Natasha must have given him is ruined. It looks like two bullets were fired, because there's a large hole in the back of the coat and also, much more horrible to look at, a large hole in the back of his head. It's a dreadful, gut-wrenching sight. I've seen my share of violent death, but it's always been traffic or farm accidents or, at the worst, suicide. Even after twenty-four years in uniform, this is the first murder I've witnessed close up. Ballycarrick isn't exactly the crime capital of the world.

Poor young Bernard Carmody – I'll call him Blades from now on; it's the least I can do – is clearly dead. I get to my feet and move back. We'd better not touch anything before forensics get here. I try to encourage Natasha to stand up, but she refuses to move. She's not fit to tell me what happened, and I don't want to push her. I get back on the phone to Nicola, who assures me there are two ambulances on the way, and minutes later I hear more sirens and they arrive. Two paramedics usher Natasha into the back of one of them and take her off to Galway hospital to be treated for shock. I ring Galway Station, asking them to send guards to meet the ambulance and make sure Natasha is protected.

The other ambulance waits beside the roundabout; any attempt to resuscitate Blades is clearly pointless, and they can't move his body until forensics arrive. One of the paramedics releases the horse, which staggers to its feet; a member of the public who seems to know what to do with distressed horses soothes the animal and appears to have it under control. I take my notebook and go around to the cars all stopped in a haphazard manner on the roundabout. No one has seen the Mercedes or its occupants before, and no one took its number. Apparently the car just caught up with the sulky and the front-seat passenger stuck a gun out of the window and shot Blades twice before the car roared on.

After I've taken the name and number of every driver so we can interview them again later, Darren and Cathal arrive and direct each car past the accident, up the hard shoulder.

The phone rings in my pocket. Duckie.

'Sergeant Munroe speaking.'

'Mags, I hear from Leo you need some backup with a traffic incident involving a Traveller –' He's in high good humour. Silly Mags and her pro-Traveller ways, and not able to cope with a simple traffic violation.

'It's not a traffic "incident". It's a murder,' I interrupt him.

A brief pause. Then he barks, 'What? Oh. Right... OK... Well, take witness statements, find out whatever you can, interview anyone who saw the Traveller involved...'

I sigh inwardly. I have been a guard for a long time; I do know how to handle a crime scene.

'The Traveller involved is dead, Donal, and I've work to do,' I say, and ring off.

The next hour goes by. Nicola and Leo turn up to help as well, also directing traffic and assisting someone from the county council animal welfare section, who have arrived with a horsebox to take the poor animal away to safety. I'm glad Delia isn't on duty at the station today – she's helping out at a nearby music festival. I would hate her to be put in a position of knowing what's happened here and not be able to go straight to Dacie. That's going to be my job, as soon as I can get away.

Tim O'Halloran from Galway forensics arrives. 'Well, if it isn't

Sergeant Munroe. How's things, Mags?' He grins and winks as if we're meeting in the pub, not the scene of a murder.

I know you can't take every case on emotionally – if you did, you'd be a nervous wreck after a month in his sort of job – but I can't feel the same way myself. I knew Blades too well, and Natasha too.

'Grand, Tim,' I say. 'How's Esther?'

'Up the spout again.' He guffaws. 'I know, I know…I'm an awful man. She says that this time for sure she's sending me for the…' He makes a snipping gesture with his fingers as he crouches down over Blades.

'Congratulations anyway,' I say, unsure of how to react to this. The O'Hallorans have five – or is it six? – kids already, but surely they've chosen that? Anyway, I've enough problems to worry about as I watch him take physical samples.

Two other members of his forensic unit in their white suits check the sulky, and soon the cart is removed from the scene. And then finally, once Tim allows it, the body is loaded into the other ambulance.

There are people who have to be told, and this is my job. Blades's mother and father first, and then Natasha's parents, and Dacie, and it's all so horrible and heartbreaking and sad.

* * *

WHEN I GET HOME, I can tell by the state of the kitchen that Kieran has made the girls sausages and chips for dinner. I climb the stairs to find him lying on our bed with Ellie on one side of him and Kate on the other, and they're watching *The Simpsons*.

He is dozing but jumps up when I come in and hugs me. 'Hi, love.'

I kiss him and then go to kiss the girls.

'Hi, Mammy,' they chorus.

'Seymour Butz!' yells Moe in the tavern. 'I wanna Seymour Butz!'

My girls giggle wildly. It's their favourite bit of *The Simpsons* when Bart calls the bar and gets Moe to yell out names Bart and Lisa have made up. I.P. Freely, or Amanda Hugginkiss is another one. Has them in hysterics.

'Sorry I'm so late,' I say to Kieran, although he's knows what I've been doing – I've phoned him with a rough outline, though we can't talk about it in front of the girls.

He says, 'Cuppa tea? We had sausages, but there's a frozen lasagne in the freezer I can put on for you if you want?'

'I'm grand. I'll just have some toast. I'm starving and the lasagne would take too long.'

The girls are back enthralled by Bart and Lisa, so Kieran and I go downstairs. He puts the kettle on and scoops the remains of the girls' tea into the bin. I put two slices of bread in the toaster. Kieran seems not to know what to say. I suppose it's not often your wife is witness to a murder, not even when she's a guard – especially not a small-town community guard like me.

'I'm sorry I'm so late,' I say again, meaninglessly.

'Ah, Mags, stop that...'

'I had to go and tell Bernard Carmody's parents he was dead, and then Natasha's parents, and Dacie...' Out of nowhere, I'm crying. I've been focused on putting one step in front of the other all day, but the memory of all those grief-stricken faces... Huge extended families, one mourning the dead and the other terrified by the danger their girl is in. Hot tears slide down my face, and my throat is burning.

'Ah, Mags, don't cry, love...' He pulls me into a hug, and I can feel his arms around me. I rest my face against his chest and feel less hopeless and despairing of the world. Kieran is my safe place.

He holds me as I sob.

CHAPTER 10

*W*e've had a lazy Saturday morning, the girls and I, and it's been restful. It's a shame Kieran's got some big job on, which he couldn't postpone, but the girls came into my bed when they woke up, and we watched *Dancing with the Stars* on catch-up TV. Then Ellie made us all tea and toast, and we ate that in bed while watching the worst auditions on *Britain's Got Talent*. It was so nice just to hang out with them; it made me feel a bit better after the tragedy of yesterday. I haven't talked to them about what happened of course, but I think they can sense I need comforting.

Now I'm in the kitchen, a hoodie on over my pyjama pants, waiting for the kids to finish with their showers. The place is like a bomb hit it, but I'll get to it in a minute. I need to get the girls out first. Everyone has rallied round to take the pressure off me. Ellie is going to her friend's house for a sleepover, and Kate is going to Orla's, Kieran's sister's place. Orla's daughter, Evie, and Kate are inseparable.

My own two sisters left Ballycarrick years ago. The eldest, Jenny, went to go nursing in the Middle East, where she met and married Ahmed Amari, from Dubai. They have three boys, and we see them every second year. We FaceTime and send birthday presents, but we're not that close. Ahmed finds Ireland bewildering, and to be honest, the feeling's mutual, we don't get him either. He works for Emirates, the airline, and so he's well travelled and all of that, but he has nothing to say to us nor we to him. No animosity from either side, but it's just like two different species or something. I tried lots of times – I'm fascinated by other cultures – but he seems to find my questions mystifying, and I always get the impression from Jenny, without her saying anything, that by asking about his life and his beliefs, I'm offending him in some way, so I've stopped doing it. He's a devout Muslim and prays several times a day. Jenny didn't convert, and it's a testament to him that he didn't allow her to be forced to do so by social pressure, but the boys are card-carrying Muslims too and so it's all a bit...I don't know...awkward or something.

My younger sister, Delores, now called Lori, lives on a commune in Montana, way up in the Rockies. She's got a guy, Hopi, who she calls her soulmate. I've seen a picture of him, all hair and beard and tie-dye – he's like an extra from a Woodstock film. He's never left the commune because he is living a carbon-neutral life so can't fly. She comes home every summer, though, all dreadlocks and hippie clothes, and asks where I keep my tahini. I'm fond of her, in small doses, and Kieran and the girls are mad about her. She introduced my husband to marijuana two years ago. I nearly lost my mind, her bringing that into my house. I came home from work to find the girls in bed, the living room stinking of weed and the two of them giggling like eejits and eating all around them.

Kieran was so sorry, and for ages after; he knew I could have lost my job. And Delores went to stay with Mam for the rest of the trip. I'm over it now. I wasn't being a goody two shoes or whatever, but I am a guard, and having illegal drugs in the house and my husband and sister stoned off their heads in my front room wasn't exactly ideal, you know?

So for years now, it's just been Mam and me.

Mam was keen to shut up shop to spend the day with me, but I said not to because it's not fair on her. She's worked so hard to keep that place going, and Saturday is her best day. So I told her I needed some space, and it's true. I need to process what happened to poor Blades, and Natasha.

THROUGH THE FUZZ of my thoughts, I hear a car pull up outside. It's not Kieran's van, I know the sound of that, and Mam is busy in the shop with mother-of-the-bride outfits being delivered in anticipation of all the local nuptials coming up. So who...?

My heart sinks as Ellie calls downstairs, 'Mam, Nana Nora's here.' I close the laptop and start loading the dishwasher, throwing in plates so fast it's a surprise they don't break.

I need my monster-in-law in my life right now like I need a hole in the head. She only ever calls when she's got a bee in her bonnet about something.

She walks in and scans the manky kitchen. Most of last night's dinnerware is still on the table, as well as the breakfast things from this morning. Kieran must have made himself a sandwich for work, so the collateral damage of that culinary operation is in evidence too. As she inspects the mess, I feel a bit like a useless servant and she's the mistress of the manor. Nora gave us the deposit for this place fifteen years ago, and she never lets me forget it. I suppose in my heart of hearts, I feel like she kind of still owns it a bit. I often say we should just save up and pay her back, but then a holiday is so alluring and she never asks for it and we blow the cash on that instead. Kieran says he did much more than that amount in work on his parents' house over the years and that if anything she owes us, but I hate her having something over us, you know?

Nora Munroe never hides her disappointment that Kieran married me. He went out with Róisín Duggan for years. Her father is a gynaecologist in the private maternity clinic in Galway and the president of the golf club and her mother is a GP, and Nora was delighted with her. Kieran and Róisín lived in America together and everything, although Kieran came back to Ireland on every excuse – Communions, birthdays, christenings, even the christenings of children of distant cousins. Róisín never seemed to want to come home with him; she loved New York and all her friends were there. So when he came home one Christmas, alone as usual, we bumped into each other out in the pub, and we had such a laugh. I'd known him for years, kind of casually – everyone around here knows everyone else – but I was being written off by everyone in Ballycarrick as a bad job, thirty years old and still no man, the spinster of the parish. But something about him – I don't know, he was gas, I suppose, and gorgeous in an understated way, and I'm a sucker for funny – drew me to him, and him to me.

Looking back, it was very romantic. He came to find me the very next day and said that he was mad about me, that he'd always liked me and almost asked me out years ago before he went to America but never got up the courage. He said he wanted to go out with me and hopefully get married. Just like that.

He flew back to talk to Róisín, and she was very understanding about it all. She knew he'd been homesick for a long, long time, but she was set on staying in America and said he must do what he had to do. So then Kieran Munroe left his swanky apartment in Manhattan and the bright lights of New York City for the last time and stayed in Ballycarrick with me. We got married and had the girls. Easy. Except for Nora; she nearly had a stroke. She'd envisaged a future hobnobbing with the Duggans and bragging about her solicitor daughter-in-law, not a guard and the daughter of poor Marie Kelleher, lowly shopkeeper.

Róisín still sees Kieran for a drink when she comes home, and she and her partner, a very charming and sweet Mexican American called Joel Sanchez who works in the New York Senate, took us to dinner when we visited with the kids. She was lovely. She booked a table at the Top of the Rock with views over the whole city as the sun went down, and the girls loved it. She sends them presents at Christmas and photos of her and Joel's dog, a tiny Pekinese, dressed in a Santa costume. Everyone is grand about it, except the Wicked Witch of the West standing before me now.

She gasps as she enters, like an actual theatrical gasp, like she's about to faint at the sight of a plate with the remains of spaghetti bolognaise on it. 'Mags, my God, were you sick or something? The place is in a right state.'

I can't help myself, and it's all my own fault. Kieran says I wind her up on purpose, and he's right, but she always gets my back up, that woman, and I behave not like myself.

'No, not sick, Nora, hung-over.' I smile sweetly, although I've not had a drink since the day of Kate's Communion, not even last night when I was in such distress.

She just purses her lips and wrinkles her nose like someone had shoved a smelly sock under it, and glares. I give in and take Kate's jumper and the local magazine off the chair myself so she can sit down.

'Will you have a cuppa?' I ask cheerfully.

She glances around again, the look expressing her fear at contracting typhoid by consuming anything in my filthy kitchen. Her own house is spotless, and like a shrine to her kids. Photos everywhere, every cup they ever won, every certificate, every medal. Placed there to make the girls' husbands and me aware of how blessed we are to have had marriage to a Munroe bestowed upon our unworthy heads.

'No. I'd better not...' she says. The unspoken ending to the sentence is, 'for fear of my life.'

'So, Nora,' I say, using my best placating guard voice, reserved for confused drunks and people who are all worked up over something, 'what can I do for you? If you're looking for Kieran, I'm afraid he's at work, but I can ask him to call.'

'It's you I came to see, Mags.' Her voice is like a hot blade through butter.

I brace myself but say patiently, 'Well, here I am.'

'Look, I might as well get straight to the point. I'm very worried about my son.'

'Why, what's wrong with him?' I feel a shock of alarm, and my heart races with panic. Is there something awful the matter with Kieran, some fatal illness he hasn't told me about and that's why he's been going around all quiet and slightly unhappy looking? And that is why Nora is here, because he won't tell me himself?

'What's *wrong* with him?' Nora looks astonished that I would even ask. 'I'll tell you what's wrong with him! A man should be a king in his own castle, and he feels he's being treated as a bread earner and nothing more. He's out there in all weather, slaving away, working his fingers to the bone, and when he gets home, it's to this.' She waves her hand around with an expression of disgust. 'He's a wonderful husband and father, and he deserves a woman who looks after him properly. He works so hard for you!'

I'm gripping the edge of the worktop, shaking. I'm so, so glad my darling husband isn't ill, but now that I've recovered from that shock, my distressed mind has already raced to another awful possibility. Is Kieran really unhappy with me? Has he really complained to his mother about me, and the hours I work, and the sloppy housekeeping? He's been on edge lately and not like himself, but he surely would never talk about our marriage with anyone, let alone Nora?

I say in a trembling voice, 'I work hard too, Nora, and I was just about to clean up the house –'

She cuts across me again. 'Work hard? Sitting on your – I'm just going to say it, Mags – ever-expanding bottom, down in the station issuing dog licences? *My son* is the main breadwinner of this family, as you well know, and for him to have to put up with living in this, this...*squalor*. And on top of that' – she pauses and eyes me, her gimlet eye glinting like a baddie in a film, taking in the hoodie and elastic-waisted PJs that do a poor job of hiding my curves – 'having to put up with a wife who has clearly let herself go.'

Oh God. It's just what Sharon has been warning me about. I wish I was all toned and tanned and skinny, though Kieran says he doesn't find that attractive. And to be fair, he always likes actresses with 'a bit of meat on their bones', as he says, but still.

I felt I'd won the jackpot when Kieran asked me to marry him. He was so good-looking and hunky. After we married it was all setting up house and him starting his business and me progressing to sergeant, then trying for kids, then briefly worrying about not having kids, then having kids and all that entailed, and then me getting *my* career back on track... When I finally looked up again, I was in my forties with crow's feet, stretch marks and grey roots.

'I think it's better you leave now, Nora...' I whisper, my voice barely audible.

She bridles, like I've roared at her to get out. 'This is not your house, Mags, it's my son's house. I put the deposit on it for *him*, not you, so I most certainly will not leave!'

'Nora, *please* leave!' This time I do sort of shout at her, because it's that or burst into tears.

Ellie and Kate arrive at the kitchen door, drawn by the sound of raised voices, their faces pale. Seeing them, Nora pretends to look all sad, picks up her bag and walks out of the house, passing them, saying nothing.

I just wait, my hand on the worktop, the blood pounding in my ears. I'm trying really hard not to cry. I refuse to believe Kieran has gone to his mother about me, saying I've let myself go. But it's horrible; it's like she's planted this poisonous seed in my brain and it's already sprouting. I have to get rid of it, pluck it out by the roots...

Kate runs to me, tears in her eyes as well. Silently I put my arm around her. I beckon Ellie over, but she shakes her head.

'What, Ellie?' I say, trying to get my voice back to normal. 'Look, you know Nana can be a bit of a dragon, but she loves us all.' I make a funny face, and Kate giggles. 'She'll calm down soon.'

'You shouldn't have shouted at her. She's Dad's mammy.'

'I know that, but I was upset.' I try to keep the hurt out of my voice. I can't bear it if Ellie takes her side. 'She was very rude to me.'

'She just said the place was a mess.' My daughter looks straight at me; clearly, she was listening. 'And it is – she's right.'

'Ellie!' Now I really am going to cry. I swallow like mad. 'That's not fair. We all live here, we all mess it...'

'Jess's house is never like ours – it's always tidy. And her mam works too. And Dad is tired all the time and fed up, and you're never here, or if you are, you're reading, and it's just crap for us. Nana was just trying to make you see.'

I can't believe this. First, my husband betrays me, and now my darling daughter is turning on me.

'Ellie, stop being mean!' Kate shouts, and as she does, Jess's mother, the saintly Holly who keeps her house so clean even though she works two whole mornings a week for Violetta in the local florist's, beeps her horn outside. Ellie grabs her bag; it looks heavy.

'Let me carry that out to the car for you...' I start to say.

But she screams, 'No! I'll carry it myself!' and runs out and slams the front door. The second dramatic departure in as many minutes.

Kate hugs me hard, and I bury my face in her silky hair and breathe, and then I tell her everything is OK and it must be a full moon, and we laugh. Then my little nine-year-old champion helps me finish loading the dishwasher and even offers to cancel her play date with her cousin so she can stay and look after me, but I roll my eyes and tell her I'm made of sterner stuff.

An hour later, Orla pulls up in her car. As Kate leaves, she hugs me again. 'Ellie didn't mean it, Mam. Some girl in school is picking on her, and she's being mean to us because she's upset about it. She made me promise not to say anything, but that's why she was so horrible.'

My sweet girl is so loyal to her sister. I can see how hard it is for her to tell me this, and I hug her back gratefully. 'It's OK, love. I'll sort everything out, OK? I promise. Just you go on over to Auntie Orla's and have a nice time, and she'll drop you home later, OK?'

'Are you sure?' Kate looks so torn, my heart breaks for her.

'Of course I'm sure. Go on – it'll all be fine.'

She goes to the door and picks up her Harry Potter bag, with her beloved Beanie Boo teddies hanging off it. 'You and Daddy won't get a divorce, will you?' I see the tears brim in her eyes again.

'Ah, Kate, will you stop?' I smile and gather her in my arms again and then go down on my hunkers so I'm eye level. 'Listen to me, Kate Munroe. Me and Dad are fine. We love each other very much, and we love you girls too.'

She swallows and whispers, 'Nana Nora is a mean old bully.'

I smile and sigh and opt for honesty over a transparent lie. 'I don't like Nana Nora much right now either, pet, but she's Daddy's mam so we're kinda stuck with her. We'll have to manage her somehow. Don't worry, everything will work out.'

'I love you, Mammy,' she whispers.

'I love you too, pet. Now go on off and have a great day playing with Evie. See you later.'

I wave to Kieran's sister from the front door, and I wonder what she'd think if she knew what just happened between me and her mother. Orla seems close to Nora, but it's hard to tell how close because she's deep. The best in the world honestly. If you need a favour, she'll be there in a heartbeat, and she's really lovely to the girls and everything. But even after a glass or two of wine, she never lets the guard down. She's blonde and slim, with straight white teeth and a genuine smile. I like her. I do. She's married to Fergus, who's 'high up in the bank', and they have a boy and a girl, Evie and Tom. And they have a lovely, clean house and a flawless marriage.

She waves back and calls, 'See you later! I just met Deirdre, and they have Irish dancing from five to seven this week. She's texting everyone later. And I promised Evie they could watch *Frozen* and get a pizza afterwards.'

'Thanks, Orla!'

She drives off in her BMW people carrier and with her perfect highlights, and I feel a stab of envy as I smile and wave after her.

As I shut the door, my phone pings. A message from Gearoid. Of all the Munroe family, I get on best with him. He was only twelve when Kieran and I started going out, the youngest of all of them and cheeky with it. He's doing a PhD in music but still lives at home because accommodation in Galway is ridiculous, as expensive as Dublin. He loves his mother but is under no illusions about her. What nobody knows, not even Kieran, is that Gearoid is gay and has a boyfriend in Galway. I only know because this poor chap was beaten up one night and the case came up on a day I was giving evidence about something else. Gearoid was there because the victim of the assault was his fella, and I spotted him but said nothing. Later that week he met me for lunch and told me, but asked me not to say. Seems mad to me in this day and age. Like, Kieran wouldn't care, and neither would the rest of them, I'd say – well, the mother would pass out and the father would say nothing as usual – but he just doesn't want the drama. Fair enough. It's his business. Because of my job, there are lots of things I don't tell Kieran, so I'm grand with it. It's not my business or my story to tell. But since then, me and Gearoid are kind of allies.

I read the text.

Don't mind her. I know whatever happened, it can't be your fault because you're fab and she's like a cut cat this week for some reason. Gerry messed up the highlights, is my guess. x

I smile. Nora must have told him what happened, only very much from her point of view. Nora's highlights, as she calls the battle against the grey, are the bane of Gerry's life, I'd say. She's been going to him for years, but she always complains to anyone who'll listen.

Thanks. xxx, I text back. At least I have Gearoid on my side.

And there's that horrible seed, throwing out another poisonous shoot: *Is Kieran on my side?*

Of course he is. I don't believe for a moment my husband ever complained about me to his mother. He's a typical Irish fella, he loves his Mam but never tells her anything. So much so that I'd often say something in conversation with her and she'd have no clue and I'd have assumed Kieran had told her. He calls to her once a week, for a cup of tea and she fusses over him and runs him through all the latest illnesses of the inhabitants of Ballycarrick, from the terminal, through chronic, to major but treatable, and finally minor. He listens with half an ear, I've seen him actually scrolling on his phone as she rambles on, and then he finishes his tea and leaves until next week. Like, he fixes things around the house for his parents, or is on hand for any jobs or help they need, but the idea of him sitting at the kitchen table pouring his heart out about the state of our marriage just doesn't ring true.

The place is tidy enough now, so I shower. I don't know where I'll go but I need to talk to someone about ordinary things. There's nothing I can do about Blade's murder until the forensic reports are in, and even then I don't know if Galway will want me involved. I decide to give Sharon a call and she says she'll meet me in town for an early lunch.

After I've dried myself off, I pull on the new jeans my mother gave me back in March. I've been afraid to try them on because they look so small, but it turns out they are magic. They have some kind of webbing stuff that goes around the worst of the flab, sucking me in and rounding me off. I even dare risk a tucked-in shirt, another present from Mam that came extra in a delivery last week. It's silk and a lovely emerald green, and she's always said that colour is lovely on me.

I refuse to let myself go.

CHAPTER 11

'Wow, you look nice!' Sharon seems genuinely surprised when I pull up behind her on Main Street and get out of my car to meet her on the pavement. 'You're wearing make-up! And I like those black boots.'

It feels like a bit of a back-handed compliment, like up to now I've been only fit to frighten the horses. I say, 'Thanks, Shar. Where do you want to eat? Teresa's Bakery?' Teresa has a little sit-down part out back where you can get coffee and amazing sausage rolls, pies and cakes.

'I'm on keto,' Sharon says in the same tone you might use to suggest you were about to have a root canal with a rusty nail.

Teresa's café is the downfall of every diet in Ballycarrick. Elaine from the slimming club even calls it the Pit of Despair, which tells you how bad it is. The aroma of baking, coffee, that heady combination of sugar and fat combined into mouthwatering confection, will test even the most determined dieter.

'How about the Samovar then? Tatiana's very helpful with the menu. If you ask, she'll do you a plain salad without the chips or the mash, and she won't even force a single baked potato on you or insist you have crisps.'

Tatiana, being Russian, thinks we are all a bunch of overindulged, soft-as-butter, hopeless cases. She wears t-shirts in five degrees and had to be convinced that nobody would come to her pub in the winter if she didn't turn the heat on. I suppose after Vladivostok, Ballycarrick must seem tropical.

'The Samovar it is.' She locks her car and we head for the pub.

Sharon and I have been friends since third class. She stood up for me when Sister Consuela wanted to lock me in the cupboard because Mam bought my copybooks in town and not from the nun who had a side hustle going on selling the exact same copybooks with a huge markup. Sharon stood in front of the cupboard and said she would report Sister Consuela to the bishop. It was a running joke between us that the long arm of the law was one thing but the bishop was on a whole other level. A childhood in an Irish primary school can cement a friendship in a way few other institutions can. We were inseparable through secondary too. Sharon was the first person I told when I got my first period, first kiss, first drink, first everything really.

'And they have wine,' I say with a grin.

'It's not even midday! Do you think I'm some kind of an alco?' she asks, mock horrified.

'Err...' I nudge her as we enter the pub.

It's early yet, and apart from the few my mam calls the 'God Help Us', the dedicated drinkers of the parish – including Frank Mooney, who gives me a cheery wave – the place is deserted. Tatiana is crouched behind the counter, busy stocking shelves.

'Hi, Tatiana,' calls Sharon to the top of the Russian woman's head. 'Can we get two coffees please? Americanos. And the menu.'

'No problem.' Tatiana rises magnificently into a standing position. 'I'll bring the coffees down to you.' A minute later, she delivers them with two of these tiny biscuits that taste of cinnamon in little plastic wrappings.

'Take my biscuit away, Tatiana. I'll savage it if it's there.' Sharon is nothing if not dramatic. Her weight is a source of constant struggle – well, it is for everyone really, but Sharon is one for extreme diets. At one stage she was only eating spuds, literally nothing else, but that was just insane, and now she has swung completely the other way and won't touch a potato to save her life.

'So wait till I tell you,' she begins as she absentmindedly unwraps my biscuit and then swallows it whole. I know where this is going. 'He's only after putting my house on the market.' She pauses for effect.

I take a moment to get my head around things. It's very hard to go from worrying about a murder to worrying about property prices. I had wanted something to distract me from Blades, and Sharon certainly doesn't seem to be interested in his murder even though it took place only a few miles away. Still, I wish the distraction didn't have to be about Danny.

And here we go again. Don't get me wrong, I can see why she's hurt, but the house she's on about isn't even half her house any more, he bought her out in the divorce, and she got a lump sum as a deposit for her own place, which is lovely. So, her mentally clinging to Danny's house, incidentally built on his mother's land and with his sisters living all around, is really bad for her state of mind. But pointing this out right now would serve no purpose whatsoever, because that's not really what this is about. So I wait.

'He rang to tell me…as a *courtesy*.' Her voice quivers at this bit. 'He doesn't know the meaning of the word! But anyway, apparently that little trollop feels like the house is too much to my taste and so they're moving to – wait for this – Castlepark!' Castlepark is a nice, ordinary housing estate behind the primary school. 'I mean, *Castlepark*!' she repeats.

Clearly in my puzzlement, I've failed to look outraged enough. I roll my eyes and groan. OK, that will do, and she's off again.

'No wonder my house is too much for her, and she coming out of that poky place in the terrace. But you'd think she'd be like the cat that got the cream in my architecturally designed home, the granite work-tops, the bespoke island, the Lloyd Loom patio furniture, that mirror – remember the one I got shipped in from Paris? And she's turning her little tinker nose up at my house? The cheek of her.'

'Ah, well,' I say soothingly, 'you've got your own lovely place now, and you and Sean are happy out, so let him off – he's not worth it.

You're so much better off without him in your life, and you know it.' This is my mantra with Shar since Danny left her for 'Chloe from the chipper', as she will forever be known.

Sharon makes a brief effort to agree with me. 'I know that, and she's welcome to him...' But then she slips back into misery and hurt pride again. 'But how could anyone in their right mind want to leave my house, decorated with such taste and class, detached on its own grounds, for a house in an estate? I don't understand it, Mags. I mean, I know she has no class – she took Danny after all – but still... And you know what he was wearing last Friday? He was taking Sean out for his tea, which means no nutrition whatsoever, only greasy pizza and chips, but he was wearing that grey Tommy Hilfiger jumper, the one that's too long in the arms and makes him look ridiculous.'

Sharon loves interior magazines and always notices if someone has a designer purse or handbag, things about which I haven't a clue. But this endless grief isn't about the house, or the clothes. It is about the hurt and humiliation Danny makes her endure in a small town, where a bit of juicy gossip goes a long way. The truth is, she still adores Danny, eejit as he is, and she misses him so much, but she can't admit that on top of the humiliation, so she rants about Chloe and houses and clothes instead.

I need her to find a way out of this, even if it's hard, and what kind of a rubbish friend doesn't have the hard conversation? I read somewhere once that how successful a person is can be judged by the number of awkward conversations they're willing to have. But it's her success I'm after, not mine.

'Sharon, listen to me. I mean really listen now.' I fix her with a firm gaze. 'You need to get over this. I know it's awful, but you need to admit to yourself that you're not upset over the house or the holiday or the fact that he was late picking Sean up, but that you're hurt by him leaving. That you loved him, and he betrayed you and embarrassed you in front of the whole place – that's where this is coming from. But you can't begin to get over it or feel better until you see this for what it really is.'

'Ah, for God's sake, Mags, don't start psychobabbling me now, you of all people. I just think –'

I interrupt her. I'm not letting it go again. She has to at least begin to move on. 'You're my best friend since we were nine, so I have to tell you – you're not doing you or Sean any good by dwelling on this, living your life through Danny's, going mad over every stupid thing he wears or place he goes. What he did to you was rotten, and he was in the wrong, but he was always and ever that way. He's just a cheat, and you're better off without him, but it hurts and that's all there is to it.'

She gulps her coffee with tears in her eyes. 'Don't start all that again, Mags. I know you think you're helping by telling me he was unfaithful, but you're not. It's so not like him, this behaviour. She is such a little trollop. If she hadn't tricked him… He never looked at anyone before, I told you – it's just everyone in this town loves spreading rumours. You know what I heard them laughing about in the post office this morning?'

Again I wait, feeling so sad for her, the way she refuses to see him as he is and thinks if only Chloe takes her hooks out of him, all will be well.

'That old one behind the counter was telling Mrs Burke that Judy O'Halloran's new baby is the spitting image of Danny! How mad is that? They shut up as soon as they saw me standing there. They were mortified to be caught talking total rubbish.'

Judy O'Halloran is the PE teacher in the local school, and I've personally seen her and Danny out driving together, even after Chloe. I don't say anything, but the look I have on my face must be enough to let Sharon know what I really think, because she goes white, stands up and grabs her bag. 'It's not true!' she hisses, even though I've said nothing. And then she storms out, and we haven't even ordered yet.

I gather my things, pay for the coffees, and follow her, feeling sick. I've made a mistake. I should have said, 'No, no, it couldn't be Danny's,' but the fact is, it could. Poor, poor Sharon.

CHAPTER 12

By the time I get out into the street, Sharon has already driven off. I climb into my car and navigate out into the Saturday lunchtime traffic.

All the way back home, I debate calling to Holly's, even though Ellie is staying there overnight. I just want to make sure my girl is all right. I know my daughter, and she'll be all upset now, having fought with me. She hates falling out with anyone. I think about what Kate said, that some girl is picking on her at school.

Why? I wonder. Not that bullies need a reason; it's just how they are. They get it from home, either from being bullied themselves or watching the people around them bully others. But why didn't Ellie tell me?

Holly and James live in the new *development* on the way out of Ballycarrick towards Galway. The development, which Sharon has advised me must under no circumstances be called a housing estate like Castlepark, is a collection of architecturally designed customised family homes, each with its own character and flair. Or so the massive billboard outside it says anyway.

In fact, they are all more or less identical, inside and outside. They're huge, with white masonry and grey windows that form right angles on the front and gables. That's all the go nowadays apparently. Any eejit can put a window in the middle of a wall, but ones that wrap around a corner, now that's really showing the world you're something special. I grin.

Inside they're decorated in whites and creams, marble islands the size of snooker tables in the middle of the kitchens, huge range cookers that are never used.

I swing in the large marble driveway, complete with electric gates, thankfully open, and pillars with eagles on top, the works. Ellie might be furious at me for checking up on her, but hopefully she won't be. I'm not sure how much more rejection I can take today, but I need to check that my girl is alright.

James answers the door. He's an accountant and works for one of the big multinationals in Shannon. He's seemed nice the few times we've met. He's also very good-looking; geek-chic, Sharon tells me it's called. He's too small for me. His hair is cut in a style, rather than just cut short like most men, and he wears heavy-rimmed square glasses.

'Mags, hi. Is everything alright?' His brow furrows. 'I thought Ellie was staying the night?'

I smile. 'She is, thanks for having her. But I just wondered if I could see her for a sec?' I keep my voice light.

He gives me the slightest of quizzical looks, but I don't elaborate – it's a guard trick.

I can see straight through an enormous porthole window in the back wall of the gigantic reception area, a window large enough for a grown man to step through, and they are doing a barbeque out in the perfectly landscaped garden. There's a spotlessly white Maltese terrier and an elaborate swing set, and standing at the fanciest of the Weber barbeques is Jess's mother, Holly. She looks amazing in cut-off denim shorts and a white top, her tanned and toned body perfect. Behind her, Jess and another school friend, Sarah, are bouncing on a trampoline. I can't see Ellie, but no wonder she loves it here; the whole family looks like something from a magazine.

'Sure, I'll just get her,' says James, disappearing into the interior.

Moments later Ellie appears alone, looking terrified. 'What happened?' she asks, her face pale.

'Nothing,' I reassure her, 'nothing at all. I just wanted to swing by to make sure you were OK.'

She looks puzzled for a minute. So much for me worrying that she was mithering over our fight.

'After this morning?' I prompt.

Her blue eyes fill with tears. 'Oh, oh, I...I'm sorry, Mam, I didn't mean...'

'I know, pet, and I shouldn't have shouted at Nana.' I draw her in for a hug and kiss her dark curls.

'You're right, though, she can be horrible,' Ellie whispers. 'She was saying something mean about you last week and Daddy heard her, and he went mad at her.'

'What? When?' I ask, my heart lifting.

'Oh, we were with Daddy last week – he picked us up from gymnastics – and he called in to Nana on the way home to fix the leaking tap in the downstairs bathroom. Kate and me were in the kitchen, and Nana said to Grandad that Daddy looked tired and it was probably from eating frozen food and living in a dirty house. And Daddy heard her and came in and told us to go out to the car, but we had the window down and we could hear him telling her that you worked really hard and that you earned more money than he did and that you were a brilliant mother and a brilliant wife and that if she was going to ever say another bad word about you, she could find someone else to fix her taps. And then he just walked out.'

A rush of love for my big, kind husband floods through me, mixed with guilt that I'd let Nora's poison seed take root at all. Of course he would never have discussed me with his mother. 'He's a good one, your dad.' I give her a squeeze and hold her back from me. I look into her lovely face and wipe her eyes with my thumbs. 'Now, get back to your buddies and I'll see you tomorrow.'

She hesitates for a split second.

'Is everything alright, Els?' I ask. I desperately want to ask her about this girl who is picking on her, but I don't want to betray Kate, and also I know Ellie will just clam up and deny anything is wrong because that's the way she is. I'll just have to keep watch and try to be there for her when she feels ready to tell me. At least she has Jess and Sarah, and they're very popular girls so they must afford her some kind of protection.

The tears threaten again, but she blinks them away. 'Fine, see you tomorrow,' she says, and turns and runs back to the Perfect Home catalogue scene.

Back in the car, I text Kieran.

I'm sorry for being a bit of a wagon lately – you don't deserve it. If you're home in time, will we go out for our tea? Ellie staying with Jess, and Kate at Orla's till late. Love you xxx

Not exactly a romantic night in, but it's something.

I wait. One blue tick. Two. He's read it. Then the three dots. He's replying.

You're not a wagon. You're lovely. Gearoid rang me. Don't mind my mother, Mags, she's like a briar these days. We'll stay out of her way for a while. Yeah, let's go out.

I'm about to reply when there is another text from him.

I love you too and always will. You are the best person I know. xxx

And then:

I hope you're not unhappy. I know you lie awake half the night, and I'm sorry I laugh at you worrying. I'm just not sure what to say. I wish I was better at helping. xxx

My heart breaks. Has Kieran been worrying about me being unhappy, and is that what's making him unhappy?

But I'm not unhappy. I'm just... Menopausal. And I need to tell him.

CHAPTER 13

*A*t nine o'clock on Monday morning, I'm experiencing a jumble of thoughts and emotions as I drive along the quays in Galway on my way to a top-level meeting in Garda Western Region HQ about the murder of Blades Carmody.

First and foremost, I want whoever murdered Blades to be brought to justice. He might have been one of those annoying, revolving-door types, constantly in and out of prison for lifting stuff off building sites – in fact he was the kind who'd leave poor Kieran tearing his hair out, that's true – but he didn't deserve what happened to him. I get the feeling – and maybe I'm wrong about this – that my colleagues would be more concerned about his murder if he wasn't a Traveller. I mentally prepare to fight the battle, and as I say, maybe I'm wronging them. They're not all like Duckie; that much is true thankfully.

Poor old Blades. I keep seeing him in my mind, in a pool of his own blood, his lovely new jacket destroyed. And Natasha so distraught. He would have liked to have been seen as a major crime figure – that would have suited his ego – but that just wasn't the case. He wasn't involved with the drugs trade or sex trafficking or any of the deeply horrible stuff that the Dublin gangs get involved in. He was just a Traveller kid with a big attitude that hid all kinds of inferiority complexes and insecurities.

I'd suspected all along there was something odd about Natasha buying that jacket, and now it's clear she was secretly going out with Blades Carmody. There's no way that relationship would have been sanctioned by her family.

Not that I think that is anything to do with Blades getting shot. Dacie McGovern would never allow a murder, not in a million years. He might have got a warning if they found out about it, and a bit of a hiding isn't beyond them either, to be fair, but they'd never go beyond that. The young lad Natasha is officially intended for, Joseph Ward, would never do such a thing either, it would seem. Delia has explained to me that the Wards are just like the McGoverns – except they're ruled by the grandfather, and keep their heads down around the law and get on with their business as best they can. So they're not behind this, that's for sure. I wish I'd had a chance to see inside the car that was chasing Blades, but the windows were tinted.

Natasha had nothing useful to tell the guards about the shooting. I heard from Delia this morning that they came to the hospital to interview her after the attack; they'd kept her in overnight as she was so shaken. The detectives who spoke to her made her go over and over what happened until she was nearly hysterical. They seemed to think she wasn't telling them the full truth, but according to Delia, Natasha is as much in the dark about what happened as everyone else. All she knows is that Blades was teaching her how to drive his sulky on a quiet back road when suddenly he jumped up beside her, grabbed the reins, yelled at her to hold tight, cracked the whip and took off like a bullet. She didn't even see the Mercedes properly until it caught up with them. She doesn't know anyone he's associated with apart from his own family, but that doesn't surprise me. Traveller men tend to not share things with their wives, let alone girlfriends; it's just not the way things are done.

Natasha is back home now, and Delia is keeping an eye on her. Darren, our new community guard, is parked most of each day outside the site, watching out for an unknown black Mercedes or anything else unusual. I can tell Delia really appreciates Darren's support; she gave him one of her very rare smiles when he offered to do it as I was divvying up the various jobs to do with the investigation.

We've gathered as much evidence as there is available, I think. We spoke to the Carmodys, the McGoverns and a few other stragglers around who would be on the shady side, but nobody had a clue and I believe them. I wish I had more, but we got as much out of the Travellers as anyone could, certainly more than if the detectives had arrived from Galway.

As I get nearer to Galway Garda station, my heart sinks a bit. This is the first time I've been here since they turned me down for detective sergeant, and the guys who interviewed me are likely to be at the meeting today. And much worse, Duckie is going to be there as well, wearing his DS civvies while I'm still in uniform. I groan. But I have to be at this meeting. Detective Inspector Ronan Brady, who is leading the investigation, asked me to come, as I'm a witness and I've done all the preliminary investigations and interviews. I'm just feeling a bit insecure, and I imagine they'll all be sharing glances when I talk about the investigation so far.

I heard Duckie told some of the other lads that I thought I was like your man in America, the horse whisperer... What's his name? Monty Roberts, was it? Only that I think I'm a Traveller whisperer. I don't care. If he would only realise you don't need to be an anything whisperer, you just need to treat people as individuals and with a bit of courtesy and respect and not assume the worst before you know anything.

Knowing I'm in the right doesn't make walking in there and presenting to them less daunting, though.

Stop worrying about your own feelings, I tell myself. *The important thing is to find out who killed Blades Carmody.*

There's a barrier for the Garda station car park, but I don't have a fob. I drive up to the barrier and press the buzzer.

'Hello?' says a male voice.

'Hi, I am... I've a meeting here today... Well, I've been asked by

Detective Inspector Brady...' Oh God, I sound like a total rookie. 'I don't have a fob. Can you let me in, please?'

'Name?'

'Sergeant Mags Munroe.'

'One moment, Sergeant, you're expected.'

He clicks off and the barrier lifts. I find a space and park.

Inside, I approach the desk. There's no receptionist in sight, but a young woman in uniform appears.

'Sergeant Mags Munroe to see DI Brady, please.'

'Certainly, Sergeant, one moment. Have a seat.'

I cross the enormous white and glass foyer of the station. While I'm waiting, my skin starts to itch and I scratch at my thighs through my uniform trousers. I've started on HRT, but it's only been two days and it's not doing anything yet; it will take a couple of weeks to feel the effects apparently. Meanwhile, I'm still itchy and irritable, I've been awake half the night again, and this morning I even had a hot flush.

There's a fella on the TV, a famous architect, who does up people's houses, and all he ever seems to do is stick huge glass boxes onto the sides of perfectly ordinary bungalows. Generally I think, they look ridiculous, but what do I know? All right if you live in Australia or California, but all that glass, like this place, with huge high ceilings, must be a nightmare to heat in the winter. One whole wall of the station foyer is taken up with an art installation, suspended by rope wire. It's a huge thing, ten feet square, and it looks like a patchwork quilt made of glass, different colours and shapes, all abstract. It's lovely.

A door opens and Ronan Brady appears. I'm pleased to see him because I've always liked him. He's a bit serious, but you can't blame him for that. His wife died of breast cancer four or five years ago – she was only forty-two – and he's been heartbroken ever since, the poor man. I met her a few times; she was lovely. The day of her funeral, he was not stoic as everyone expected him to be. He was distraught. Honestly, wild-eyed and almost deranged with grief, he was, and though someone had done their best to dress him in a dark suit, he looked dishevelled. I won't ever forget him that day. We all stood helplessly, watching his heart break in front of our eyes as the coffin was lowered down into the dark hole.

I remember saying to Kieran in the car on the way home that maybe the whole box into the grave thing was too brutal, and wondered if people are better off without that bit, but he disagreed. He thought people needed to see it, to actually watch it happen, that it was part of the process of accepting that the person was gone. I don't know. Maybe he's right. But that day, Ronan Brady was as close to falling into the grave on top of her as I'd ever seen. They had no children either, so it was just him on his own. He has a brother, I think, who came home from Australia for the funeral, and an elderly mother, but he looked so lost that day, poor man. It was this time of year too, summertime.

'Mags, welcome,' he says, shaking my hand. 'Some detectives just arrived from Dublin, so we'll get cracking in the next few minutes. Can I get you a coffee?'

'Ah, no, I'm grand, thanks,' I manage, trying to sound breezy. So Dublin are taking an interest in Blades Carmody's murder. That's good, but I'm a bit intimidated.

I follow him through several security doors – he taps the fob hanging on a lanyard around his neck at each one – until we reach the lift. He calls it and gestures that I should enter before him into the small space. The door closes and we're alone in the lift.

As he punches the button for the third floor, I find myself looking at him in the lift mirror. He's carrying a file of notes. He's wearing a navy suit with a slight pinstripe, a pale-blue shirt and dark-green tie, and his dark curly hair is oiled back from his forehead. He looks so smart, I'm beginning to wonder if he has a new woman in his life, when he meets my eyes in the mirror and smiles. I feel awkward at being caught looking, and then the worst possible thing happens – another hot flush. And I know I'm going to go red, beginning from under my collar, then rising up my neck into my cheeks. I'm going to look like a teenager with a crush. Hot flushes really are evil; you look mortified to begin with, then you get mortified at everyone noticing, and so you're hot and embarrassed at the same time.

Before it gets too bad, I'm saved by a loud *ping* and the doors open onto a very long, brightly lit corridor. I lag behind, waiting for my flush to subside, before catching up with Ronan and following him through a large pair of oak double doors. Inside, there is a long table that could easily seat twenty people, like you'd see in boardrooms on TV, I was never in an actual boardroom before. There is a huge screen at the top. A few people are already gathered, one being Duckie, who has dressed for the occasion in the 'uniform' the younger detectives always wear, jeans and a dark, nondescript hoodie. I'm childishly delighted at how ridiculous he looks and can't help glancing at Ronan with a grin.

'Mutton dressed as lamb', as my mother would say.

Ronan grins back at me. 'Don't let him rise you,' he murmurs in my ear before he walks to the top of the room, and I take a seat at the table, feeling pleased that Ronan Brady understands the situation with Duckie and is on my side.

Duckie is engrossed on his phone so hasn't seen me yet. Seconds later he looks up. 'Ah, Mags, 'tis yourself,' he says, mock effusive. 'Taking a break from dog licences and noisy neighbours? No harm too, that would drive you daft. I don't know how you stick it.'

He was doing the exact same job himself up until last month, but to hear him, you'd swear he was high-ranking Interpol. I take Ronan's advice and don't let him get under my skin. If I do, he wins.

The other men at the table look at me then, and one of them is part of the panel that interviewed me. I realise I'm the only woman in the room, and also the only guard in uniform, and it feels like my first day at school. Then the man from the panel says, 'Sergeant Munroe, it's great to have you here,' and the door opens again and two out of the three people who enter are women, and I begin to feel less like the odd one out. I pull out my notepad and prepare to take notes.

After everyone is seated, Ronan addresses the meeting. 'Thanks for coming, everyone. Before we go any further, I know there are some new faces here, so I'll quickly introduce everyone. I'm Detective

Inspector Ronan Brady, and I'm leading the investigation. Here on my left is Detective Sergeant Donal Cassidy, beside him is Detective Garda Tony Mullins and Detective Garda Fiachra Dillon, all attached to my team. On my right, we have Inspector Martin Mulcahy from the Criminal Assets Bureau. Below Martin is DI Julie Deane and her colleagues from Harcourt Street in Dublin, DS Hazel O'Flynn and Detective Garda Tom Butler. And there at the end is Sergeant Mags Munroe of Ballycarrick. I've specifically invited Mags to this investigation because of the huge work she's done in community policing over a long many years and in particular because she knows the Carmody family. That, and the fact that she was first on the scene. So that's everyone.'

He looks down at his notes. 'Now, the story so far is that a Traveller called Bernard Carmody, who goes by the nickname "Blades"' – Ronan allows himself a small smile and there is a titter in the room, which bothers me a bit even though I've been as bad as any of them about his name in the past – 'was shot and killed while driving a sulky up the dual carriageway. Bernard was not long out of prison, and he had a girl with him, Natasha McGovern, another Traveller.'

With a quick look at the Dublin detectives, Ronan continues. 'While this is of course first and foremost a murder investigation, I know our CAB and Dublin colleagues are most interested to investigate the possibility of a link between Carmody and Dublin drug gang boss Alan Keogh. Keogh's nephew Barry Keogh was a fellow inmate of Carmody in prison, so they might have set something up while they were incarcerated together.

'This is supposition for now, but it looks like Carmody may have run off with some cash, because this shooting has every sign of a professional gangland hit. Forensics examined the sulky and Carmody's body, and also checked Natasha McGovern's clothes while she was in the hospital overnight, but no traces of class A drugs or large sums of money were found. So whatever reason the gang was after Carmody, it wasn't anything to do with what he had on him at the time.'

Ronan pauses again, and the CAB inspector says quietly, 'We have an extensive file on Keogh. We won't circulate it, but any queries pertaining to the investigation, direct them to me and we can assist.'

The CAB are notoriously secretive. Since their inception in 1996, after a journalist was gunned down on the orders of a gang boss, they've been very successful in depriving gang leaders of the proceeds of their crimes. It is becoming increasingly difficult to launder money in Ireland, and they are by far the biggest thorn in the side of organised crime in the state.

DI Julie Deane from the Harcourt Street team nods. 'Good, and we can run computer analysis in Dublin, mobile phone data, phone mast information, anything else technical that can track Alan and Barry Keogh's movements in the days leading up to and subsequent to the killing of Carmody. The more information we can find to link the Keogh crime family and the Carmody crime family, the better it will be.'

I'm listening closely and beginning to wonder if maybe the detectives from Dublin are barking up the wrong tree here. I know all about the Keoghs; everyone does. They're a huge Dublin crime family up to their elbows in drug running, heroin and crack cocaine. They're absolutely infamous in Ireland, and Dublin is always trying to get them one way or another.

Chunkie Keogh, Alan's older brother and a real flash Harry, lives mostly on the Costa del Sol. The Spanish authorities provide a safe haven for Irish criminal types; they're known for not really caring who lives in their country so long as they are kept out of it. The introduction of international arrest warrants in 2006 has made them buck their ideas up a bit, but still, it isn't ideal. The Costa del Crime is very much on the Irish force's radar.

Meanwhile, Chunkie runs the entire Keogh operation from there and is universally feared. He has links to all the main drug gangs of the world and really fancies himself as the next Al Capone. He is a stocky man, dripping in heavy gold bracelets and medallions, theatrically short, and a painful death is meted out to anyone who remarks upon his small stature. He has greased-back mousey-brown hair, and in pictures he is much more hirsute now than ten years ago, so he probably went to Turkey for hair plugs. That's what they all do these days, even ordinary fellas. Apparently, the flight from Izmir to Dublin goes out with a load of baldies and comes back with a planeful of Irish lads looking like those Troll Dolls that Kate used to love when she was small.

I'd never let Kieran do that, even if he did go bald. And he wouldn't want to; he's just not that vain.

Alan Keogh is the younger brother, who keeps an eye on things here in Ireland. He's very different from Chunkie. Although he's probably had a lot of 'work done', as they say in celebrity circles, he's genuinely handsome. He's in his thirties, and looks a bit like Daniel Craig – you know, the lad who plays James Bond? A bit like him anyway. He frequently features in Gerry the hairdresser's extensive magazine library at the races or at fancy events in Dublin. He makes sure to keep his nose clean. CAB watch him like a hawk, but he's slippery and clever.

He likes the fine things in life, yachts, champagne, fancy restaurants and that sort of thing, where Chunkie is a low life and wouldn't know an hors d'oeuvre from a bag of chips. Alan Keogh always looks relaxed and charming, sunning himself in Saint-Tropez or at Cheltenham races backing a winner, and is never seen not dressed to the nines. He has a thing about handmade suits and Italian shoes. He's just taken over the Dublin operations of the family after the elder Keogh was shot in Belgium last year. Interpol is dealing with it; it was a million-euro heroin deal gone bad. So, you know, not nice people.

I can see why Dublin and CAB are desperate to find a link between anyone and the Keoghs, a thread on which they can pull to bring the whole thing down.

But it's hard to see how the Carmodys can be that link. In the first place, to refer to the Carmodys as a 'crime family' is ridiculous, even if they do have more than their fair share of petty thieves among them. Also, I've never known any Traveller family to get into drug running. It's not that they're angels, far from it; it's just not their thing. And Delia is adamant that no one in either the Carmody or McGovern family has any idea why Blades was murdered, and I believe her.

Ronan is speaking again. 'So this brings us to Ballycarrick and the scene of the murder. We're grateful to have Sergeant Mags Munroe with us, so if you could fill us in on what you know, Mags, that would be very helpful. You've known the Carmodys for some time. Can you give us a rundown of their criminal activities?'

I didn't realise this was going to happen, and I force down a slight panic, trying to gather my thoughts while all eyes are on me.

'Do all the Carmodys have links to organised drug crime, or just the murdered man?' asks the inspector from CAB.

I shake my head. 'I'd say organised crime is the wrong word where the Carmodys are concerned. Or organised anything, to be honest. I mean, a lot of the Carmodys do have convictions, that's true, but they're not for anything to do with drugs. We're talking things like stripping the lead off church roofs, which Jimmy and Neil Carmody are both in prison for at the moment. And Blades...' – I stop myself as Duckie smirks – 'I mean Bernard, the murder victim, well, he was only released a couple of weeks ago, as Ronan said. He was doing time for repeatedly robbing tools off building sites.'

'But that's before Carmody met Barry Keogh in prison, of course,' points out the top Dublin detective, DI Julie Deane.

'True, but even if Blad...Bernard did cross paths in prison with Barry, it's unlikely they'd become friendly since the Keoghs aren't Travellers, and Travellers and settled people don't mix, even in prison.'

She looks unconvinced by my explanation and shoots her colleagues a superior look. 'So, Sergeant Munroe,' she says, 'with your extensive local knowledge, do *you* have a better theory about why Bernard Carmody was killed in a gangland-style hit while out for an evening drive in a horse cart with his girlfriend?'

Duckie titters, and to my horror, I can feel another hot flush hovering. Luckily there are jugs of iced water on the table, so I pour myself a glass and gulp it down. 'I'm not saying it's not a gangland hit. It's just I don't think he'd work with the Keoghs and I don't think he'd run drugs.' Then I add, 'And Natasha McGovern isn't – wasn't – his girlfriend. She's engaged to someone else.'

DI Julie Deane and Garda Tom Butler look a bit annoyed, and I realise I've made a mistake. I, a humble country guard, have accused the 'top brass' from Dublin of getting things wrong. Still, the other female detective, DS Hazel O'Flynn, seems interested.

'So,' she says, 'you're saying Natasha McGovern was sexually involved with Carmody while engaged to someone else?'

'Oh no, not "sexually involved",' I say firmly. 'Traveller girls never have sex before marriage –'

Duckie interrupts me in his hideous booming voice. 'Course they do. Look at the way they dress, like Page Three girls, with it all hanging out and their short skirts.'

My blood boils. I've had to listen in court to cases where what the woman was wearing is entered in evidence, and it makes me furious because it's irrelevant. She could be wearing a bikini, or nothing. She could be stark naked wandering around SuperValu doing her shopping, and it's still illegal to lay a hand on a person without their consent. But if a clever barrister can convince a jury that the girl was 'looking for it' by the way she was dressed and his client was an innocent, a poor misled man who 'misread the signals', then he'll most likely get off. It happens over and over. No wonder women are reluctant to report sexual assaults. I'm a guard, and I'm not sure even I would if it happened to me. Until we live in a world where a woman's underwear, or how much she had to drink, or where she was walking alone can't be used as evidence or mitigating factors in court, we are wasting our time.

'DETECTIVE SERGEANT –' I try to stop him, but he has the bit between his teeth.

'And I'm telling you, no Traveller worth his salt would ever put up with another fella stealing his old doll – they'd beat the living daylights out of him for even giving her the eye. So I will say this – I'm sure it's drugs, but if it's not, it's internal Traveller violence. Carmody was probably warned off that young one and didn't listen, so he was then killed. And if that's the case, we'll never find out who did it, because even if they hate each other, they hate us more, and they'll never rat each other out, no matter what the grievance between them. That's what they're like, rats.'

My heart sinks, right into my Gardai-issue boots. Duckie has just handed everyone around the table the perfect reason to wash their hands of the whole thing if they don't find a connection with drug running. The problem is, Irish guards just aren't interested in 'in-Traveller' violence, like the way they used to turn a blind eye to domestic violence. They never really try to solve crimes that happen *inside* the Travelling community, and for that they blame the community themselves for 'never ratting on their own'. To be honest, they aren't wrong. The trouble with Travellers is they are notoriously tight-lipped. They are generally suspicious of authority anyway, and in a police interview room, you can't get a word out of them.

'Detective Sergeant Cassidy,' I say, 'the McGoverns aren't gangland-style hitmen. They're not murderers at all. And the Longford man Natasha was engaged to, they're not that type either –'

'Oh, come on, Mags,' Duckie interrupts rudely. 'I know you're all knacker-friendly and you let them off with a load of stuff, no motor tax, shoplifting. Sure, the jacket that *Blades,* as you call him' – he grins around the table for effect – 'was wearing was stolen from Dillon's menswear shop, you know yourself, and you did nothing about it even though I reported it to you.'

I stay calm. 'I checked with Joe Dillon, and that jacket was fully paid for by Natasha McGovern.'

He scoffs. 'Sure, your mother's *manfriend* says whatever you want him to say, surprise, surprise.'

I can't believe my ears. I feel myself go white with fury. I'm not exactly shocked or even bothered that there's gossip in Ballycarrick about Mam and Joe – there's chat about every unmarried or widowed man and woman who have lunch together – but for Duckie to repeat small-town rumours in a top-level meeting... I want to kill him. Instead, I quietly gather my notepad and pen. I remember reading a line in a book – someone was quoting Napoleon, I think, when he said to never interrupt your enemy when he is making a mistake.

'Detective Cassidy, I think we've heard enough of your theories on the matter.' Ronan's stern voice causes Duckie to swing around on his chair in alarm. 'I'd be grateful if you would come to my office at four today. We need to talk.'

Duckie blushes puce under his tanning lotion. 'Ah, Ronan, I was just saying that –'

'See you at four,' Ronan interrupts coldly, then stands, gathers up his own notes and addresses the rest of us. 'The Carmody funeral will be tomorrow. I know the Galway and Dublin teams will each have someone there undercover. Mags, I assume, will be there anyway as it's her beat – right, Mags?'

I nod.

'Good,' says Ronan. 'So that's the local knowledge covered.'

Duckie clears his throat. 'I'll be there as well, Ronan. I'm from just down the road in Dromanane, so I have a lot of that sort of knowledge myself.'

Ronan smiles blandly at him. 'Thanks for the offer, but I want to keep this tight. If I need you to be there, I'll definitely shout, but for now anyway, I think we're fine. We have a great team gathered and so...' The last words hang in the air unsaid.

Duckie has no choice. 'Ah, right, no problem. You know where I am if you need anything.' He is seething and mortified. He'd hate to be spoken to like that in any circumstances, but it happening in front of me must really put the tin hat on it. *No harm to him*, I think uncharitably.

'Great, thanks everyone,' says Ronan. And the meeting is over, much sooner than I'd expected.

CHAPTER 14

I don't often find myself in Galway with a bit of time to spare, but I'm not due back in the Ballycarrick office until lunchtime, so I decide to buy Kieran a new jumper. He loves those handmade Aran ones you can only get in Galway. His old one is so full of holes it's like a string vest, but he won't stop wearing it. I used to think they were desperate altogether, only for tourists, and I don't let him wear the cream ones for that very reason, but he actually looks great in the grey one, very rugged and handsome.

I leave my car in the Garda station car park because it's impossible to park in Eyre Square. It's a fifteen-minute walk into the city. Also, you have to be very careful driving around Galway. Every second car is a rental with a tourist at the wheel, so it's full of nervous people driving on narrow medieval streets for the first time, often on the wrong side of the road for them.

I enjoy the walk anyway. Galway is one of those places that just lifts your heart. The shops, the cafes, the people milling around, buskers everywhere. After Duckie's performance, this is just what I need, something to soothe the soul. I'm happily walking down Shop Street towards the Woollen Mills when I hear the band. A bunch of buskers – there must be ten of them all playing different instruments

– are belting out the Rolling Stones song 'You Can't Always Get What You Want'. Isn't that the truth.

I stop and listen. There's a girl with wavy blonde hair almost to her waist singing with them, like one straight out of an ashram. Galway is so hippy-dippy. She's all floaty dress and those big farmer boots underneath. If she wasn't absolutely breathtakingly beautiful, she'd look ridiculous.

I sing along quietly to the lyrics, about not always being able to get the thing you want most of all.

And then I see him, Ronan Brady, on the other side of the crowd, and he raises his hand and waves. I wave back. Should I go over to him? I don't know. I've never really spoken to him outside of work. Plus I've only just seen him in the meeting, so what else is there to say? Then I decide it would be totally ridiculous not to go over and say hello, so I move around the crowd enjoying the music and stand beside him.

'Mags, hi.' He smiles down at me. 'You're taking your coffee break in Galway?'

I smile back. 'I thought I'd take advantage of being here and do a bit of shopping, soak up the atmosphere, have a bit of lunch. It won't do me any harm to give the local bakery in Ballycarrick a rest for one day.'

'Dead right too. All work and no play makes us very boring law enforcement officers. I might even join you – I've a bit of time to kill. I walked in to pick up some flowers for Evelyn's grave, but Dee the florist won't have them ready for the next hour. It's Ev's anniversary on Friday. Five years.'

'Oh, Ronan, I'm so sorry...' I begin foolishly.

'Don't be daft, why would you remember the date?' He has a nice smile. 'Now, where will we go?'

The band are belting out 'I'm Shipping Up to Boston' as we stroll amicably down the street.

There's some kind of street performance going on further down, a big bunch of teenagers rapping and dancing. I read the banner:

Galway Youth Theatre. Pity Galway's so far away and I don't have more time – Ellie would love to be in a theatre group.

'We could try the new place down by the Spanish Arch?' I suggest. I remember Sharon saying she was in there a few weeks ago and it was lovely.

'Grand.' He shoves his hands in his pockets, and we walk along. He's taken off the tie and jacket and has opened the top button of his shirt. It makes him look instantly younger and more carefree.

Tourists are soaking up the atmosphere, and the shops are doing a roaring trade.

'What do you think about the meeting?' I ask, and immediately regret it. It's his wife's anniversary; he probably doesn't want to talk shop.

He doesn't seem to mind; maybe it takes his mind off things. 'I thought you had an interesting point. Maybe you're right. Maybe it is nothing to do with the Keoghs and their drug racket. It's true what you say that Travellers won't mix with settled people even in prison, so maybe we're grasping at straws here.'

I feel pleased he listened to me, although I'm not sure what to say next. We skirt around a guy with dreadlocks and an enormous beard swallowing mouthfuls of petrol and then setting fire to his breath, much to the delight of the gathered tourists. Ronan walks ahead, making a space in the crowd for me.

'I was actually going to ring you later anyway,' he says once we are able to walk side by side again, now that the crowd has thinned out a bit. 'So this is handy to have run into you.' He holds the door of the fancy new coffee shop open for me. 'What would you like? My treat.'

'Oh, er…a decaf flat white please.' I pull a jokey face because those words still sound poncy to my ears, even though fancy coffee shops have been around in Galway for a good while now. Even in Ballycarrick it's not just a spoonful of Maxwell House anymore, the undissolved grains swirling around on top of the water. A flat white is just the lingo now for coffee. And I switched to decaf a while ago, because caffeine is the worst for the insomnia.

'Decaf flat white coming up,' he says.

The place is packed. As we queue at the counter, I look around for a possible table. The café is one of those that is trying to look like it belongs in the meat-packing district of New York, itself an affectation, since if you actually started packing dead animal flesh, the hipsters and the cool people who hang out there would most likely pass out in front of you. But nonetheless, that's the vibe, as they say. All raw wood and tubular steel and those lampshades that look like they're from some bad fifties sci-fi film. You know the kind. It is nice, though, warm and buzzy, lots of chatter going on around and people far enough away from each other that you can have a private conversation.

'Will you have a cake or something?' he asks.

'Ah, no, I'm grand, thanks.' I've just spotted a tourist couple getting up to leave from a corner seat. They have all the gear for Ireland – raincoats, waterproof trousers, hiking sticks. Nothing an Irish person would even consider owning. It makes me smile how the weather always seems to take us locals by surprise. The heavens open several times a day, and yet while the tourists are ready with all the Gore-Tex gear and proper boots, Irish people scamper around with newspapers over their heads, shocked and appalled at the sudden turn of events, their summer clothes rapidly becoming transparent.

'I'll grab that,' I say, moving away from him towards the table. I hover near the couple while trying not to look too predatory as they gather their stuff. They look at me.

'I'd be into your grave as quick.' I make the usual Irish joke, universally understood here as the thing you say when you are going to grab someone else's spot. The tall blond man and his girlfriend look at me with blank expressions.

'Thank you...for the table.' I gesture at it like a lunatic.

'It belongs to the café,' the man says in a German accent, as if I'm completely off my rocker.

'I know.' I sigh as their Gore-Tex backs head for the door.

I sit down and watch Ronan pay for the coffees. He gets two scones as well, which I'm secretly delighted about. A scone and a coffee with a colleague in a cheery café on a sunny day – what could be nicer?

'So,' he says as he lands the stuff down on the table and sits down opposite me. 'I got you a scone, even though you didn't want one, to make me feel better about having one myself.'

'So what did you want to ask me?' I say, cutting the raisin scone in half. He's got jam and butter and cream as well, really pushing the boat out, but it all looks delicious.

'Well, you know that young girl you just recruited into the Reserve, the Traveller girl?'

'Her name is Delia McGovern and she's eighteen, so I suppose she's a young woman, not a young girl.' I know I sound like a mad woolly-hatted feminist, and I brace myself for him rolling his eyes.

He doesn't. He simply says, 'I'm sorry, you're right. I shouldn't call her a girl. But she is a Traveller, isn't she?'

'She is.' I take a bite of the scone; it melts in the mouth.

'Right. Well, I was wondering if she would have any light to throw on this mess.' Ronan slathers his scone with butter and jam as he speaks.

'How'd you mean?' I ask cautiously.

'Well, you were saying it might be to do with Natasha McGovern in some way...and I know you've done some preliminary investigations already, and that Delia was part of that...' His voice trails off without him adding anything else.

'Actually, I don't think it does have anything to do with Natasha or any of her family, and even if it does, what's that got to do with Delia?' I ask, trying to keep the defensive tone out of my voice.

I feel protective of Delia – personally responsible, you might say. After that first awful morning with Duckie, she's been on her guard, which in Traveller body language comes across as plain aggressive, but she's melting slowly. Nicola has taken her under her wing and is being great. She and Delia get along well, and the two lads are warming to her, especially Darren. She does her work diligently, and whenever she goes out on patrol with any of the others, they report that she's a great help. She actually has a wicked sense of humour and is incredibly kind, attributes that make the job worth doing. Last week she stopped all the traffic going into the GAA pitch for a match to let all the old people coming out of Mass get across the road.

'Mags, am I missing something here?' Ronan is looking at me directly.

'No, why?'

'Look, I know what Duckie said about Travellers, and I'll be talking to him later. I want you to remember I'm not like him. All I'm saying here is, Delia's a member of the force and I'm asking you if you think she might be in a position to use her knowledge to help us? That's all.'

I relax. He's right. Delia McGovern is well able to fight her own battles, and anyway, what he is asking is perfectly reasonable. 'I'm sorry, Ronan, I didn't mean to come across like that. I've already spoken to her, as it happens. But she hasn't been able to tell me anything, apart from that nobody knows anything, which is interesting in itself. I don't know what more she can do?'

He looks at me. 'She can attend the funeral.'

'She'll be doing that anyway.'

'I mean in an official capacity. Not in uniform, I don't mean that, but ready to listen out for any information somebody might let slip.'

I know he's being reasonable and that it's the correct thing to do, yet something doesn't feel right about it. 'I'll ask,' I manage.

'OK, what's the problem?' His smile takes the sting out of the words.

'There's no problem. I'll ask her,' I repeat brightly.

He keeps on smiling. 'Mags, I didn't get to be a detective inspector without being able to read body language, and if you don't mind me saying, yours is exuding a fairly powerful repellent at the moment. So come on, off the record, what's up?'

I realise my armpits are sweating, and I hope it's just attitude and not body odour I'm exuding. Then the sweat prickles my neck, I feel the beads forming on my temples, a droplet running between my breasts, and...oh no, a hot flush. Here we go.

'I'll just pop to the loo,' I mumble and run.

In the bathroom, my fears are confirmed. My head is like a tomato, my chest blotchy where my V-neck t-shirt exposed it. Tears come unbidden. Poor Ronan. What must he think is going on with me? First in the lift, now in the café – he's going to think I fancy him or something awful like that. I take a piece of toilet roll and splash my face with cold water, but it does no good. I'm just so horribly hot. I need to get outside, so I leave the toilet and go out the back door of the café into a tiny brick-walled yard. The cool air is bliss, and I lean against the wall by the bins, my eyes closed and my face turned to the small blue square of sky.

'Mags?'

I open my eyes and find Ronan standing there.

'I'm sorry,' he says. 'I just thought you didn't look great, so I thought I'd check…'

'I'm fine, Ronan.' I give him a watery smile. 'Just a hot flush. I've found out I'm going through' – I make quotation marks with my fingers – 'the change'. It's a delight, let me assure you.'

He becomes even more sympathetic. 'Oh, poor you. I don't know who designed all of this, but after girls and women go through all the business with periods and everything, having babies, rearing them, feeding them, just when it's all about to end, then this gets landed on them. If it was men, you may be sure we'd be raising the roof in complaint. That was another thing Ev had to put up with. They had her on these hormone suppressant tablets, and on top of the breast cancer, she had all the symptoms of the menopause as well.'

I feel mortified again. His poor wife had cancer as well as the menopause. I'm able to take HRT, and the symptoms for me should clear up in a couple of weeks. 'I'm sorry, I shouldn't be complaining. It's nothing…'

'It's not nothing, I know that.' He rests his hand on my shoulder. 'I hope it wasn't me pushing you about Delia that brought this on.'

'Of course not,' I say weakly.

'Let's finish our coffees?'

We make our way back to the table, and once we've fought off a couple of tourists who are trying to get our unfinished coffees and scones removed, I explain. 'I think I'm just a bit protective of Delia, that's all. It was hard for someone like her to come to us. We're not to be trusted as far as the Traveller families are concerned, even ones that stay out of trouble like the McGoverns, but she did it, you know? She braved them all, faced down her parents even – and in their world, that's a huge deal – because she wanted to be a guard, and so I hate the idea of using her to get to her family or even the Carmodys.'

Ronan sits back in his chair, his face a mask, and I can hear my heart thumping. Though he is special branch and I am not directly under him in the organisation, he is still my superior. There is collaboration between detective units and the rank and file, but they are horses of a very different colour. Have I overstepped the mark?

He says slowly, 'But you said it yourself, she wants to be a guard. So let her be one. I get why you care, Mags, but in this business, you are either on our side or against us. If she's against us, she should never have been allowed past the front door. But we'll assume she's with us, so why not let her do what she fought so hard to do?'

He's right. I'm making assumptions about Delia every bit as much as Duckie is, for all my championing of her. We can't wrap her up in cotton wool, and as police, we are expected to use everything at our disposal to solve crime and bring criminals to justice. I wouldn't think twice about asking one of the others if they had some inside track on something; it's part of the job. Never off duty and all of that.

'You're right.' I find myself smiling. 'I'm being a bit of an old mother hen about her, I suppose, but that won't do her or the force any good. I'll make sure she's there at the funeral and knows what has to be done.'

'Thanks. I appreciate it.' He drains his coffee and checks his watch.

'Is it time to collect your flowers?'

'Ten minutes. You alright until then?'

'Of course I am.' I like that he wants me to wait with him.

'I don't want to rush the lovely Dee,' he says.

'I'm sure she's making you the perfect wreath.'

'Not a wreath, a bouquet. Dee makes the same one every year. She made Ev's wedding bouquet for her, and Ev joked that she loved it so much she had no notion of throwing it to anyone. She didn't either. She kept it and got the flowers pressed into a frame, and hung it over the fireplace. So I get a wedding bouquet made every year for her grave.'

'Oh, Ronan...' Once more, I hardly know what to say.

'Ah, Mags, don't look so worried.' He grins. 'I was a mess when Evelyn died, you saw me, but it was five years ago. I miss her every day and I wish she were still here, but I'm not broken anymore. She'd have come back and haunted me if I kept that up. I just do the bouquets as...I don't know...a way to mark it, I suppose, but it's not as tragic as it sounds.' He reaches over and puts his hand on mine, giving it a quick squeeze before releasing it.

'So you're doing okay these days?' I ask.

He nods. 'Yeah, mostly fine. The lads think I should be out there, as they say, looking to meet someone, but I don't know. Sometimes I think it would be nice, but then I can't really picture it, y'know?'

'I do, I suppose. I've been with Kieran for years, so the idea of meeting someone new... Well, I wouldn't have a clue for starters. Elton John and Queen were in the charts the last time I went dancing.'

'Exactly.' I notice that he talks with his hands, an unusual trait in an Irish man; I always associate it more with Italians or something. 'What am I going to do? Take myself off to a disco like some creepy old guy? Or go online dating and have every criminal in the country taking the mick? Nah. I reckon if it's meant to be, it will happen, and in the meantime, I'm surviving.'

'I'm glad. I often thought of you in those months after. I nearly rang a few times, but...' I stop. Why does everything I say sound so silly and pointless?

'Thanks. Yeah, that first year was a blur, to be honest. But it gets easier. The process is slow and painful, but it turns out my mam was right – time does heal all wounds.'

'Evelyn was so young, and so beautiful.'

He smiles, a slow, sad smile that tugs at my heart. 'She had the BRCA gene mutation but never knew it until it was too late. Evelyn was adopted so had no idea of her family history. Maybe if she'd been raised by her birth family, she could have been checked, but that wasn't how it was. She found – well, actually I found it – a lump one day, and despite a full year of radiotherapy and chemo, surgery and those hormone suppressants, it was no good.' He exhaled. 'She was so brave, Mags, honestly. I know people say that all the time about people who are sick, but I swear she was a lioness, never giving up. But in the end, it's not about being strong or not being strong. It's about what kind of tumour you have, how aggressive it is, how early they catch it – those are the deciding factors, nothing else.'

I nod. 'I remember hearing a fella on the radio a while back, some sports person, talking about how he was so strong he beat cancer, and it made me so cross. Like does that mean that people who die are weak? Or don't want to live badly enough? That's so wrong to say.'

'You're a wise woman, Mags.'

'My dad died when I was seven. He was only thirty-eight. Leukaemia.' I want him to know I kind of get it.

'Even younger than Ev. That was hard for you,' he sympathises. 'Do you remember him?'

'I never remember him being well, to be honest with you. Mam had a clothes shop, and me and my sisters spent most of our child-hoods in there because Dad was sleeping.' Memories long suppressed of endless boring days in the shop come unbidden.

'And did your mam ever remarry?' Ronan asks gently.

'No, she never did. I wish she had. Even now, I'd love her to meet someone.' I wink. 'I don't suppose you have a thing for older ladies who like social dancing and Daniel O'Donnell, do you?'

He chuckles. 'I used to, but I had to give them up – they wore me out.' He checks his watch again. 'Oops, that's more than ten minutes. I'm going to be late.'

We stand up and squeeze through the tables, and he holds the door for me as we emerge into the bright sunshine.

I say, 'I'll talk to Delia later and give you a ring.'

'Great. Talk to you then, Mags. And don't worry, I'll give Duckie a good talking-to this afternoon.'

I smile; I don't know what to say really. 'Thanks.' I know he's not just doing it on my behalf, but it's lovely to feel someone important is on my side. 'I appreciate it.'

'No problem.' For a second I think he's going to give me a hug, but we both seem to realise at the same time that that would be weird, so he just waves and walks away.

CHAPTER 15

J'm back in Ballycarrick before I remember that I meant to buy Kieran a new jumper. Oh well. He'd probably never wear it anyway; he loves the old holey one too much.

I rang Delia before leaving Galway to ask her to come in for a meeting, and here she is, standing in front of my desk, her chin jutting out, looking belligerent, like she thinks she's in trouble. I know it's her default position, but still, like Ronan, I suddenly want to tell her that I'm not the enemy here.

'How are you getting on, Delia?' I ask, gesturing that she should sit. She takes the seat opposite. I don't really like having this desk between us – I've never really liked it – but it's how it is, and the chain of command is important in a police force. You can't be friends with your commanding officer – that's the mantra.

'Grand, thanks, Sergeant Munroe,' she replies, her eyes never meeting mine.

'How's Natasha? Is she feeling any better since…?'

'Yes, Sergeant, she's grand.' She's being tight-lipped.

I sit back. 'Delia, I promise you can be open with me. I know there will always be some people, both on within the Gardai and in the community, who will treat you differently because you're a Traveller, but I hope you know I'll never do that. You are a member of the Garda Reserve and therefore part of this station, so it's important you feel you can be open with me. And that you can come to me if you feel anyone else is treating you differently.'

I see the shadow of a smile cross her face.

'What?' I ask.

'Nothing. I'm grand, Sergeant.'

'Please, tell me.' I cock my head sideways to meet her downcast eyes.

She pauses, and I can see her considering whether it's wise to speak. Eventually, she does. 'Well, it's just funny, like, that you want me to tell you if people treat me different like, 'cause I don't know what it is to be not treated different. Different to what? I've been called names, spat at, thrown out of shops, refused service in places, my whole life, since I was a child, and all my family the same. So I'm not saying it's not happening now – it is of course – but it's all I've ever known. And I know you're a nice woman and all and that you're trying to help, but like, you're not going to change the world. To most of them' – she jerks her chin towards the window – 'I'm a knacker and all belonging to me are the same, steal the eye out of your head, battering their wives and kids, mistreating animals, all the stereotypes of Travellers. One of us does something wrong, and we're all the same, bad to the bones. One of us does something good, then we're the exception. That's how they see us, always have and always will. That's what they see when they see me, and it doesn't matter about this uniform, or what you tell them to do – nobody can change it.'

I am amazed by her honesty. 'So why join the guards?'

'Because I want to.' She shrugs. 'Sergeant, people will think what they're gonna think anyway. I can't change that. I can't control other people. But I can control my own life, or at least I want to try to.'

For any young woman to be so astute would be interesting, but for someone of her background, where women have very little control of their own fate, it is remarkable. She is an unusual girl.

I sometimes look at my lovely daughters, Kate and Ellie, and I wonder what they will do when they grow up and if they will get interesting jobs that are worthy of their hard work and intellect. I think they will. They are all about encouraging girls into the sciences, and there's a programme on TV about keeping girls in sport as they enter the teenage years. Things are so much better now, and I hope my daughters won't ever even consider their gender when it comes to choosing a career.

My daughters will have to be strong, but Delia will have to be even stronger. She has a mountain to climb.

'I agree with you, Delia. And now I need to ask you something in return. You understand that anything we discuss in here is entirely confidential?'

She nods. 'I do.'

'OK. In some ways I'm doing the very thing I don't want others to do to you, but here goes. How comfortable are you in using the fact that you are a Traveller, and therefore on the inside as it were, to help us with the investigation into Blades Carmody's murder?'

The atmosphere in the room becomes heavy. She doesn't reply.

I want to take it back, say it doesn't matter. But I remind myself of Ronan's rationale. Either she's with us completely, no more or less than we'd expect from any member of the force, or she's not. And if she's not, then she has no business in the Garda Síochána.

And the truth is that when we recruit from different communities, while the officers are chosen on merit, they're also chosen because they have a way into those communities that the rest of us would struggle with. We've recruited members from as many diverse groups as possible in the years since Ireland opened up to the world, so the ethnically diverse officers are expected to step up when members of the public from those backgrounds need help or are under investigation. By that token, Delia should be no different.

'You want me to spy on my own?' Her words hang heavily in the air.

'No.' I'm matter-of-fact. 'You're not a spy, you're a member of the Gardai and therefore expected to use all the skills at your disposal to assist us, your fellow officers, in applying the law.' I'm being less conciliatory now, I know, but Ronan is right – if she doesn't get that, then she's wasting everyone's time.

'OK, what do you need me to do?' She seems decisive and I'm relieved.

'At the funeral tomorrow, I want you to be there for your cousin Natasha. But I met with some detectives from Dublin and an inspector from the Criminal Assets Bureau this morning, and they are currently operating under the assumption that Blades Carmody was murdered by some henchman of Alan Keogh's.'

I pause, and Delia looks at me politely but blankly, clearly not knowing what or who I am talking about.

'Alan Keogh and his brother Chunkie run the Keogh drug crime family, which is based between Dublin and Spain,' I say. 'They're one of the biggest drug gangs in Ireland, and Barry Keogh, Alan's son, apparently crossed paths with Blades in prison, so the Dublin officers investigating the Keoghs assumed Barry recruited Blades into their drug-running operation, and then perhaps Blades ran off with some money.'

Delia frowns. 'But the Keoghs aren't Travellers?'

'No, they're not.' I watch for her reaction.

She averts her eyes and says nothing, so it's obvious what she's thinking – that the Dublin detectives don't know much if they think Blades Carmody would get in deep with a settled person.

I carry on. 'Both Dublin and Galway Special Branch are going to have undercover agents at the funeral, listening out for information. I'd like you to do the same.'

Her lips twitch with humour. 'You want me to go undercover as a Traveller, Sergeant?'

I smile as well. 'OK, sorry – I mean, just keep your ears and eyes open for any clues that might help us solve this.'

She thinks hard. 'I don't usually talk to any Carmodys, not even at funerals. Nana won't let us have anything to do with them – nothing but trouble, she says, and based on recent events, she's not wrong. Natasha hasn't a clue, I'm certain of that, but my cousin Geraldine works in the Traveller centre in Ennis and so does Michelle Carmody, who's married to Paddy Carmody, Blades's brother. She'll be at the funeral, and I'll have a reason to talk to her because of Geraldine. She might know something through Paddy.'

'That would be great, but, Delia, be careful...'

She gives a snort of derision. 'The day I'm scared of a Carmody will be a day for Ireland.'

She's right. They're prize eejits and generally not to be feared, but it's just marginally possible they have got themselves accidentally mixed up with some very dangerous people.

'All the same, we are dealing with a murder enquiry, and rightly or wrongly, Blades was the target. We don't know why yet, so be careful. And now go and help Darren keep watch at the site, and if you see that black Mercedes...'

'Don't go near them, call straight into the station, get Nicola to order backup from Galway...' she rattles off, with a smile that lights up her whole face as she leaves the office.

I pick up the phone to Ronan, happy to report that I have done my duty, and we agree to meet after the funeral tomorrow to go through what, if anything, we find out.

CHAPTER 16

I get home in time to make dinner, pork sausages and buttery mash with apple sauce and gravy, everyone's favourite. I ignore this week's weeds looking balefully at me from the bottom of the fridge. Potatoes are vegetables, and my kids won't die of scurvy if they don't eat the purple sprouting broccoli or rainbow chard or whatever the green stuff is this week. There's a couple out the road, they're lovely hippie types and she came round a month ago asking if we'd be interested in getting a box of organic vegetables each Monday. I said we'd love it of course, and signed up to the tenner a week and I did try to cook the kale with lemon juice and garlic but Kate said it tasted like weeds from the side of the road and she wasn't wrong, although I still haven't had the heart to cancel the order. So each week I'm looking at some green leafy thing and puzzling over it. My kids like peas, carrots and broccoli. Rainbow chard and artichokes are a bit beyond the Munroe daily fare, I'm afraid.

Kate is full of a school project to do with rabbits, and I think that at least if we got a rabbit, I wouldn't feel so guilty about all this greenery because the bunny could munch away. But that would mean we'd have a rabbit, which I need like a hole in the head. Better to tell the lovely hippy couple we're not really a kale kind of family, but it's admitting defeat, so my pride won't let me. I'm an eejit, I know.

So I keep trying to find space for the Minions yoghurts among all the green leaves going slimy in bottom of the fridge and wondering what the hell to do with lemongrass.

OF COURSE I do know I have to do my bit for climate change. Like, the thing would terrify you, wouldn't it? The trouble is, I don't know how to make a difference to something so huge. I wash out the milk bottles and take my own bags to the supermarket, but does it help really?

That Greta Thunberg – you know, the young girl who's famous now as the Swedish climate change activist – she's so serious and so worried, she freaks me out. I should listen to her more, and I do sometimes, but I'm no more good after it. Then I get a fit of guilt because I still drive a diesel car and we fly away in a plane once or twice a year, to places that have that big yellow yoke in the sky... What's it called again? 'The sun'? Carbon emissions are bad, but if you ever did five months of solid drizzle in an Irish winter, you'd understand. It's like Chinese water torture – *drip, drip, drip.*

There was some fella on the radio the other day, some celebrity – don't ask me what he was famous for as I never heard of him – and he said it was irresponsible to bring children into such a flawed and doomed world. He actually used that word, 'doomed'.

Sometimes, at three in the morning, I wonder if he was right, and the world really is doomed. I love the girls both so much and the idea that they are coming into a doomed world makes me want to cry.

So yes, I do recycle plastic and cardboard, but it's a drop in the ocean of what needs to be done. Tiny me, in tiny Ireland, recycling milk cartons. People criticise the politicians for not doing enough, but I don't think that's fair; I think they must care about the planet. They are fathers and husbands – now I come to think of it; there are a few women but mostly men – but they haven't a clue about the future, no more than I have. So they're like me and you and everyone else, preferring to deal with the day-to-day stuff, the things we can control, and trying to put the polar bears and the ice caps to the back of our minds.

I pay the TV licence, and they negotiate an interest rate with the Central Bank; I pay the tax for the car, and they produce a green paper on access to greenways for cyclists. We're all the same, dealing with the small stuff because the big stuff is too terrifying.

Kieran laughs when I tell him what I'm worried about, and though I should be annoyed, it makes me smile. He can always make me laugh at myself. I'm getting all apocalyptic, he says. And then the things that seem insurmountable between three and five in the morning seem not too bad and I feel like an eejit for getting myself into such a state.

I pray the world will not be doomed for my girls. They're so fabulous. I mean, I know every mother says that about their kids, and they should, but Kate and Ellie are smashing; they're the exact right mixture of funny and smart and kind.

If I go up to bed earlier than Kieran, I'll go into their rooms to watch them sleeping.

Kate still kicks off the duvet – she's done it since she was a baby – and when I touch her foot that she's thrown out the side of the bed, it's ice-cold. I cover her up, but in the morning, when she comes in for a sneaky cuddle as she calls it, she's freezing again. She used to wear those cute sleepsuits with the feet in them, but she's too grown up for them now she tells me. I love to see them growing up strong, confident and happy, but a part of my heart breaks too. That lovely baby smell, that cuddly body – they're being replaced by long limbs like a gazelle and contraband sparkly lip gloss.

Ellie is the opposite. She buries deep in a pile of duvet and pillows and cuddly toys. All you can see are her dark-brown curls. She's different to her sister, deeper or something. She is artistic and sensitive and so clever sometimes it scares me.

She is in her last year of primary, going to secondary school next year, and I'm lying awake these days thinking about that. At least it's a relatively new anxiety, which gives poor Greta Thunberg and David Attenborough a break, but I'm worried sick about her. Mam says I'm getting myself up in a hoop over nothing. She fits the entire convent school with their uniforms, and she says they are lovely girls, but they would be to Mam, a woman in her sixties who every single family in town knows. But will they be nice to my little girl?

Ellie is a sensitive child. She's clever and musical, and I know – I know – I sound like one of those painful mothers like Elsie Flanagan: 'Well, my daughter is in an orchestra, and makes her own hummus, and has been chosen to represent Ireland at the blah blah blah…' But honestly I swear I'm not like that. Ellie is good at most subjects at school, though she's not keen on Irish, and she plays piano and does ballet, but I'm not bothered about any of that. I'm worried that she's not very cool. There, I've said it.

I wasn't one of the cool girls going to school either, but I wasn't a nerd – I was kind of in the middle. Delores was cool, and for 'cool', read 'always in trouble', and Jenny was a swot. I won't worry about Kate the same way – she's a tougher kid, better able for the world or something – but Ellie comes out with things some days, and I just find myself praying that she doesn't say that in school or they'll crucify her.

Like last weekend she was helping Mam to tidy the storeroom in the shop for a bit of pocket money when she says, 'I really prefer Daniel O'Donnell to a lot of modern music.'

Now if you don't know who Daniel O'Donnell is… Well, if you're Irish, you'll definitely know him, but if not, he's a singer of 'lovely' songs from what Kate calls the 'olden days'. That means any time pre-2000, by the way. He puts glitter in his hair and wears a suit and is very clean-cut. He's like Ireland's answer to Cliff Richard or Jim Reeves or something. Once a year he hosts a tea party in his hometown of Donegal. He's a dote, genuinely a lovely man. He and his wife do shows on the telly, and they'd have you in stitches laughing at them, but Daniel is for grannies, not young girls. Even he'd admit that himself. If Ellie goes into school and says she likes Daniel O'Donnell, she might as well stick her own head down the toilet. So you can see my dilemma. That's only one example; I could give you fifty more. Like she always hugs and kisses me or Kieran when we pick her up from school. It's adorable and I'd hate her to stop, but she can't be coming out of secondary school and running into my or Kieran's arms. But how do you make a child cooler? Should you even try? I've no idea.

Mam says adversity builds character, and I know she's right. She says not to wish a life of ease on your kids, that it makes them weak and vulnerable to collapse when things go wrong, as invariably they do. Instead, as they overcome each little hurdle, they get stronger and learn more, making them better able for the next thing life throws at them. I told her she's like the Dalai Lama, she's so wise.

'Didn't he say that if you think you're too small to make a difference, try sleeping with a mosquito?'

'He did,' I said.

Ellie is subdued this evening, creating lakes and islands with her mash and gravy, and I make a note that I must get her alone and see if she'll open up to me about this girl at school.

Kieran is as happy as Kate. He's explaining to any of us who will listen how he has just bought an extortionately expensive communication system so his roofing team can connect over a large area without taking out their phones. They have little transmitters they wear on their shirts, and they can talk to their fellow roofers even if they can't see them. The range is longer than any walkie-talkie and is hands-free. Kieran is a stickler for health and safety, and this means his staff has both hands free at all times, much safer apparently. 'You should have one,' he says to me happily. 'You never know when it might come in handy if you want to contact me.'

'In case I need a roofer in a hurry?' I tease.

'You might have a slate that needs fixing.' He winks and Kate laughs.

After dinner, I see the girls off up to bed, and when I come back down, he's settled in front of the telly with a beer. I cuddle up beside him on the couch, and he puts his arm around me.

'How was your day, love?'

I tell him what I can without giving away too many confidential details. I roll my eyes over the 'top brass' obsessing about gang warfare and drugs, and about Duckie and the 'in-Traveller violence' thing.

Kieran turns to look at me, alarmed. 'They think there might be a criminal gang behind that killing?'

'Maybe...'

'If it is, they're not going to take kindly to someone poking about their business.'

'Well, it's either we poke around their business or they get away with it and wreak havoc on the whole place,' I say, amused. 'I mean, we are supposed to be the police, you do know that? Poking around in baddie business is kind of what we do. In charge of law and order and all that kind of stuff.'

He's clearly worried. 'Well, it's your decision obviously, but...'

This is one of those occasions when I realise my husband still can't quite wrap his head around the fact that I am a Garda sergeant by day, even if I'm a wife and mother by night. 'Actually, no, it's not my decision, Kieran. I am a guard, that's what I'm paid for, and I can't pick and choose what case to get involved in or not.' I can't help sounding a bit annoyed, and he winces.

'Ah, Mags, give me a break, will you? I know you're a huge asset, but you're my wife and the girls' mam, so the idea of you getting up in the business of seriously bad people is a bit scary, that's all I'm saying. I can't help being worried for you.' He tightens his arm around me.

I sigh and lean against him. Probably he secretly wishes I worked two mornings a week for Violetta in the florist's, like Jess's mother, Holly.

'Don't go thinking I'm not proud of you and what you do,' he says quickly, as if he's read my thoughts. 'It's just I'm...'

I smile up at him from inside the protective circle of his arm. 'Worried. I know. But you don't have to worry. I'll be fine. None of this is down to us anyway – it's totally in the hands of the teams from Dublin and Galway. They have their own undercovers on the job, and they only wanted to talk to me to get a bit of local knowledge and because I was a witness at the scene. The fact is, you're in way more danger than I am every time you climb up onto a roof.'

He beams down at me with relief. 'Well, that's all right then, but Mags, just humour me here, will you take one of the transmitters anyway? The range on them is amazing. They use 4G, but even if there's no mobile phone coverage, these things will pick up a signal.'

'Fine.' I reply and then I tune out. It's true what they say, boys never really grow up, their toys just become more expensive.

CHAPTER 17

The next morning dawns bright and clear. I've slept better than I have for a long time, and I feel a lot livelier as a result. Maybe the HRT is kicking in already. Kieran tells me I'm 'looking beautiful this morning' before he rushes out the door to take advantage of the weather, but I'm so preoccupied that I don't answer right away, and then he's gone before I can say something equally nice back. Never mind, I'll make it up to him later. I wish I'd bought him that jumper now.

For now, there's Blades Carmody's funeral to prepare for, and I whizz around the house cleaning up before Mam gets here to mind the girls, not that she would say anything even if the house was on fire and underwater at the same time – she's no Nora Munroe – but just because I want to. Kieran's already given the girls breakfast, Rice Krispies in front of the telly. After I've cleaned up and showered, I get into my uniform and make sure it's spotless. Myself, Darren, Cathal and Nicola will all be in uniform, but Delia will be in her own clothes and sticking close to Natasha.

When Mam arrives, I give her a big hug and say, 'Sorry you had to close the shop on a Saturday to mind the girls, Mam.'

'Oh, don't worry, pet. Most of the town is closed today – nobody's doing any shopping.'

We don't say any more about it, but we both know that's the way small towns carry on when there's a Traveller funeral coming through, like the mourners might suddenly stop mourning and set fire to the place after robbing it blind.

I kiss the girls and get into my car and drive into Ballycarrick. Uniformed guards won't be going to the church – that would be intrusive – but we'll wait in the town for the funeral to go through on its way to the cemetery. Our presence will calm the natives, and we'll hold our Garda hats in our hands as the funeral procession passes to show the proper respect.

I put on the menopause podcast again. The cheerful, soothing voice tells me the menopause can be a wonderful thing, a new start to life and all that. It's a time of choice and should be about finding out what I want in life. Far from being the end of the road, the menopause can be a new beginning. Apparently it all depends on my attitude.

Have I got the right attitude, I wonder anxiously? Well, I'm still not sorry not to be whizzing around the place being a detective sergeant and seeing even less of my family. And I love my job, I do. But at the same time, I certainly haven't managed to find a new beginning, and I suppose now part of me is worried it will be same old, same old until I retire.

Darren, Cathal and Nicola are ready for me on the station steps, their uniforms pristine and boots shined. Michael is staying behind to man the desk. The four of us climb into the squad car, drive up the town and park it discreetly out of sight in the marketplace before taking up our positions on Main Street.

The Carmodys have already held the rosary at the funeral home, and the removal was yesterday evening. While the coffin was brought to the church, the town was inundated with Traveller families; it is the done thing to go to funerals of even distant relatives, so hundreds of people nobody recognised were milling around. You could feel the tension. People were wary anyway, but the fact that Blades was murdered made people even more jumpy. Mam was right – today most of the shops are closed and windows shuttered.

All night, Blades Carmody's body has been lying in Ballycarrick church, the same church where his niece and nephew, Julianna and Billy, made their Communion only a couple of weeks ago. His funeral Mass started at eleven, and it's nearly another hour before we see the local undertaker, Ernie Caffrey, and his son Thomas, who works for him, finally walking towards us down Main Street. They're wearing long black overcoats and black top hats, and behind them at a steady pace comes the huge black funeral carriage, drawn by four magnificent black horses with nodding black plumes of feathers. Inside the carriage, surrounded by extravagant flower arrangements reading 'LOVED FOREVER', 'SPECIAL UNCLE', 'BEST FRIEND', 'BROTHER', 'DARLING SON', lies Blades Carmody in a lead-lined mahogany coffin with gold handles, which must have cost ten thousand euro at least.

Traveller funerals are as lavish as their weddings and Communions, and the gravestone that goes up for Blades will be a white marble palace guarded by weeping angels. It outraged Ernie Caffrey three years ago when the local council passed a by-law restricting the height of gravestones. I can't remember on what pretext they passed it, but it was clearly aimed at the Traveller graves, which Ernie makes a fortune from. He's found a way round the problem, though; he sells the Travellers a few neighbouring plots and spreads the marble memorials out sideways instead of building up. Depictions of *The Last Supper* have become popular as a result.

After the funeral hearse comes another horse-drawn carriage carrying Blades's parents and brothers Jimmy and Neil, out of prison on compassionate release, and a sobbing girl I don't recognise. Blades's many other siblings walk beside the carriage in smart black suits and beautiful black dresses because, unlike people in the settled community, no Traveller attends a funeral in their ordinary clothes.

Next is every single member of the extended family, every Carmody from all over Ireland, even from warring factions, and then other Travelling families from the Galway area, including the McGoverns. Dacie is walking with a stick and wearing a black veil, and then comes Natasha, wedged between her father and two of her brothers, and another man I don't recognise who I assume is her intended, Joseph Ward from Longford. Natasha isn't wearing make-up, and she's white as a sheet. Delia is hovering near to Natasha, looking really beautiful in a slim black dress that comes down to her knees. She doesn't wear much make-up and the dress is classic and flattering. The other young Traveller girls have gone all out, in very revealing and dramatic outfits, which must have taken hours to put together. A funeral was a big day out. I hear Darren beside me take a breath when he sees Delia, and I hope he doesn't imagine he has a chance with a Traveller girl.

The procession seems endless but finally it does end, and my colleagues and I turn and bring up the rear, marching side by side at the same slow pace until the high iron gates of the cemetery finally loom ahead, standing open to the road.

The carriage turns in, the huge heavy coffin is lifted out by eight strong men and lowered with great effort into the grave, and Father Doyle begins a decade of the rosary, the five sorrowful mysteries. Like a play, everyone knows what to do, where to stand, what to say, and everyone there responds to the prayers by rote, an age-old ritual of burying the dead.

Once the prayers are finished and the men have all used the spade to put some earth on Blades's coffin, the women throw in lots of white roses. The crowd begins to slowly disperse, walking and talking in small groups as they make their way out of the cemetery.

Delia takes the opportunity to come up to me where I'm standing alone. 'You see your man there? I don't like the look of him,' she says. She doesn't help me by pointing anybody out, just lifts her chin slightly to the left. I look around in vain for a suspicious character. 'Your man by the Costello grave,' she says, 'standing beside my Uncle Ted, staring at Natasha. Tall. Skinny.'

I think I know who she means now, even though he's dressed exactly like all the rest. 'He's not a McGovern?'

'He's no relative of mine.'

I'm amused by her certainty. 'Delia, you must have hundreds of cousins, so how can you tell?'

'He's got no look of us. We're nothing like him,' she says seriously.

'OK. Maybe he belongs to a different family, come to pay their respects?'

'Then why isn't he with them?'

I have a thought; I don't know why I didn't think of it before. 'He must be one of the undercovers, from Dublin or Galway.'

Her mouth twitches, as it does when she's politely trying not to smile. 'No.'

'How do you know he's not?'

She looks at me for a moment, then graciously explains. 'You know how a settled person can spot a Traveller, even if that Traveller is trying to pass as settled?'

It's an uncomfortable question, but this young woman is so honest with me that I return the favour. 'Yes, I do.'

'It's the same with us and cops. There's no such thing as an under-cover cop to a Traveller – we can spot one at a hundred paces. You see over there? He's one.'

I look where she indicated and see a bit of a clear space in the crowd, in the middle of which stands a man, dressed in a black suit, reading the inscription on the headstone.

'And there's another one...'

Another bit of clear space around a woman who to my eye looks exactly like any other Traveller woman at a funeral. I'm fascinated. 'How does everyone know who they are?'

She shrugs. 'I don't know, really. How do you spot a Traveller if they're dressed exactly like a settled person?'

It's a great question. I suppose there's a look, or sometimes just certain cues, a way of walking, a way of talking...

Delia's mouth twitches again. 'I'm going to talk to Michelle Carmody,' she says, and walks away.

I continue to keep my eye on the man Delia was suspicious of. He's not one of ours, and he's not a Traveller, so then who is he and what's he doing here? He continues to stare at Natasha, and I circle a little nearer, pulling my phone out of my pocket and taking a few discreet photos just in case Delia is right and he's something to do with Blades's murder and not just a man fascinated by a sad, beautiful girl.

Eventually, the skinny man peels away from the crowd and walks towards the cemetery gates. I stroll after him, keeping a long way back as I don't want to give myself away. I'm not going to lose him, because there's no cars for him to escape in; everyone has walked here. Then a black Mercedes pulls up to the gates, and the man sprints the last ten yards. I'm too far away to catch him, but I already have my phone in my hand, switched to camera, so I manage to snatch a photo of the car before he jumps in and is gone.

I kick myself. Why didn't I just arrest him on the spot? Although it's hard to see on what grounds.

I get straight onto Michael at the station and tell him to get onto Galway about a black Mercedes that might be the one involved in the Carmody murder. Then I call Ronan on his mobile, and while I'm waiting for him to pick up, I enlarge the image on my phone as much as I can, trying to make out the Mercedes's registration. It's blurry but it's probably a Dublin plate, and maybe forensics can enlarge it more. And at least I have the skinny man's picture.

Ronan picks up, and I tell him what's happened. He says he'll take over, notify the traffic cops, and I should forward him the photos then stay on at the cemetery, keeping a lookout for any other odd behaviour. 'Stay safe, Mags,' he says with real concern in his voice, 'and be careful. There's a couple of undercover detectives there, but even if they see anything, they won't be able to intervene because it will blow their cover, and it's important that the Travelling community never finds out who they are.'

It doesn't seem like a good time to tell him what Delia has just pointed out to me, so I say, 'I understand.'

'Great work, Mags,' he says. Then, just before he rings off, he adds, 'Well done,' which is heart-warming but seems like far too much praise in the circumstances.

After sending the photos to Ronan, I look around for Delia. She's deep in conversation with another young woman, whom I assume is

Michelle Carmody. I still feel angry with myself for letting the man get away. I try to tell myself maybe the make of car was a coincidence – there are a lot of black Mercedes in the world – but I don't find myself very convincing.

'There's no justification for taking a life,' murmurs a voice from not much higher than my elbow. 'It's a mortal sin.' It's Dacie McGovern, who has come to stand beside me.

I look down at her. 'I'm so sorry, Dacie. It's heartbreaking. And poor Natasha – what a terrible experience.'

'I won't pretend I had much time for him, I didn't, but what happened to him was wrong, God be good to him. And sure, Natasha got a terrible shock.' She nods, glancing towards her granddaughter, who is weeping into her handkerchief while surrounded by her father, brothers and fiancé, Joseph. 'She'll come around to Joseph,' she says in her quiet voice. 'My marriage was a match. My mother's marriage was a match, and her mother's before her. It all works out fine in the end. The older people know us better than we know ourselves.'

A woman passes us, sobbing loudly, two older women either side of her. I recognise her as the one who was in the carriage with Blades's parents.

We let them pass. Dacie bows her head respectfully, so I do the same. Once they're out of earshot, she murmurs to me, 'That's Mary McCarthy. She was intended for Blades, and she was mad about him. She's savage with Natasha now, fearing people thought that he was with her instead of Mary. So we'll have to keep them apart for a while. The sooner we get our girl up the aisle, the better at this stage.'

The idea of the heartbroken Natasha being frogmarched into a church to tie herself for life to a man she doesn't love isn't something I can do anything about, so I try to put it to the back of my mind.

'Mrs McGovern?' I ask quietly. 'Was Blades stuck in anything he shouldn't have been, do you know? Apart from the usual?'

She looks up at me, her intelligent eyes unreadable. 'Sure, how would I know that, Mags?'

She smiles to show there are no hard feelings, but Duckie is right about one thing: They will tell you nothing.

CHAPTER 18

*B*ack at the station after the funeral, we have a meeting where I update everyone on the appearance of the black Mercedes and show them the photos. Like Delia, nobody recognises the skinny man. I apologise to her for letting him get away, but she shrugs good-naturedly. 'What were you going to do? Traveller funerals aren't the best places to shout, "Stop! Police!"' Then she rolls her eyes and says, 'Joke,' because we're sitting there like stuffed dummies not knowing whether we're allowed to laugh or not, but by then it's too late to laugh spontaneously.

I opt for smiling instead. 'So did Michelle Carmody have anything interesting to say?'

Delia's face closes up for a moment. She glances around at Darren, Cathal and Nicola, then decides she's in safe company. 'Michelle knew Blades was having second thoughts about marrying Mary McCarthy. He was mad about Natasha. Everyone knew it below in the jail in Limerick – he had pictures of her up on the wall for everyone to see. Mary was rippin' over it and was threatening she was gonna bate the tar out of Natasha for taking her fella. But Michelle's certain what happened to Blades was nothing to do with the McCarthy family, no more than it was to do with the Wards or the McGoverns. Nobody in

129

any of the families has any idea why he was killed, only...' She stops. A faint blush creeps over her cheeks, making her look even more beautiful in her black funeral outfit.

'What, Delia?' I ask.

Darren is leaning forward in his chair, his eyes fixed on the Traveller girl, while Nicola is taking notes and Cathal is sitting back with his arms folded.

Delia's cheeks are bright red, and she puts her face in her hands.

I say gently, 'Delia, we're trying to solve a murder here. And maybe stop another.'

She whispers through her palms. 'Blades told Michelle he was worried Natasha might be in danger because she's a... She's a...'

'Delia?'

'A virgin,' she says in a very small voice.

We all look at each other, and then back at her. Cathal clears his throat and says, 'Do you mean it's because she's *supposed* to be a virgin but she and Blades...'

Delia flushes even brighter red, this time with fury. 'No, that's not what I mean, Cathal!'

I say quickly, 'Delia, Cathal...'

She's furious. 'I know what you all think about us, but it's not true! Blades said she's in danger because she's never been with a fella, and before you ask, Michelle has no idea what he meant about it being dangerous and neither do I!'

Cathal has the grace to apologise and manages to sound sincere, and Delia settles down, though she's still shooting him dirty looks. Darren volunteers again to help keep a watch at the McGovern site, especially now since it looks like Natasha might be in even more danger. As soon as he and Delia have gone, I ring Ronan.

'Mags, hi!' His deep voice sounds cheerful.

'Hi, Ronan. I just wanted to check in regarding what we discussed? And I have some more information from –'

'I'd rather not talk more than necessary over the phone,' he cuts in.

I understand. It seems ridiculous that the crime gangs are somehow monitoring our communications, but the guards are increasingly wary of technology. It's invaluable in crime detection, but equally, we know first-hand how a text message or an email never really dies and can be plucked like a rabbit from a hat at the most inopportune time.

'Shaw's, at five thirty?' he asks, naming a pub out on the Dublin road, halfway from Ballycarrick to Galway.

I've told Kieran I'll be home early tonight. He's going out to a meeting at seven about the importance of getting the town a new defibrillator.

'Leave it with me. I need to juggle some things.'

'Chainsaws?' He chuckles.

'No, small girls,' I reply with a smile. 'I'll text you if I can't be there. Take it that I will be.'

'Grand.' He hangs up.

I text Kieran.

Can you have girls later? Know you were going to go to that meeting, but I need to work. It's very important. xxx

The reply is instant.

Can you ask your mother? I really need to go to that meeting. Sorry. On roof. Talk later. xxx

In a fit of annoyance, I throw the phone on the desk. Why is the care of our kids my job to sort out? He's their father, but I need to ask him if he can mind them. Nobody ever asks me if it suits. He texted me two weeks ago to ask me where Kate's socks were. Could he not hazard a guess? Even in a total stranger's house, you'd look for socks in a drawer in a bedroom, wouldn't you? Not the fridge or the garden shed. Sometimes – and I know he's lovely and all of that – I could happily choke him.

I take a few deep breaths, pick the phone up again and call my mother. 'Mam, it's me. Could you stay on for longer this evening? I've a really important work meeting, and Kieran is insisting on going to that thing about the defibrillator.'

'I can, of course, love, no problem.'

Of course it's a problem. Mam's a very active woman, and she goes social dancing every Friday and Saturday night with a group of her friends. I feel guilty for asking her to mind the girls instead, and hugely grateful for her unquestioning support. 'Thanks so much, Mam. I shouldn't be too late, or maybe Kieran will get back from his very important meeting before I do.'

She picks up on the acid in my voice and says soothingly, 'Isn't it great Kieran is so community-minded, no more than you are. This town would be so much the worse for not having him. Sure, wasn't it him who saved Chrissy Foley that time with the kiss of life, and look at the way he organises the first aid courses for the trainers of the football teams and everything.'

I smile reluctantly. Kieran is rightly obsessed with people knowing first aid; he has seen so many accidents on building sites and football pitches all his life. He arranges free courses every year in the parish hall. And he did save Chrissy's life; he kept her going for an hour with CPR until the ambulance got there, and three stents later she's up and about, good as new. We get a free-range turkey from the Foleys every Christmas as a result. Still, my irritation with him hasn't quite melted yet. 'Yeah, he's a marvel, Mam. An absolute angel.'

I hear her chuckling. 'Oh, 'tis like that, is it? I'll stay well out of it so. See you later, love.'

I smile wider. 'Bye, Mam. Thanks.'

CHAPTER 19

I don't want to walk into Shaw's pub wearing my uniform – it would put the heart sideways in everyone – and luckily I have a pair of jeans and a t-shirt in my locker. Unfortunately, I don't have any other shoes so have to wear my black clunky Garda-issue ones. I have no make-up, and I have hat hair from being under the hard-rimmed police hat earlier. Those cops on the telly never seem to have a flat ring of hair around their heads whenever they take off their hats, but I certainly do and I look a fright, not that it matters. Never mind, it's only a quick meeting with Ronan to fill him in, and then I'll be home for a bath and bed.

On the way to Shaw's, I put on an audio book. I love listening to books as well as podcasts, especially old books set in a time when no one worried about the end of the world and the bleaching of the Great Barrier Reef in Australia didn't enter into it. Dickens and Austen are great, and I'm listening to *Crime and Punishment* by Dostoevsky at the moment.

Once Danny, Sharon, Kieran and I won a table quiz because I got all the answers on literature. Danny looked at me like I had ten heads. Kieran said he made a smart remark at the bar about Google being a great thing, insinuating I cheated – even though I was on his team!

Danny is not a great believer in women having brains. Though you'd have to question the reasoning of any woman who'd go within a donkey's roar of Danny.

I met my old English teacher in the library one day. I was in with the girls – they love reading too – and while they were on the bean-bags in the kids' section, I was browsing the classics. I was actually going to check out Hardy's *The Mayor of Casterbridge* when she comes up behind me, peers over my shoulder and says, 'And to think I had to drag you by the hair of your head through *The Wind in the Willows.*' And laughing away at her own great joke, she wandered off.

I remember when she went out on extended sick leave and a replacement teacher came in for her, a man in his twenties. He sat on the desk, not behind it, and opened our minds to literature. He told us something I never forgot. He asked if any of us had ever read James Joyce, and we said we hadn't.

'You can all read, can't you?'

We nodded, wondering where this was going.

'Then no matter what it is, a novel, a law book, an engineering manual, a great piece of classic literature, a banned book even – in fact they are usually worth a read – you can read it. There's no barrier once you can read, except the ones we put on ourselves, so read whatever you like – there are no rules.'

I took that to heart and never thought a book was too hard, or too above me, from that day to this. I often think of him. If I ever see him again, I'll tell him his words allowed me to discover a lifetime of pleasure.

In Shaw's, I have to walk around for a while before I spot Ronan sitting in an alcove a long way from the bar. It must be a detective thing to always pick a private spot – less chance of being overheard, I suppose. I wave, and as I walk to join him, a waitress passes me with a plate of lasagne; the aroma hits my nostrils, making my tummy grumble.

'Have you eaten?' Ronan asks cheerfully as I slide in opposite him.

'No, actually. I skipped lunch, and I've not had a chance to eat.'

'Me neither. We might as well have something.' Ronan peruses the menu on the table thoughtfully. 'I think I'll have the Greek salad and a baked potato. And for you? My treat.'

'Lasagne,' I reply without looking at the menu at all.

'And drinks?'

'Just a sparkling water for me.'

Ronan goes up to the bar to order the drinks and food. I check my phone. Still no word from Kieran. I'd sent him a rather pointed text once I'd arranged Mam to have the girls, but he didn't reply; he prefers to keep his distance when I'm being pointed.

A friendly hum of conversation fills the pub, people everywhere eating and chatting. But the old man sitting at the table opposite our alcove is alone. He's about seventy, in an old suit, with more hair in his ears and nose than on his head, and he's missing two teeth on the bottom. A half-eaten plate of shepherd's pie sits in front of him. He catches my eye and sees his chance. I'm too late to look away.

'Did you hear about the priest that goes into a bar?' he asks.

I smile patiently and maintain eye contact. If I've learned anything in life, it's that no amount of social cues, verbal or non-verbal, work in stopping a joke teller in their tracks. They are like a freight train. Best let him get on with it. The poor old divil probably had nobody to talk to all day.

He perks up. 'Well, he goes up to the first fella and says, "Pat, do you want to go to heaven?" "I do, Father," sez he. "Right," says the priest, "stand over there by the wall so."

'Then he goes to the next fella at the bar and says, "Mikey, do you want to go to heaven?" "I definitely do, Father," he says, and so the priest tells him to stand over beside Pat.

'Then he goes to the third fella at the bar. "And so, Gerry, do you want to go to heaven?" he asks. "No thanks, Father," Gerry replies.

'"What?" says the priest, appalled. "You don't want to go to heaven when you die?" "Oh, I do, Father, I'd love to go when I die, but I thought you were rounding up a gang to go now."'

The man finds his own joke hilarious and slaps his knee in delight.

I don't know if it's the joke, or the stress of what happened at the graveside, or of Delia's row with Cathal, but whatever it is, I find myself laughing uncontrollably too.

Ronan appears at the table to find us both wiping our eyes with mirth.

The old guy stands, drains his pint, tips his cap and is gone.

'Well?' Ronan asks, bemused. 'What's so funny?' He places a glass of sparkling water with ice and lemon wedges in front of me.

'Nothing, honestly,' and I dissolve into helpless giggles again. The laughter must be infectious, because then he's laughing too. I pull myself together; he must think I'm actually insane.

'Thanks,' I say, taking a long draft of the cold drink. It's lovely.

While we wait for our food to arrive, we exchange notes. Now that the joker is gone, there's nobody within earshot of us, but Ronan still keeps his voice to a murmur. Force of habit, I suppose.

He tells me the Galway traffic cops had a checkpoint already set up on the Dublin road for motor tax. Several black Mercedes came through, but there were no passengers matching the photo of the skinny man, which he'd forwarded on to them. Forensics couldn't capture the car's registration from the photo. It's not like in the films; once you blow up a real image too large, it disappears into a fog of dots. They'd entered the skinny man's picture into the police computer, but nothing came back, so he hasn't got a police record.

'Maybe the man is a reporter,' suggests Ronan, something I hadn't even thought about – you can tell I'm no detective. So the whole thing at the cemetery really could have been a coincidence.

I tell him about the conversation with Delia, and the information about Blades saying Natasha was in danger because she's never been with a man. Ronan looks thoughtful, and I worry he's thinking like Cathal, that we're back to the in-Traveller violence thing, that Ronan now thinks Blades has been murdered for having a relationship with Natasha and spoiling her for marriage.

'Mm,' he says.

The food arrives, and he tucks into his salad and potato.

'Do you have any idea what he might have meant?' I ask. There's a nagging feeling in my mind, like somewhere deep down I know the answer, but nothing's coming to me. It's like a pub quiz after a glass of wine too many.

Ronan shrugs. 'The undercovers didn't hear a word about Keogh or drugs at the funeral, so Dublin is beginning to think maybe the whole thing was an argument within the Travelling community after all, like Duckie said. That Carmody was warned about Natasha, and then killed.'

I take another mouthful of lasagne, but suddenly it's not nice; it's sand in my mouth.

He looks up at me over a forkful of salad. 'Look, I'm not saying this investigation is over, Mags. We'll get there. It's just…it's complicated. I think Dublin is losing interest because nothing's showing up on the radar about Keogh. But you and me…we'll get to the bottom of it. I'm going to wait a few days before interviewing the Carmodys again, give them time to get over their son's funeral. And I'll send someone to talk to Natasha again. I know the guards who interviewed her in the hospital thought she was keeping something back.'

'Not according to Delia,' I say. 'And Delia's honest.'

He nods. 'If you say so.'

But I suspect – and I don't blame him for this – that he has his doubts about Delia, that he thinks she's bound to be prejudiced in favour of her cousin.

He adds, 'I know your station is keeping an eye on the McGoverns' halting site. Just call me if you need backup.'

'I will, of course.'

There's nothing more to be said about the case, so while we're finishing our food, I tell him how I was listening to *Crime and Punishment* by Dostoevsky in the car on the way here. I say how I think it doesn't matter if you are Rodion Raskolnikov or Alan Keogh or whoever killed Blades Carmody, I truly believe that somewhere in the deep recesses in the human spirit of the murderer is a sense of self-loathing. To take a life, another person's potential, to plunge their loved ones into a life of grief, surely you couldn't do that and just go on your merry way?

It turns out Ronan has read *Crime and Punishment* and it's one of his favourite books, but he doesn't agree. He says most killers in his opinion are sociopaths who are entirely devoid of empathy or compassion for anyone, including themselves. Mind you, he says, they are all cowards, that is the uniting feature. Once convicted, they'll cry like babies when they are sent to prison, scared out of their wits of the type they'll meet inside now that they are just another prisoner. Their trappings of wealth and power just mask how inadequate they really feel inside.

It's a great conversation. It's fun to talk to someone who is as interested in the philosophy of the job as I am, although of course his job is a lot more important than mine. I try him out with my theory of scoring points for good deeds.

'You are a very unusual woman, Mags Munroe, do you know that?' He grins.

'For unusual, read mental.' I grin back.

'No, not at all. Quite the opposite. Sane as they come, but I've never met anyone like you.'

'Aren't you lucky.' I chuckle.

'I am,' he says, and there's no hint of a smile. He gazes at me intently.

CHAPTER 20

*W*ednesday morning is taken up with the neighbourhood watch group, which is made up mostly of decent people trying to do good for the town but has a few curtain-twitching wannabe Miss Marples. Today they are exercised about the town having been full of Travellers last Saturday, due to the Carmody funeral.

Lavinia, Willie the postmaster's wife, is convinced one of them robbed the basket of flowers that usually hangs outside the post office. 'As sure as I sit here, right off the wall while I was inside serving Mrs Burke. Isn't that right, Joanna?'

'There one minute and gone the next, just as the funeral was passing,' agrees Joanna Burke, the doctor's receptionist, who seems to spend all her spare time in the post office, otherwise known as Gossip Central. There are other members of the neighbourhood watch as well, but they are bullied into submission by the formidable duo of Mrs Burke and Lavinia and nobody risks putting their head above the parapet.

Lavinia is on a roll now. 'And Gemma O'Flaherty, you know, married to Phillip from the garage, said three bales of briquettes went missing from their forecourt, and Fiona Griffin's daughter's pink bike was taken from their front garden.'

I am writing it all down; it doesn't do not to be seen to treat these things seriously. 'A basket of flowers, three bales of briquettes, a child's bicycle...'

Annette Deasy, a woman with big brown eyes and curly charcoal hair, raises her hand. She must be in her fifties, and she's wearing a mad long yellow dress embroidered with red flowers and red leather handmade shoes.

I smile at her encouragingly, ready to add another missing object to the list. 'Yes, Annette?'

She smiles back at me. 'I just wanted to say, I saw a big lad of eleven or twelve this morning riding a very small pink bike around Castlepark housing estate, and I did rather suspect it wasn't his, so I said it to him and he threw it in the bushes and ran off. I didn't like to take possession of it in case the owner came back for it, but I'm sure it's still there. If someone can tell me where Fiona Griffin lives, I'll bring it back to her.'

'Thank you, Annette. That would be great. I'll give you Fiona's address at the end of the meeting.' I remind myself yet again not to judge a book by its cover. Annette might be dressed like an eccentric hippy, but she's refreshingly sensible.

Lavinia looks more put out than pleased by the successful solving of the bicycle crime. 'Well, well, I suppose you haven't seen my flowers about the town, Annette?'

'No, Lavinia, I don't know about your flowers, but I doubt if it was any of the *mourners* who took the basket. They surely had enough flowers already. Did you see the size of those beautiful wreaths? Magnificent.'

'Must have cost thousands,' mutters Joanna Burke, and one or two others nod their agreement.

Settled people think it's shocking the way Travellers spend so much on the dead. I wonder if the Travellers think we are shocking for spending so little. Annette catches my eye and drops me a tiny wink, and I realise I like her. Neighbourhood watch meetings are going to be a lot more fun now she's decided to join.

I nearly pop down to Mam at lunchtime but remember it's her day for Irish stew in the Samovar with Joe. I could join them, I suppose, but I don't think I will. I stroll down to Teresa's for a scone and tea instead.

After lunch, I give Ronan a ring and he offers to meet early evening again, but even though he won't talk about it directly over the phone, it's clear there's nothing new to report since Saturday, so I say I'll call him later in the week. I've hours of paperwork to catch up on, and I want to devote this evening to Ellie. She was like her old self on Sunday, but this morning on the way to school she looked so miserable, my heart broke for her. Something bad is going on, and I need to get it out of her before it gets worse.

I leave early, but on the way home, I take a detour to the halting site where Darren is still sitting patiently in the squad car a short distance up the road, keeping an eye on the comings and goings.

The McGoverns were very suspicious about him being there at first, thinking he was spying on them, but Delia explained it to Dacie, that it was about protection, not spying, and now every so often one of the kids appears with a cup of tea and sandwich and they let him use their toilet block. He was even playing football with some of the teenage lads the other day.

I stay a bit longer at the site than I should because Dacie is worried about Natasha, who is spending her time in bed crying when she should be getting ready for her wedding. I suggest victim counselling, and wonder why she's not been offered it already; it's terrible what happened to her. But Dacie shakes her head sharply. Counselling is another institution of the settled world that the old lady is suspicious of.

I'm just turning into my road when I get a call from the station.

'Hi, what's up?' I answer the call through the car speaker.

'Hi, Sarge. Sorry to bother you, but I thought you'd like to know – we were called to an altercation up at Danny Boylan's place.' Michael's voice tells me all I need to know.

'Sharon?' I ask, my heart sinking.

'We have her here now, and she's refusing to speak to anyone. I asked her if I should call you, but she, ah...she didn't want me to, but I thought...'

'Don't worry, Michael, you did right to call me. I'm on the way in.'

I call home. The phone rings and Ellie picks up.

'Hi, pet, it's me. I was nearly home but need to go back into work for a while, there's an emergency. So can you tell Dad I'll be late?'

'But I need you to help me with my book report. You said you'd do it tonight, and I have to have it done for tomorrow –'

I cut across her. 'Ellie.' My head is full of Sharon; I'm terrified of what she might have done. 'I need to get back to work, darling. Can you ask Dad?'

'But you said *you'd* do it... Dad's hopeless at that stuff.'

'Well then, leave it on the kitchen table and I'll have a look when I get home, alright?'

'But that's no good. I can't change it in the morning – it will be too late...' I hear the break in her voice; she's moments from tears.

I hear Kieran's voice in the background, asking what the matter is, and then he comes on the phone. 'Mags? Is everything all right?'

'Not really. I was nearly home, but then I got a call from the station and I need to go back in. I'm so sorry.' I can't tell him why. It's Sharon, I don't know what's happened, and it's police business so it's confidential.

'Ah, for God's sake, Mags, what now,' he snaps.

I stare at the car speaker in astonishment. I know Kieran prefers me to be home in the evening – *I* prefer me to be home in the evening – but I've never heard him sound angry about it before. Disappointed, yes. Grumpy, yes. But never coldly angry like he sounds now.

'I'm sorry, it's just something really important came up that only I can deal with...'

'Bye, Mags.' The line goes dead.

I feel tears threatening and swallow hard. I'm a terrible wife, a terrible mother, I'm old and fat, Kieran would be better off leaving me and marrying a young one... It's awful. It's like I have Nora Munroe in my head, screaming her poison at me. I know, I *know*, Kieran never complained to his mother about me. But what if, like most mothers can, she'd just sensed what her son was thinking and feeling?

The station is quiet when I get in, and Michael looks up from the desk as I enter.

'How is she?' I ask. 'What happened?'

He slides a report across the desk at me. 'She's calmed down now, but she did a fair bit of damage up at her ex-husband's place. She had a hurley, so she came prepared. She battered the car before using a Stanley knife to slash his tyres, and keyed the paintwork, broke the front window of the house, gave Boylan a nasty scratch on his face when he came out to stop her, and when his new woman tried to intervene, she got a right clatter as well. She resisted arrest and gave myself and Cathal a job to get her in the car. She was out of control.' He's not looking pleased.

'Are Danny and Chloe going to press charges?' I ask, reading the report with a sinking heart.

'I'd say so. They were raging. The car is wrecked and Boylan loved it. A Jaguar. I'd say she's after doing ferocious damage.'

'Did she hurt Chloe?'

'Well, she was screaming like she was hurt, so we had to phone the doctor – the ambulance was gone to Ballinasloe – but I think she was only frightened really.'

'And is Sharon all right?'

'Apart from being like a demented lunatic, yeah, I'd say she's grand.' Michael is cross, clearly no love lost there.

'And who has her son?'

'Her mother. Nicola called her and she said she'd keep him.'

The report in my hand, I walk down the corridor to the left, to where we have three cells, and open the flap on the one with the locked door. Sure enough, there is my best friend, sitting on the bed, her back to the wall. Her mascara has run and her face is blotchy.

I unlock the door and bring her down the corridor into my office and sit her in the chair facing the desk. 'Tea?' I offer.

'No.'

I perch on the edge of the desk. I don't want to act too formal; she's my best friend, even if she is technically my prisoner right now. 'Shar, I can't help you if you won't talk to me.'

Her eyes flicker. 'I don't need your help, Mags. I'm tired. I just want to go home and see Sean and forget this ever happened.' She goes to stand up, and while my heart breaks for the pain she's in, she needs to understand the severity of her actions.

'Sharon, sit back down. You can't just walk out of here. You've been arrested. You're looking at GBH, criminal damage, trespass. If Danny and Chloe press charges – and it sounds like they will – you could be facing actual prison time.'

She shakes her head. 'He won't. He wouldn't do that to me.'

I can't believe what I'm hearing. 'Sharon, listen to yourself. You assaulted his girlfriend, you destroyed the car he loves, you attacked him – he's almost certainly going to take this further. Don't kid yourself.'

'He won't, he loves me. Chloe was a mistake – he knows it and I know it.'

I stare at her. The Sharon I know isn't crazy – she's kind and warm and funny – but this woman isn't the Sharon I know. 'Sharon, what *are* you on about? You keep thinking Chloe is the problem. She isn't, Shar, she just *isn't*. Danny is a two-timing rat and not worth any woman's energy. It's hard, I know, but it's the truth. He was never faithful, not from the start – he's not capable or something. But who cares? I don't give a monkey's about him, but I care deeply about you and Sean, and you're playing with fire here. Please believe me when I tell you these are not insignificant charges.'

She won't meet my eyes and is gazing at the wall above my head.

I raise my voice, trying to get through. 'You have to go up there now and apologise. I'll go with you. You have to tell Danny you'll pay to repair the damage, and you have to apologise profusely to Chloe for hitting her, and we need to go now, before he comes in here all guns blazing with his lawyer.'

She laughs, not the lovely happy laugh she and I have shared so many millions of times. This is a harsh, angry bark. 'I'll go to jail before I apologise to that tramp.'

I slip off the desk, cross to the chair and go on my hunkers beside her. 'Shar, listen to me, please? You're my best friend. I love you. If the last forty years of friendship mean anything, then listen to me now. If Danny presses charges, this will go to court, and everything – and I mean everything – can change in a moment there. If you can't be sensible for yourself, then at least be sensible for Sean.'

Her eyes are unreadable; I need to do more.

'It's a possibility that you could go to prison, Shar, if we don't try to reverse this immediately, and where would Sean end up then? Not with your mam, or me, but with his father, of course, and Chloe. Is that what you want? You in Mountjoy and Sean living with them? Sean being brought to visit you once a fortnight?'

That image is the one that finally penetrates the hard shell of bitter resentment. Tears pool in her eyes, and within seconds she is sobbing, trembling in my arms.

I pat her back soothingly. 'Come on, let's get this over with. To hell with Danny – we're doing this for Sean, all right?'

My arm around her, I lead her out of the station to the squad car and settle her into the passenger seat.

'I haven't the money to pay to fix the Jaguar, or the window,' she says as I climb into the driver's seat, her voice quavering.

'I'll give it to you. Don't worry, we'll figure something out.' I reverse and pull out onto the road and head for Boylan's.

A LOT of people don't understand how difficult it still is for women after divorce. The women are usually left to mind the children, and it's a lot harder for them to recover their feet financially. Even Kieran doesn't get it. I've tried to explain, but his eyes glaze over. He thinks the equality war is over. Women have all the rights now, he says, and reminds me again how John Holohan has to pay sixteen hundred euro a month maintenance to his missus who cheated on him and is only allowed access to his kids once a week. I can't tell Kieran that John has to be chased to pay, and how his wife, Daniele, lived in dread of the emotional abuse he meted out to her and the children year in, year out because it was confidential, but anyway, he wouldn't believe it.

Coercive control, that's what John Holohan was doing to his wife. It's a crime only recently on the books, and it's great that it is. A brave woman and a guard in Dublin took a case all the way to the High Court last year. The husband wasn't battering her, but he controlled all the money, alienated her from her friends and family, dictated what she wore and who she saw, and a judge ruled that it was an offence and your man got put away for it. It was a great day for women.

But according to everyone in Ballycarrick, John is a grand man, he never hurt a hair on her head, she was the one who did the dirt, and it is all so unfair on poor John. The man Daniele Holohan is with now was her neighbour and a teacher in the secondary school, and the one who gave evidence of the unreasonable behaviours her husband subjected her to: making her wash windows in the rain, ordering her to weed the garden in the depths of winter, humiliating her in front of others, undermining her with the kids' teachers at school, dictating everything, where she could go, who she could see. The truth is he's a sadist, but because he never hit her, he's a grand man.

The neighbour seems nice, and I wish them both well.

I digress, but you know what I mean. It's still a man's world.

* * *

BOTH CARS ARE THERE, and the lights are on as we pull up. Paudie Lenihan's van is also there – he's the local handyman – so he must be fixing the window.

I tell Sharon to stay in the squad car for now while I talk to Danny. She nods and grips my hand for a split second.

Standing at the door, I put my hat on – I'm here as a local sergeant, not as the best friend of the perpetrator – and ring the bell. I hear footsteps and then the door opens and there is Danny, with a blood-streaked scrawl on his cheek.

'Good evening, Mr Boylan,' I say. 'I'm here with your ex-wife, who wants to apologise and offer to pay for any damage.'

His eyes flash past me to where Sharon is sitting in the squad car, and he takes a step back into the hall. 'Get her away from my house, Mags. She's mental, wants locking up. I mean it now. I'm coming down to ye in the morning to make a statement, and I will press charges. She wrecked my car, and that window is going to cost a fortune, and she hurt Chloe, and look at the state of me.' He points to his scratched cheek.

'That's your prerogative, of course, Danny, but if you would just hear her out...'

'I have no interest in anything that mad old wagon has to say! She came here, attacked my car, put a brick through my window, attacked me, attacked Chloe –'

I interrupt him quietly. Plan A of Sharon apologising isn't going to work, clearly. Time to resort to plan B. There are no witnesses, Chloe is inside, and Paudie is too far away. Still, I keep my voice down. 'Danny, we both know there are aspects of your personal life that you'd rather stayed secret. It would do neither you nor Sharon any good to have made public the results of your previous relationships around the town. You have lied and cheated through your entire marriage. By all means press charges, but once you open that can of worms, there's no way of stopping the entire story coming out. Do you think Ted Canovan would still use your accounting practice if he knew what went on between his wife and you? What about Phillip O'Flaherty from the garage if he heard about *his* wife? That's another account gone. We both know that's just for starters. So my advice to you would be to let this go.'

If it weren't so serious, it would be funny. Danny stands before me, his mouth opening, then closing again, like a stupid fish.

'She can't come up here, wreck my property, threaten my family...' he begins again, but there's less force behind his words now. We both know he's beaten.

'And she's sorry about that, but come on, Danny. If anyone is at fault here, it's not Sharon. She thought she was getting a faithful husband, you have a son together, and you have robbed her of the future she thought she was getting, her and Sean. And then for her to hear in the post office that you fathered Judy O'Halloran's child…'

That hits home. 'You're an interfering old cow, Mags Munroe, that's all you are. I'm sure the Guards aren't supposed to get stuck into people's private business. Come to think of it, I wonder what the chief super would think about you coming up here and threatening me…' He is warming to his theme now.

'I'm not threatening you. I'm explaining what could happen and making you aware of the potential fallout from a hasty decision. That's my legal duty. And anyway, it's my word against yours, and who is a court going to believe, Danny? A serial philanderer and liar? Or an upstanding member of the Gardai with an impeccable record? So don't let's bother with that road, eh?'

'But she wrecked my car and hurt my face,' he whines. The fact that the thump she gave Chloe is barely mentioned says a lot about him.

'She did, but that's the price you pay. Now what are we going to do here?' I face him down. Thankfully Sharon is still in the car; at this stage that's the best thing.

'It's not fair, Mags…' He's still whingeing.

'No, Danny, it's not. Nor is it fair that you'd get up on a gust of wind, it's not fair on Sean that everyone in the place knows what his father is like, it's not fair on Sharon that she had to leave her lovely home and that you moved a girl young enough to be your daughter in here, it's not fair that she's had to endure the pity of this place – none of it is fair and it's all your own doing.'

'But…'

I'm losing patience. 'Are you pressing charges or not, Danny? Yes or no? I need to get home.'

'If I do, you'll make sure that everyone knows my private business by teatime tomorrow, is that it?'

I lock eyes with him, saying nothing, but yes, that's exactly what I'll do.

After what feels like an interminable delay, he sighs. 'Fine, but you stay away from me, do you hear me?' He points his finger to Sharon in the car and shouts, 'She needs locking up.'

I pray Shar stays where she is, and to her credit, she does.

'We'll leave it there so,' I say.

Back in the car I drive down the avenue. Sharon is frozen in silence beside me as I tell her Danny won't be needing her apology and won't be pressing charges. And I tell her why. She's never believed me about Danny before, but now I suppose she'll have to accept it as the truth, because why else would he back off at the threat of it all being confirmed? I pull up outside her place.

'Do you want me to come in?' I ask.

She shakes her head, then turns to me. 'I'm sorry, Mags, for every-thing, for putting you to all this trouble today. And I'm so sorry for walking out on you in the Samovar and not calling you since. I should have known you were right all along, and I don't blame you if you don't want to be my friend anymore...'

'He's not worth it, Shar. We've stuck together for forty years – we won't let a miserable toad like Danny Boylan come between us.' I give her a smile, and she returns it with a watery one.

'Night, Mags. You were brilliant back there.'

'Yerra, that's all in a day's work.' I smile. 'I'll see you tomorrow.' And I drive back to the station, let Michael know there'll be no charges and pick up my own car.

CHAPTER 21

$\mathcal{I}$ am just about to put my key in the lock when I feel my phone buzz in my pocket. I take it out.

Hey, Mags. Need to meet to discuss case tomorrow. Shaw's again, 5:30? R

I hesitate before I reply. Kieran won't be happy, but Ronan is my superior and this is a murder case.

I'll be there. M

Kieran is nowhere to be seen, but the girls are watching *Strictly Come Dancing*; the whirling dervish of cerise spandex and spangles seems to mesmerise them.

'Hi, girls.' I stick my head around the living room door.

'Hi, Mam.' Kate smiles at me.

Ellie says hi but stays looking at the screen.

'How was your day? Did you get your book report done, Els?' I ask, deliberately keeping my tone light. 'Do you want me to look at it?'

'No,' she replies, her eyes still on the telly. 'Dad helped me.'

I sit down on the couch beside Kate. 'How on earth did he get into that get-up?' I ask her, pointing at a fella in turquoise body suit that looks like it was spray-painted onto him.

She giggles and whispers, 'I hope he doesn't need to pee.' She is nine and finds all toilet humour hilarious.

'Or worse.' I wink, and she dissolves into peals of helpless laughter.

'So, Els, any news?' I try with my eldest again.

'No, nothing. I need twenty euro tomorrow because we're going to Galway to see a film in Irish about the famine.'

By the tone of her voice, it sounds like she'd rather live through the actual famine than go to that. I feel her pain. Ireland has a tragic history, no doubt about it, wars and revolutions and famine and all the rest of it, but I suppose for our children, it's over and done with, and they must wonder why we all have to keep banging on about it. When I was in school, we used to have to read the writings of this mad old one who lived on an island off the coast of Kerry years ago. Many of her children died, and even as a teenager, I used to think she must be a very careless mother to say they all fell off cliffs or drowned or starved or whatever it was that happened to them. Maybe I'm heartless, but honestly, the misery industry in this country would drive you to drink. What on earth is the point of taking a gang of twelve-year-olds to a film about a whole country starving to death? In Irish? Seriously? To depress them? To make them feel grateful for what they have? Or guilty? The schools nowadays are forever banging the mental health drum, and rightly so, as most crimes committed have some element of poor mental health about them. So on the one hand, they are trying to keep our kids happy and not self-harming or doing drugs, and on the other hand, we're making them sit through two hours of the misery of the Potato Famine, in Irish? Still, I don't want to undermine the teacher; she probably means well.

'Really? That sounds…interesting,' I manage.

'It won't be,' Ellie replies. I feel a pang of loss for my sunny, bubbly girl. Where has she gone?

'Have you had your dinner yet?' I ask.

'Not yet,' Kate says. 'Dad was going to make a pizza after he's had his shower.'

'Then how about we go for pizza to Luigi's?' I suggest. Luigi, despite first impressions, is not from Milan but from Mullingar and is really called Leonard. But he does make nice pizza, and his place is all checked tablecloths and wine bottles as candleholders.

'And ice cream?' Kate asks enthusiastically.

'Of course ice cream!' I agree, hoping for a reaction from Ellie.

She glances at me and I see it, the tiny glimmer of her old self. She's a sucker for a her favourite ice cream sundae, the Knickerbocker Glory. 'And Dad?' she asks, looking worried. She must have heard Kieran barking at me on the phone earlier.

'Of course Dad. Sure, who'll pay for the pizza if we leave him at home?' I laugh and she sort of smiles too, but she still looks sad. 'Righto, Kate,' I say, 'go upstairs and tell moneybags what's happening. Tell him to dress in his Sunday best and bring his wallet.'

As Kate thunders upstairs, I shut the living room door and go to stand in front of my daughter. 'I know you don't want to tell me what's wrong, Els. I never wanted to tell Granny Marie anything either. I thought she'd make everything worse. But she never did, and I always felt better for talking to her.'

'There's nothing wrong,' she says, her eyes on the floor.

'Please tell me, Els, or I'll imagine much worse.'

She stands then and tries to get past me.

I place my hands on her narrow shoulders – she's almost as tall as I am now – and I look into her deep-blue eyes. 'Els, I can't sleep, I'm so worried about you. We used to talk about everything, but now I know something is bothering you, and you're so sad, and I haven't a clue what it is?' I don't dare mention anything about school in case she suspects Kate of telling and brings all holy hell down on the poor kid's head.

'I'm grand, Mam, I promise.'

'Ellie, I know you're not. Something is up, and I'm going to get to the bottom of it, one way or another. I'm a guard, after all, so my powers of investigation are pretty good.' I grin, and she rewards me with a tiny smile. 'So here's what we're going to do. We are all going to Luigi's, and we're going to stuff our faces with pizza and Knickerbocker Glories and have a laugh as a family, and then when we get home, you and me are going to have a chat. I don't want to have to use my thumbscrews or the electric cattle prod, but I will get it out of you.' I smile, though she knows I'm joking. 'And I swear to you, when you tell me, I can help. I can make it better, I promise you.'

She looks doubtful.

'Do you know how I know I can?' I ask her.

She shakes her head.

'Because since you were a teeny-tiny tot, I've been able to make you better. Whether it was food or wind or a dirty nappy...'

She rolls her eyes, mortified, but I'm relentless.

'And later, when Noah Walsh kept taking Hoppy from you in the playschool, and even later when Mrs O'Donovan was really mean to you and said you were too clumsy to play the concertina. Or the time in fourth class that Jane O'Keeffe took your homework and copied it and told the teacher you had copied her and she won the prize. Or the time nobody picked you for the basketball team. Didn't I make it better every single time?'

'But that was when I was a child!'

Dear God in heaven, you're still a child! I want to scream, but I know that won't help.

'You're growing up now, I know that, but you are still my daughter and you'll be that when you're fifty, and I'll still be fixing things for you. So please, my love, tell me and I will fix it, I swear.'

'Mam, come on, we're ready ages!' Kate yells from the hallway, and I hug Ellie briefly and fiercely.

'Later?' I ask.

'Later,' she says with a weary sigh.

* * *

DINNER BEGINS PERFECTLY, just us four having fun and chatting. Kieran isn't talking to me much, but he is having fun with the girls. Kate is full of the Irish dancing competition next weekend, and I try to arrange my face into a mask of delighted enthusiasm for what will surely be an afternoon of unadulterated torture. A whole five hours in the parish hall, watching small girls hop around like demented frogs in hard banging shoes, as Deirdre Hickey, the dance teacher, who must be ninety-five if she's a day, bellows instructions. The mothers will sit together in miserable solidarity, with their flasks of tea and biscuits, feigning glee when their offspring come over brandishing a silver medal in the two-hand reel or whatever it is. Each child has to pay a tenner to enter, and the whole parish goes. The hall is free, and so every penny of it goes into Hickey's pocket. A complete racket.

'Will you come, Daddy? I'm after getting really good at the hornpipe, and Miss Hickey says I might get the gold this year?' Kate's face is smeared with tomato sauce from her Hawaiian pizza; she looks adorable.

'Will you, Daddy? You'd love it,' I say, and wink at Ellie; she knows the score.

Trapped, Kieran casts around for an excuse. 'I would love to, pet, but I have to work, you see, and I've this big job on, and the man that owns the house is very scary – well, he's not too bad but his wife is terrifying...' He lowers his voice and makes a funny face, and they both laugh.

'But it's on Sunday, Dad, and you don't work on Sundays.' Kate is triumphant.

'Well, isn't that the best stroke of luck ever?' I exclaim. 'Daddy doesn't work on Sundays, so he will be free to go to the competition for the whole afternoon, every bit of it, from one o'clock all the way to the end at six.' I'm loving Kieran's look of incredulous horror.

'Well, how about I go for your dance...' he begins.

'Oh, you can't do that,' Kate announces breezily. 'Miss Hickey doesn't tell any of the parents who is going on when. She says it's only common courtesy to watch all the dancers, not just your own child, and that people who just want to stay for a few minutes when their own girl is dancing are very rude.'

'Well, doesn't Miss Hickey have a lot of opinions for a woman who has no dealings whatsoever with the Revenue,' Kieran mutters darkly.

'Who are the Revenue, Daddy?' Kate asks, her high-pitched voice heard by everyone in the tiny restaurant.

'The government department in charge of paying tax. You have to pay tax to the government on money you earn, and Daddy doesn't think Miss Hickey pays her taxes,' Ellie explains helpfully, just as Don Hurley passes our table, returning to his wife, Martha. Don catches my eye, and I smile apologetically. Hopefully it won't get out that the Munroes are questioning the dance teacher's legal taxation status.

'Dad doesn't think that, Ellie,' I say loudly.

'But he said...'

'Ellie!'

'So you'll come on Sunday, Dad?' Kate sees her chance.

'I will. I'll be there, Kit Kat.' He ruffles her silky hair.

Luigi allows the kids as many flavours as can fit in the glass for their sundae, so they both go up to the counter to choose, leaving me alone with Kieran.

'You better not think *you're* getting away with not going to the dancing,' he says with a half-smile, topping me up with the end of the bottle of red.

'I wouldn't miss it for the world,' I lie cheerfully.

It looks like he's forgiven me for being late. He must know he was being unfair; he was just tired probably. I decide to tell him now about tomorrow's meeting with Ronan rather than spring it on him at the last moment. 'Kieran, I'm sorry about being late tonight, and I'll explain another time, but I need to tell you, I've got another meeting after work tomorrow. I'll be home as quick as I can, but it won't be before seven.'

There's silence. He lowers the bottle to the table and sits staring at it. I feel a twinge of annoyance. I'm investigating a murder – well, I'm not the lead investigator, that's Ronan, but I have local knowledge and I want to help him as much as I can. 'Kieran...'

He raises his head and meets my eyes. 'And this meeting involves having dinner and drinks with some fella in Shaw's, does it, Mags?'

I'm thrown completely off balance. 'If by some fella you mean Ronan Brady, actually it does, although I'm not planning to eat this time. It's just I...'

'Why not? Sounds like you were having a great time with him the other day? Laughing away, the two of you, in between whispering to each other?'

Oh God, what's he saying? Why does he look so hurt? My heart is racing. I press my hands to my burning cheeks. Please, not a hot flush, not now. I glance towards the girls. They're still choosing sprinkles and jellies for their ice creams and have been joined by two other kids they seem to know. 'We weren't whispering, Kieran, we were only keeping our voices down because we were discussing a murder case and didn't want the whole parish to hear. Just as well, as it turns out. Obviously there were plenty of eyes on us, not that we were trying not to be seen...'

'Weren't you? I heard you were in a hidden alcove a long way from the bar. And if you want to know who told me that, it was Gemma O'Flaherty, who passed you by on her way to the ladies'. I was paying for diesel at the garage this afternoon, and there she was, wanting to know if you had a cousin or a brother visiting, as you and this good-looking fella in Shaw's seemed so close. I felt about six inches tall. I didn't know what to say. I just told her you'd been meeting a work colleague and got out of there.'

I feel like killing Gemma. And her own track record with Danny Boylan is not exactly squeaky clean, so who does she think she is? I wonder for a minute if Danny said something to her about me knowing they had an affair and she wanted to stir things up for me. Honestly, sometimes life in a small place would drive you daft. I wonder if people who live in London or New York have to put up with this kind of rubbish or whether it's just part of the universal human condition. Either way, it's very frustrating.

'And you said exactly the right thing, Kieran. That's precisely what I *was* doing. Ronan's my boss – well, in this case he is anyway – and we only met in Shaw's because it's halfway between here and Galway so it's convenient. And I was eating because I hadn't managed to have lunch with the funeral and everything. We can't discuss sensitive details of the case on the phone because of the hacking risk, so it's either he comes to Ballycarrick Station or I drive all the way to Galway.'

I see a flicker of something in his eyes. Hope? Or distrust? 'Seriously, Mags, it really was just a work thing? You seem so distracted these days, and he rings and you just tear off right away. I don't know…I just feel…'

'Oh, come on, Kieran – what did you think it was?' I am amazed at the idea he could imagine me having an affair, because that's obviously what he's been thinking since bloody Gemma put it into his head with her sly gossip. 'You don't really think it would be any other kind of meeting? Seriously? Me? I haven't got eyes for anyone but you, you know that – not since that Christmas when you came home and everyone had given me up as a bad job. I love you, you big eejit.' I smile and he rewards me with a small grin. 'I always have and I always will, and I'd never cheat on you. You're my gorgeous husband and their dad, and I have no interest whatsoever in anyone else. I thought you'd know that.' It's true, he's gorgeous, even now while he's looking all miserable.

He cheers up a bit more at that, and says, 'It doesn't stop him having a notion of you, though.'

I scoff. 'Ah, Kieran, would you stop it and have sense. Ronan Brady fancying me? Are you mad?'

Now he looks amazed himself, and then he says something so wonderful, it makes me want to cry. 'Why wouldn't any fella have eyes for you, Mags? You're lovely and funny and kind and smart and gorgeous, and I wish you realised that. Although I'm kind of glad you don't, because if you did, you might wake up one day and realise if anyone is boxing above their weight here, it's me.' He runs his hand through his hair, and I see the tension begin to leave him. 'When your one Gemma said that, I don't know, it all seemed to make sense, in my head anyway, why things have been a bit off with us lately. You working so much, and my mother having a go at you, and me being, well, just a bit useless when I knew you were having a hard time with the menopause and not sleeping and all of that. I kept thinking what could I do to get you back, and I was so scared I'd lose you. I couldn't bear that, Mags, I just couldn't.'

'Oh, Kieran…'

But then Kate and Ellie return, and Kieran just places his hand on mine, giving it a squeeze. I squeeze back.

'Do you want a spoon of mine, Mammy?' Kate offers kindly from the lurid coloured glass full to overflowing. 'It's got bubblegum and chocolate chip and mint and raspberry ripple.'

'No thanks, pet.' I smile at her.

Kieran orders coffees from the young waitress, and the girls keep the chat going for the rest of the meal. Kieran and I keep smiling at each other, and all is well with the world.

Later on, once Kate is in bed and Kieran is in front of the football, I tackle the next problem. I gently tap on Ellie's door and enter to find her sitting up reading *Little Women*. Her hair, always tied up during the day these days, is loose, and in her Harry Potter pyjamas, she looks so much younger than her twelve years.

'Hey, Miss Ellie,' I say, sitting on the bed.

'Hi, Mam.' She sounds like she has the weight of the world on her shoulders.

'So? What's up?' I ask.

She pauses and takes a deep breath. 'You must promise you won't ring the school, or go down there, or do anything without talking to me first.' Clearly she's had time to think this through.

'Okay,' I say, not meaning it. I know they say you should always be totally honest with your kids, but in all relationships, there is room for a white lie.

'There's a girl at school, and she hates me. She's really popular, so she's after telling everyone that I'm a nerd and a swot and a loser, and that if anyone hangs around with me, they'll be the same.'

I bite my tongue and clench my hands. I want to find this little witch and rip her limb from limb.

'And so I've got no friends,' she finishes miserably. 'I used to be friends with Trish and Catriona, but she's told them that they'll get beaten up if they hang around with me. They tried to ignore her, but she ripped Trish's school coat and then threw Catriona's schoolbag in the river when we were walking home, and their mam got really mad at them 'cause their dad is out of work and they've no money for new books or coats.'

I don't quite understand. 'But Jess is your friend, and Sarah?'

'Jess isn't my friend.' She sighs. 'She only invites me around because her mother and father want her to get into that posh private school that you have to apply for and show them a portfolio of your work, and I'm the smartest in the class, so her mam told her to hang around with me and copy my projects and stuff like that. That's why I always take my schoolbooks with me when I go there.'

'Oh, Ellie...' That must be why she wouldn't let me carry her bag out to Holly's car for her last weekend. I think angrily of Holly and James and their perfect house and how they are in the process of creating their version of the perfect child, and trying to use Ellie to do it. For a moment I'm not sure if I feel more sorry for Ellie or Jess, and then I remember last weekend and Jess and Sarah bouncing on the trampoline and Ellie nowhere to be seen – probably inside putting the finishing touches to Jess's 'portfolio'.

'I can't believe Jess's parents are encouraging her to take advantage of you like that. Isn't she ashamed of herself?'

Ellie's shoulders sag. 'She says she's taking pity on me and for me not to think we're real friends, and I'm not to speak to her in school.'

'Just wait until I –'

'Please don't say anything!' begs Ellie, panic on her face.

I sigh. 'All right, if you really don't want me to. And hopefully she'll get into that awful snobby private school and you won't have to put up with her anymore when you go to the convent in September. It will be better at the convent – all these silly girls will have grown up a bit.'

She shakes her head. 'No, Mam, it'll be just the same at the convent, worse probably. The other girl will be there, and even if she isn't, the problem is me, not the school.'

'Els...'

Ellie goes on. 'Like, I am a weirdo, and nobody else in the class is like me either. I'm reading *Little Women*, for God's sake. I should be on TikTok and trying to get someone to maul me.'

'Maul you?' I try to hide the horror from my voice, imagining wild animals attacking my darling girl.

'Mam.' She sighs exasperatedly. 'Kissing, you know, boys and girls?'

'You're only twelve!' I gasp, knowing I sound just like my mother.

'I'm nearly thirteen, and that's not the point. I'm a complete eejit and haven't a clue. I don't listen to the right music or anything...and I never say the cool things.'

I hug her and feel her hot salty tears on my cheek. What I say next is critical. I compose my thoughts. 'When I was in first year at the convent, so twelve or thirteen, there was a girl called Jackie O'Halloran, and she sounds like your enemy. She was cool – she looked like Rizzo from *Grease*.'

She gives me a lopsided grin – *Grease* is one of our guilty pleasures.

'She was a year older than the rest of us and had a boyfriend, and she was allowed to go to discos that Granny Marie would have had a stroke if I even asked to go to. The others in the class didn't like her so much, as they were scared of her, and so they looked like her gang. Sharon was in the other class – the nuns thought it would be a good idea to separate us because we talked all the time to each other. Anyway, one day I got my period unexpectedly, and we were doing PE so I had on white football shorts.'

Ellie's horrified face almost makes me laugh. She had her first period a couple of months back, and while she couldn't wait for it to happen, the novelty has well and truly worn off.

'So as you can imagine, the shorts were all blood, and I was mortified, and she was laughing at me, and she called me Jammy Dodger for the rest of the year. I used to wait until everyone had left the school before walking home because I didn't want Mam to see them calling me names. I was so embarrassed, and she would yell it across the street if she saw me anywhere.'

'Oh, Mam, you poor thing. That's awful.'

'She tormented me for a whole year. And I was totally miserable. Sharon couldn't help because her dad always picked her up in the car, so I had no one to walk with.'

'Did you tell Sharon?' Ellie's eyes are wide.

'No, I didn't. I was so embarrassed about it, I just endured it. There was a Christmas disco in the parish hall and everyone was going, but

Sharon was away at her granny's, so I pretended to Mam I had a cold because I'd be there at Jackie and her henchwomen's mercy.'

'And did you not have other friends besides Sharon?'

I shake my head. 'Not really. I wasn't that cool either.'

'So what happened?'

'Well... And if you ever breathe a word of this, I'll have to have you arrested.' I wink at her. 'Somehow, and I've no idea how, I must ask her actually, your granny found out what was going on, and she waited one winter's evening. Jackie used to go for piano lessons up Duggan's Lane – there was a teacher up there – and Granny Marie waited behind a wall, you know the one, at the back of the pub?'

Ellie nods, enraptured.

'So Granny waited in the dark, and as Jackie walked past, she pulled her in behind the wall. Jackie was a miserable little squirt – maybe that's why she was so horrible. Anyway, Granny Marie pinned her to it and had her scissors in her hand. You know the big ones with the brown handles? Well, she clung Jackie O'Halloran to the wall and held the scissors to her neck. Now, that scissors wouldn't cut butter, but Jackie didn't know that. And Granny said, "You ever so much as look in the direction of my daughter ever again, I swear I'll make sure it's the last thing you ever do. Nobody will ever suspect me because I'm a perfectly respectable business owner and I'm on the parish council, and everyone in the town knows that you are a spiteful little brat, so be warned."'

'You're making it up!' Ellie is in equal measure horrified and thrilled.

'I'm not,' I say, and she knows I mean it.

'And did Jackie tell her mother?'

I laugh. 'She did in her eye. Granny Marie can be scary enough when she wants to be.'

'I'm not a bit scared of Granny Marie, but Nana Nora now, that's another story,' Ellie says darkly.

'She's a piece of work, all right. Anyway, the thing is, sometimes a bully only understands one thing, and that's a bigger, stronger force than them. It's not very politically correct – nowadays it's all the bully is hurting too and all that stuff, but I'm not interested in rehabilitating whoever is bullying you – but I can make her stop, if you'll trust me.'

'What will you do? Hold her at gunpoint?' Ellie asks with a sad little smile.

'No, I'd get fired for that. But if you tell me who it is, I promise I can make her stop and nobody will ever know it was me.' I make this promise having no idea whatsoever how I am going to fulfil it, but right now I need her to trust me.

'How?' The glimmer of hope is there now.

'I can't tell you that. All I can say is it won't be illegal but it will work.'

'Mam, I don't know...' She wants my help, I can feel it, but she's scared.

'Do you trust me, Els?'

She nods.

'Give me her name.'

'Rachel Mahony,' she manages.

'Bertie the butcher's daughter?'

She nods.

Relief floods through me. This I can do.

'Right, say no more, and give me a few days. And while we're at it, tell Jess you can't go to the pictures next weekend. You're not some toy she can pick up and drop when it suits her.'

'But, Mam, she'll be mad if I do that and –'

'Sweetheart, I know it's hard, but listen to me on this. We teach people how to treat us, so if we behave like a doormat, we'll be treated like one. If Jess isn't your real friend and is only using you for your brains, then use those brains and don't let her.'

'She's all I have left now, though.'

That sentence tears at my heart. I know telling Ellie that she has me and her dad and Kate is no consolation at the moment; she's at that age where it's all about friends. 'OK, I've an idea. I saw a bunch of kids from Galway Youth Theatre the other day. They were doing some kind of street performance, loads of girls and lads around your age. So what would you think about joining that? You could make new friends, and you love all that drama stuff?'

Her face lights up. 'But isn't it too far?'

It is, and already I'm racking my brains how to make it work. 'Well, we'd have to see when rehearsals were on and that, but there's me and your dad and Granny Marie, and there's a bus, so maybe together we could make it happen?'

'Oh, Mam, I'd love it, I really would love it.'

Seeing her enthusiastic and cheerful for the first time in ages cheers me up. I'll do whatever it takes to make this happen for her.

'Right, so you leave Miss Mahony to me, and you go online tomorrow and find out whatever you can about the youth theatre and I'll ring them.'

I kiss her forehead, and she wraps her arms around me and holds on tight. 'I love you, Mam,' she whispers.

'I love you too, sweetheart.'

Before I go downstairs, I check on Kate, who is out like a light.

Kieran is still engrossed in the football, but I slide in beside him on the couch and before long he turns off the television.

CHAPTER 22

I'm standing in the queue at Bertie the butcher's. I would have been here sooner, but Bertie has been off in France for the last week on a 'second honeymoon' with his missus, leaving Finbarr Deasy and Howya to manage the shop.

Howya is so called because his surname is Phelan and someone donkey's years ago thought 'Howya Phelan' was hilarious, and so it stuck. I've no idea his real name.

Now Bertie's back behind the counter, sporting a bit of a tan, and everyone is congratulating him for surprising his wife with a romantic holiday. He's the one who reads at Mass, gives out Communion and sings over everyone in the congregation too. He's cheerful and smiley, and his shop sponsors the local football club. Bertie's smoked ham, Bertie's sausage rolls, Bertie's mince – to the people of Ballycarrick, it is ambrosia. There is another butcher's at the other end of the town, but he is more or less ignored. There is almost a snobbery to getting meat in Bertie's. I can't explain it, I know it sounds mad, but there you have it.

I wait my turn and try not to look into the back where the actual chopping up of the meat happens. I'm not a vegetarian, and have no notion of becoming one, but I don't like to be reminded so starkly that we are all munching on the flesh of other sentient beings. Even as a kid, I hated when Mam made roast chicken because it looked like a chicken. Steak doesn't look like a cow, or a chop like the fluffy little lambs you'd see frolicking in the fields in the spring. Hypocritical, I know. One of my many faults.

Howya finishes with a customer and approaches me, but I tell him I'll wait for Bertie. Again, that doesn't raise an eyebrow; lots of people have a favourite butcher in the shop. Mam prefers Finbarr, says he gives the best cuts, while Sharon always goes to Howya because he trims the fat first and then weighs the meat. I'd never ask to have the fat trimmed. Maybe that's my problem.

I walk to the end of the long glass counter, under which are neatly arranged meats of all kinds. Steaks, chops, roasts, sausages, skewers, stir-fry, you name it. Bertie really jumped on the gourmet band-wagon early on, and it's paying off. People thought he was getting notions of himself at the start, a mortal sin in Ireland, with his harissa rubs and chipotle sausages, but there was a market for it. His wife puts a recipe up every weekend on their shop's Facebook page, and whatever that requires is cleaned out by the end of business on Saturday. Even Father Doyle has been known to remark in his closing blessing on a Sunday that he wished the families of Ballycar-rick a nice afternoon together and to enjoy the roast beef with horse-radish, or the Lacken-raised free-range duck with bok choy that Bertie the butcher has on special that weekend. It causes a universal titter in the church and sends everyone off for another week with a smile on their faces. Bertie Mahony is a pillar of the Ballycarrick community.

When I get to the head of the queue for Bertie, he tries to go to the woman behind me –Gerry the hairdresser's *au pair* – but Howya points me out and he is forced to approach me.

'Ah, Mags, how are you? What can I get you?' he asks, mock cheery. He's cringing. No wonder he is.

'I'll take a pound of sausages please, Bertie, and four chicken breasts, the stuffed ones,' I say.

'No bother.' He goes off to get them, and I never take my eyes off him. He is puce now. I don't smile, or even make chit-chat as everyone else does.

He arrives back, and I've moved along the counter right to the end of it, so we're fairly out of earshot now if we keep our voices down.

'Is that it?' he asks.

I nod, and as I hand him my card to pay, I say very quietly, 'Your daughter, Rachel, is bullying my Ellie, and I want you to make it stop. And if she says one word to Ellie about any of it, or it ever comes back on my daughter, I will have to act.' I have planned the little speech for days; nothing I say can be construed as a threat. His criminal activities are not something I can leverage. Officially.

He takes the card and punches in the amount I owe, not saying a word, but I can see him swallow and his ears are still pink.

'I'll speak to her.' His voice is strangled. 'I'm sorry about that. It will be sorted, I promise.'

'Good.'

I take my meat and leave, thanking my lucky stars that I personally investigated suspicious activity reported in the woods up behind the castle two years ago. Ten cars, all full of middle-aged people engaging in extra-marital activity while others watched. The mind boggles. And all arranged by and participated in fully by the local pillar of the community.

I arrested them all that night, and he begged and pleaded, mortified of course, that it not go any further. His wife, Maura, knew nothing of his woodland activities, which was no surprise. She runs the local Legion of Mary and had been almost a fully professed nun when she left the order to marry Bertie. He'd cried in the station that night, saying it would ruin him if it got out. Since everyone involved was an adult and consenting, the only charge was lewd behaviour. I explained Section 18 of the Criminal Amendment Act of 1935, which governs public decency. If a complaint had been received, then a file would had to have been prepared for the director of public prosecutions, who would then decide if a case was to be brought. We did receive a complaint but just about the peculiar activity in the woods; the person who rang us thought there might have been drug dealing going on. So it was a bit of a grey area. I sent them all home with a caution and said no more about it, but Bertie has not been able to meet my eye ever since.

I don't blame him; I'd like to forget all about that night myself. If I never again in my life have to arrest a bunch of partially clad dental nurses and county council workers in their cars getting up to all sorts with the neighbours, it will be too soon.

I decide to call in to Sharon on my way home with the meat. The girls are at football training so I have a couple of hours, and I've not spoken to my friend in person since the night at Danny Boylan's place – I've been run off my feet – so I owe her a visit.

I pick up two apple slices in Teresa's Bakery and a bag of jellies for Sean in the garage shop and head over to her place.

She opens the door a crack.

'Morning,' I say cheerily, waving the apple slices.

'Hi, Mags. Listen, it's not a great time. I just...'

'Ah, Shar, it's me. Let me in, will you, or the whole place will think we've fallen out.' I laugh, but she doesn't meet my eyes.

'I just can't, Mags...' She goes to shut the door.

After years as a cop, I instinctively place my foot in the door so she can't close it. She looks down at my runner and then at me. Gently I push the door. She gives up trying to stop me and turns and walks down the hall into the kitchen. I follow her, feeling increasingly worried. Shar's house is usually immaculate. She loves huge gold mirrors and ornate picture frames, and while the décor is a bit over the top for me, her place always looks good. Not anymore. It smells dirty, and there are fruit flies all around the kitchen. A bowl of blackening bananas is what's drawing them. The bin is overflowing, and the sink is full of cereal bowls. The TV is on, some mindless Saturday morning cooking show. There's no sign of Sean.

'Do you want tea?' she asks, plonking down on a kitchen chair. She looks wretched. Her hair is lank and pulled into a ponytail, and she is still in her pyjamas. Not that I'm anyone to judge, but while it's very like me to remain in my PJs till the afternoon, it isn't Sharon's way at all.

'No, I want to know what's going on with you,' I say, sitting beside her. 'Shar, come on, you're freaking me out. What's happened? Where's Sean?'

'He's with Danny.' Her voice is wooden. Big fat tears roll down her cheeks. 'He never loved me, Mags, never. He texted me, and I...'

She hands me her phone, and I read the text, which is from Tuesday, the day after she attacked Danny. It's long.

You are mad, you know that, right? Not mad like great craic, mad like should be locked up. The stunt you pulled at my place nearly scared poor Chloe half to death and cost me a fortune. If you weren't friends with Mags, it would have gone a whole lot worse for you. So I'm telling you now to stay away from me. I should never have got with you in the first place. Mam warned me about you but I wouldn't listen. I went with other women because you're so bloody boring. No wonder I did. And another thing, you are completely unfit to raise my son, so I'll be going for full custody and I'll get it too. He can't be raised by a lunatic, the courts will see that. I have more money and a supportive family behind me, and you have nobody and no money, so this is a fight you'll lose. Never contact me again. I'll be picking him up from school today and every day after that.

I take a second to process this. Danny's obviously had second thoughts since I threatened to ruin his reputation. I bet Chloe had a hand in this. Maybe he confessed to her and she said she'd stand by him no matter what and deny everything, and that's what's emboldened him. After all, he's used to using his charm to get away with blue murder.

'So Sean has been with Danny since when?'

'Last Tuesday,' Sharon answers miserably.

'All week?'

'Yeah.'

'Sharon, this is not right. You know that, don't you? Danny can't just take Sean like that. And he's completely wrong about how custody works.'

'He is right. He's loaded and his mother will back him anyway, and how am I supposed to fight him? I can't afford a solicitor or anything, and if it does go to court, it will all come out about him and what I did and everything, and I just couldn't...' Her voice is lost in racking sobs.

'Right.' I decide. 'There's a time for this, but now isn't it. Get upstairs, shower, get dressed, blow-dry your hair. I'll clean up down here.'

'Mags, I don't want to go anywhere. I know you mean well, but I'm heartbroken, so going out for lunch or whatever won't –'

'I've no intention of taking you for lunch, Sharon Joyce. I am taking you to get your son back. So get to it – now.'

'But Danny won't let me...'

'Let you? And since when is Danny Boylan making the law? Sean is your child. Danny left you for Chloe from the chipper' – I give her a half-smile – 'so he left the marital home. You have been very fair and reasonable regarding joint access to your son, but at no time was it ever discussed that Sean would live with his father. This is his home, with you. And this is where he will live. Danny can threaten court all he likes – and you'll get free legal aid, by the way, so don't worry about paying a solicitor – but it will get him nowhere, and pulling a stunt like this won't look good in court, I can assure you.'

'I was ringing him all week, trying to get Sean back, but he won't pick up and I didn't dare go up there after...' – she colours – 'after what I did.'

'But did you not try to collect him from school any of the days?'

'Every day, but Danny was always already at the gate with her and I didn't want Sean to see a big fight and be embarrassed. They were all there, all the mothers, and I just couldn't face it, so I every day went home again and tried ringing him. Eventually Chloe picked up and said that Sean was going to stay with them and that I was only upsetting him by all the ringing. And that she didn't need this stress now that she was pregnant.'

How dare she? I am so outraged on behalf of my friend. But this is not the time for that; we need cool heads.

'Right. No order has been made by any court, and as far as the law is concerned, Sean is ordinarily domiciled here in this house with you. Until such time as this is heard by a judge, the role of the Gardai is to maintain the status quo. Danny and Chloe have no right whatsoever to keep your son from you. And I'll be telling him that. If he wants to formalise the custody of Sean, then he will need to seek a court order to that effect. Usually the judge asks that couples enter mediation or collaborative law to come to some arrangement, but that's down the road. For now, what he's done is effectively kidnap, and he could be arrested for that. So you organise yourself and I'll straighten it up here, and let's go and get Sean.'

'I don't know, Mags. He's so angry, and…I don't want to get you in trouble either…'

I place my hands on her shoulders. 'Look at me, Shar. This is what I do. Even if we weren't friends and you arrived to the station with this story, this is what I would be doing. So I'm not pulling any stunt – I'm enforcing the law. And as for that excuse for a man being angry, well, I've dealt with angrier than him, I can assure you, so don't worry about that. But just to be totally above board, I'm going to call it into the station and have uniformed on-duty Gardai there as well. We need to do absolutely everything by the book from now on, because it will go to court and solicitors love to twist things.'

'I miss him so much.'

I know she means Sean, but I really hope she doesn't mean that toad Danny too.

'I know. So let's get it sorted out. Now clean yourself up.'

I send her upstairs and ring the station. Michael and Nicola are both there, so I tell them I'm coming into work today after all and to be ready to come out on a call with me; we're paying Danny Boylan a serious visit.

In the squad car on the way to Danny's house, I brief Nicola on the Children and Family Relationships Act of 2015 and explain to her exactly what she is to cite when speaking to him. I've decided to let her do the talking. I'm sick of even looking at Danny Boylan.

As I suspected, the sight of the squad car and the two uniformed Gardai with myself and Sharon is enough to quieten that slimeball ex-husband of hers. Nicola performs admirably, and though Danny and Chloe are seething, they have to let Sean go. The poor lad runs into

Sharon's arms, sobbing. She'll have to fight Danny in court, but that's another day's work.

When Monday comes around, I get a picture from Sharon of Sean happily having his breakfast before school and a message.

You are the best friend I could ever have wished for.

CHAPTER 23

A few days later, I drop in on Mam's boutique. She is busy steaming the new summer dresses in preparation for the summer sale. She beams at the sight of me as I set down the usual two takeaway cups of tea and couple of scones from Teresa's Bakery.

'Lovely. How are you, love? Is work all right? Has anything else happened since that poor boy's shooting? God love them. His poor mother was distraught. My heart went out to her the day of the funeral. No mother should ever have to bury her child – it's wrong.'

'I know. She's not doing great now either by all accounts. I'd love to at least be able to tell them who did it or why. But we haven't a clue. Nobody knows anything, or if they do, they're not telling us.' I'm probably speaking out of turn, but Mam is like the grave; you can tell her anything and she'll never repeat it.

I'm a bit frustrated about it all, to be honest. It's weighing on me, the silence from the investigating team. It's like the crowd above in Dublin doesn't care anymore because they can't link it to anything else, something more serious, and Galway is struggling without their support. Nothing seems to have moved on, although I've met Ronan three more times since I explained about him to Kieran, once in Shaw's the following day, once in my station when he called in as he was passing, and once in court where I was bringing charges against a farmer who shot at his neighbour over a gate. Billy Mac, as he's known, is totally barmy and shouldn't be allowed to have a water pistol let alone an actual gun, so I had to go to court to object to the renewal of his licence.

Old Judge Collins isn't far behind Billy Mac in the barmy stakes, between you and me. He's honestly about ninety-five, so it could have gone either way, but thankfully on this occasion, I was able to convince him. Ronan was sitting in court as I was explaining in a very loud voice – the judge is hard of hearing – how Billy is a danger. The gathered barristers thought it was hilarious. Billy Mac is like a briar now, of course. I sent Darren and Mike out to take the gun, and he gave them dog's abuse.

Come to think of it, I don't know why Ronan was in the courthouse that day. There weren't any other cases that involved him, as far as I know.

Anyway, neither time did he have anything useful to say about the progress of the investigation, and I got the distinct impression that it was sliding down the priority list.

He no more fancies me than the man on the moon, he's just lonely and he wants someone to talk to who gets it. Kieran is way off the mark on that one. Sure, he's gorgeous, and he's going places in the guards. I'm sure he'll make chief superintendent if he sets his mind to it. I think he likes hanging around with me because I'm safe and he can talk shop with me.

'That's the way of it, I suppose, love.' Mam brings me back to reality. 'The Travellers haven't much reason to trust any of us, do they? Just be careful, though, won't you? I'm doing the nine days prayer that you'll be safe.'

I smile. Mam is a big fan of the nine days prayer, never known to fail apparently. She finds her religion a great comfort. She's very sure God listens to her, and she loves the social side of it too, like the altar flower-arranging committee meetings after Mass on Sundays or coordinating the annual pilgrimage to Knock to the shrine there where Our Lady allegedly appeared on the gable wall of the church.

Tourists are constantly amazed by Knock. It was a microscopic village in County Mayo up to the seventies, but then a local priest decided to put it on the world pilgrimage map, it seems, and to that end, built a giant basilica and an airport no less. I'm not sure it ever reached the dizzying heights of Catholic fervour that places like Lourdes or Fatima or even Medjugorje did, but it's great for us because you can get cheap flights to the Canary Islands from the airport there.

Mam and all the faithful of the parish get a bus there every year, though it's only up the road, and they make a day out of it. Masses are offered up for various intentions, rosaries said, tea drunk, buns devoured, and generally a great day is had by all.

She's in charge of the Corpus Christi procession too every year, and she enlists me and the girls to help her prune her rose bushes so she can have the best blooms ready in time. They scatter the petals ahead of the priest carrying the Eucharist. The altar boys hold a kind of canopy over the priest's head while this goes on.

Like with the Communion, I find it all a bit mad, to be honest, but then I see the community coming together, and it's doing no harm. I know my mam wishes I was more devout, but she never says anything. Her faith is personal, and she doesn't try to ram it down anyone's throat.

Though she did bring me to Lourdes four years ago. The parish council arrange a trip once a year, and they take people who are phys-ically disabled to be washed in the baths there. I was brought along as a helper when Mona Feeny needed a knee replacement at the last minute. I can't say it meant anything to me, but some people seemed to get great comfort from it. I do remember Mam glaring at me on the last day there, though, a look I hadn't seen since childhood – you know, the 'wait till I get you home' look? She and the other members of the church choir were going to have the honour of singing at Mass in Lourdes, but the organist was a very grumpy French woman who refused to play the Irish hymn 'Our Lady of Knock', saying she was sick to death of it and the Irish for thinking they had some right to go over there and sing their own hymns. She announced imperiously that she was going to play 'Morning Has Broken' and that was all there was about it, so off she went in a right huff to the gallery where the organ was. Well, undeterred, the choir of St Enda's church, Ballycarrick, were not going to take that slur lying down, so there at Mass, in Lourdes, the organist played 'Morning Has Broken', but Mam and the others sang 'Our Lady of Knock' at the top of their lungs. It was a battle of wills that nearly sent me into paroxysms of laughter that day.

So she's sweet but determined, my mam.

'Don't worry, Mam, I'm only a tiny cog in the wheel – so I won't be going head-to-head with any major-league criminals any time soon. That would be way above my pay grade.' Like Kieran, Mam needs constant assurance about my safety.

I sip my tea, then set it down and pick up a really horrific lurid pink cardigan with white flowers embroidered on the shoulders. 'Now *this* thing is a crime, Mam. I should arrest you for this.'

'I know.' She giggles at my grimace. 'But that will fly out the door.'

'Really?' I'm amazed.

'Absolutely. No accounting for taste,' Mam says with the air of one selling clothes to the women of this town for a very long time. 'So tell me, how's Sharon doing? Not still mooning over that pup Danny Boylan, I hope?' Mam is very fond of Sharon; she was practically reared in our house. 'I spotted herself and Sean yesterday. He was out on his bike down the castle grounds, and she looked worn out, the poor girl. I went for a walk with Marion Broderick after lunch because it was so lovely. That Jack Russell cross of hers has a total clown made of her, though. Apparently Trix gets to decide the speed of the walk, and we had to stop at every lamp post for a sniff or a piddle. I told her I'll only walk with her without the dog in the future. She didn't like it a bit, but honestly, I'm too old to have my Sunday afternoon dictated by a mongrel with delusions of superiority.'

I laugh, then sigh, and tell Mam how it looks like Danny is going to take Sharon to court over custody of Sean.

Mam twitches with annoyance. As I say, she's protective of my friend. Sharon's father was not a nice man, and I didn't like to go to her house – he gave me the creeps – and Sharon seemed to prefer our place as well. Maybe it was the father who gave Sharon such bad taste in men.

'He's some piece of work, that Danny Boylan, always was, even as a young fella.' Mam takes a sip of her tea. 'I hope she's well able for him.'

'I think she'll be all right.' I finish the last of my scone. 'I'm organising free legal aid for her, and I can't see her losing custody, but she's still heartbroken over Danny. She's having to finally come to terms with the fact he was unfaithful all through their marriage, and it's breaking her heart. When she thought it was just Chloe, she could pour all the blame on her, but it's not. Though what women see in him, I'll never know. It's all him, and she knows that now for certain, so she's gutted.'

Mam snorts. 'His father, Edward, was the exact same as a young fella. No girl was safe from his wandering hands. I remember him well, "the octopus" we used to call him at the dances long ago. And that Daphne Boylan has a right mammy's boy made of her son, thinks the sun, moon and stars shine out of him. They ruined him between the pair of them.'

I wipe my hands on one of the paper napkins that came with the scones and shove the others in my uniform trousers.

'You'll pull them all out of shape doing that,' Mam admonishes me.

I roll my eyes. 'I'm not sure they ever had a shape to begin with, Mam. The women's trousers of the Gardai aren't exactly *haute couture*.'

'Still, pulling and dragging them every which way won't help.' She removes my hands from my pockets and pats my cheek playfully. 'Oh, I meant to tell you, I was in the window earlier, and who did I spot walking down to the Centra for hot chocolate? Only our Ellie, and she was with the two O'Leary girls. You know the ones – the father used to work in the tyre factory before it closed down?'

'I do, Catriona and Trish.' They are the twins who were forced to abandon my daughter under threat of violence from Bertie Mahony's daughter, Rachel.

'Well, our Ellie was with the two of them and another two girls I didn't recognise, but anyway, they were laughing and skittering away. They got their drinks and sat on the wall outside and were chatting and having a right laugh by the looks of things, and Ellie in the middle of it all. I thought you'd like to know.'

I exhaled. I'd known Ellie was a lot happier since last weekend, but to have it confirmed felt like someone had let go of a vice-like grip on my heart.

'I just waved over, and she waved back and had the biggest smile on her face, love, so don't be worrying. I know you've been anxious about her, I could tell, but she looked as happy as Larry, so whatever was wrong has worked out for the best.'

'Thanks, Mam,' I say gratefully. 'And you know, it's all down to you and your example that it worked out. I just followed in your maternal footsteps.'

Mam looks at me sharply. The only reason I know about the scissors-to-the-neck incident is because she told Kieran one night after the two of them cracked open a bottle of white wine. He and my mother are great friends. Mam isn't usually a drinker, and the wine loosened her tongue. Kieran told me but swore me to secrecy. Poor Mam had a terrible head the next day and swore she would never drink again, and I don't think she ever did.

'I mean, it's just you set me such a great example of patience and loving kindness.' I smile. 'And that's why I'm going to help you on Saturday to prune your roses. An hour will do it if we both go at it.'

She is still looking at me suspiciously as she takes a mouthful of tea and then a bite of her own scone. 'Well, I suppose you do owe me,' she says. 'Do you know who I had for forty minutes this morning?'

'Who?'

'Nell, and she going on about Trevor Lynch and his drums again. She said you were giving her no satisfaction whatsoever, so she decided the next best thing was to come in complaining to me. As if I could do something to influence you.'

'Well, all I can advise you is to tell her you have no sway with me whatsoever when it comes to the law and that she might as well be howling at the moon as try to involve you or anyone else. The judge has ruled – it's done. But sure, I'm blue in the face telling her.'

'And you know Nell, she'll surely take that on board like a

reasonable person.' My mother chuckles. 'But wait till you hear the end of the story. Annette Deasy, she came in looking at the sandals while Nell was in full flight, and after a while she turned around and suggested to Nell she sell her house to Trevor if he's that interested, make a tidy little profit and buy one of the new small houses out by the football pitch where she lives. She said they're lovely inside and no maintenance or anything, that she was glad to downsize herself and didn't want to be rattling around in a big old house at her age.'

'And what did Nell say to that?' I grin.

'Well, I've never seen her speechless before...'

At that moment my phone rings in my pocket and I take it out, expecting Kieran or maybe Nicola, who is on the desk at the station. It's Delia. 'I think I should take this, Mam. I'll see you later, so.'

'Bye, love.'

I step out into the street and take the call.

Delia speaks in a flat voice, but I can hear the underlying panic. 'Natasha's gone,' she says. 'The skinny man must have taken her. Her phone is out by the sea, near Spiddal.'

'Wait, wait...' My heart is racing. I'm already running up the street towards the station where I've left my car. 'When did this happen? How do you know she's headed for Spiddal?'

'Oh God...' She gives a little gasp, then pulls herself together again. 'Nana had a very bad turn early this morning – I don't know, a stroke or something maybe – and we were there, Natasha and me. She's not been well, so we've been taking turns to stay with her, so when she took the turn, I told Natasha to stay with her and I sent Darren to get the doctor or an ambulance. I thought they'd come quicker if a guard called it instead of one of us. But when I got back to Nana's van, Natasha was gone. Nana was on her own and she was breathing funny, so I just focused on her and talked to her until the ambulance came. Then I went to look for Nat. I thought she might have been freaked out seeing Nana sick. I've her phone linked to mine on the Find My app – we always have them linked if we're out anywhere so we can find each other – and I can see her phone on the app but it's not moving, it's just sitting there in a field by a tiny narrow road. They must have made her throw it away...'

'Send me that location, Delia,' I instruct, and as I reach the station car park, it pings on my phone. I slow down and stride towards the main doors of the station. 'So who saw the skinny man, Delia?'

'Nobody did!'

'*What?*' I come to a shocked standstill. 'Then did someone see a black Mercedes?'

'No one saw anything!' Her voice is agonised. 'But I just *know* it was him, Sergeant Munroe, I know it. I should have gone up to him at the funeral. I should have asked him what he was at staring at my cousin like that for –'

'Delia,' I interrupt sharply. 'Stop. Calm down. Think. Maybe nobody took Natasha. She's been very unhappy about Joseph, hasn't she? Maybe she's not in danger. Maybe she's just run away of her own accord to get out of the marriage...'

Her voice goes higher, angry and frustrated. 'No, no, you don't understand. We'd never defy our family like that!'

'Really?' I'm thinking of Blades Carmody, and of Natasha buying him a jacket in secret.

'No! Look, yes, I know, Blades and the jacket and everything, I know, but this is different. She wouldn't run away, she just wouldn't. You have to believe me. I know this is to do with Blades and whoever shot him. I don't know why, but I just know.'

I sigh. I have serious doubts about this, but what if Delia's right? Plus Natasha's phone is still not moving. I can see its location now. It's in a field not far from the coast, and Natasha must have been in a car to get that far so quickly. It is odd. 'OK, Delia, I'll pass it on to the investigating team, and we'll take it from there, all right?'

'No, Sergeant, we have to go and find her now! Nana's in hospital, but she'll die for sure if she finds out Natasha is in danger, and Nana asked me to look after her, and Darren's disappeared, and I need you to drive because I haven't got my licence yet...'

She's in bits, blaming herself. She needs to feel part of this. I relent. 'Look, I'll call the officer in charge of the investigation, Detective

Inspector Ronan Brady. He's a good man, and if he's thinks it's a good idea, I'll bring you to meet him and we'll decide what to do for the best.'

'But –'

I am firm. 'Delia, this is me telling you what to do, and part of this job is obeying orders. And this is an order. Wait there at the site until I've spoken to DI Brady, and then I'll be in touch.'

A pause and then she says, 'Please be quick.'

I step into the station and tell Nicola I'll be gone for a couple of hours. She tells me Darren had to go out to Billy Mac again because he is now after setting his dog on the neighbour in the absence of a gun to threaten the poor man with. The other squad car is up at the primary school with Cathal, who is giving out medals and high-vis jackets for the road safety campaign. This is aggravating because I don't even have my own car with me today; it's back in the garage because the Bluetooth is gone again, so I'm using Kieran's van. He's at work, but he travelled with one of the Polish guys today. They're actually out near Spiddal themselves at the moment, and for a second I think of calling him to ask if they've seen a black Mercedes pass by – they must have a good view from the roof of whatever house they're fixing.

But that's a ridiculous long shot.

I call Ronan, who instantly agrees to meet me at the usual place, Shaw's. For some reason I don't ask whether it's OK to bring Delia; I just decide it's a good idea. I drive to the halting site. The ambulance has been and gone, taking Dacie with it, and everyone from adult to toddler is milling around outside Dacie's caravan, looking anxious and sad. Delia dashes over when she sees it's me in the van and jumps into the passenger seat, then out again as she realises she's sat on one of Kieran's transmitters.

'I'm so sorry…'

'Don't worry, you haven't broken it. It's just a transmitter for use on a building site. Kieran uses it to contact the lads on the roof if there's no mobile signal or something. I don't know. I kind of tune out when he's going on about it, to be honest. Boys and their toys. Pop it in the glove compartment there.'

She does and gets back in. 'I've not said anything to anybody,' she tells me as we drive away. 'I don't want Nana finding out.' Then she takes out her iPhone and finds Natasha's phone again. She groans in panic. 'It's still not moved. I'm right – that man's made her throw it away.' Her own phone is pink and sparkly and covered in stickers, and I realise with a pang just how young and vulnerable she is. I think how Natasha, even if she is a little madam who needs reining in, is even younger, and suddenly I'm as worried about her as Delia, even if she has only run away. They're so innocent, these girls.

'We will find her, I promise,' I say, and Delia gives me a brave, watery smile.

Just as we reach Shaw's, Ronan's car pulls up, a sleek BMW 5 Series. It's spotless, very different from Kieran's battered and muddy old van. He doesn't notice me at first, just sits there on his phone. By the time my phone rings, it's him, I am out of the van and standing at his window.

When he sees me, he smiles, showing all his perfectly straight white teeth, but then he glances behind me and the smile fades at the sight of Delia. He wasn't expecting her, and I realise I should have asked him if it was OK to bring her. Frowning now, he gets out of the BMW, and before he closes the door, I can smell the leather and hear the sound of Bruce Springsteen playing quietly. The three of us stand in the late-morning sunshine as I show him the location of Natasha's phone and explain how it hasn't moved for a while.

He looks exasperated. 'So this girl and whoever she's with are sitting, or lying, in a field?'

'What would she be doing lying in a field?' snaps Delia. I glance at her; this is no way to address a superior officer.

He throws her a cynical amused look. 'Well, I don't know, but in my experience, young girls and their boyfriends...'

Delia's eyes shadow, and that old wary resentment is back.

'Ronan,' I interrupt hastily, not wanting her to explode at him like she did at Cathal, 'we really think it's been there too long, and Delia is very, very sure Natasha wouldn't run away. We're worried this is to do with the man at the funeral.'

'OK.' He gives Delia another look, then pulls me aside. 'Listen, Mags, the undercovers kept a close eye at the funeral. This so-called "skinny man" is not on Dublin's radar. They saw no sign of any representation from the Keogh side at the funeral either – Alan isn't moving from Dublin, Chunkie is in Spain. The drugs squad in Limerick and the one here haven't come across anything, and they'd know within a few days if there was a big drop, so we know there's nothing happening in this area.'

'But that doesn't mean Natasha McGovern doesn't need help?'

He shrugs. 'Whatever your young friend here says, this Natasha girl is clearly a bit of a tearaway. Maybe she isn't with her phone anymore, but if she isn't, I'd say she lost it in the grass or something simple like that. She was going behind her family's back with Bernard Carmody and hates that Ward fella, and the more I look at this, the more I think Joseph Ward or even her own family is behind the attack on Carmody and that Duckie is right – the whole thing is an inside job and we'll never get to the bottom of it. So you take Delia home and put her back to the proper work she should be doing as a Reserve guard, because otherwise you're doing her no favours. The other young one will turn up – they always do.'

'Ronan, Delia is sure –'

He cuts across me. 'She's not your daughter, Mags, and you can't let your emotions affect your judgement. I love the way you're so caring and involved in your community, but you need to keep a cool head.' All the time he's talking, he's got his hand on my arm and he's looking into my eyes.

'I've got an idea,' he says. 'Why don't you drop Delia home and then come back here and let me buy you lunch? It's Evelyn's birthday, and I could do with some company.'

I step away from him. 'I can't today,' I say apologetically. 'I really can't. I'm sorry.'

This time, instead of looking disappointed, he looks slightly angry. 'Mags, I don't know what you're planning, but I can't give you the green light to go using police time to chase around the country after a sixteen-year-old girl who hasn't even been reported missing.' I hear the implicit order just as clearly as if he's given it directly.

I don't know what to say. He raised his voice, so Delia heard him. I'm not going to argue with a superior officer; it would set a terrible example to her as a Reserve guard. Instead, I say quietly, 'Right.' I indicate for Delia to get back in the van and follow her to the vehicle.

He comes after me to the driver's side. 'Mags...'

I turn. 'Yeah?'

He looks at me, then says, 'Nothing,' and walks back to his own car.

I get in behind the wheel of the van and pull out of the car park, heading back towards Ballycarrick. It starts to rain, and a wind whips up. It's not such a nice day anymore.

Delia sits bolt upright in the passenger seat; her eyes are red-rimmed and her jaw more jutty than ever. After two miles of silence apart from the wipers and the hiss of tyres on the wet road, she asks heavily, 'So was that your detective inspector who is such a "good man"?'

'He *is* a good man,' I say firmly. I have to stick by my Garda colleagues; I mustn't break ranks.

'He's good to you,' she says, her eyes sliding towards me.

I focus on the road.

'But not to me, he isn't, or to Natasha. He's just like the rest of them.' Then the bitterness that is never far from the surface of her comes spilling out. 'He thinks my cousin isn't important. She's just a Traveller girl. He doesn't even want us to try to save her "on police time". She's not worthy of police time, according to him. It's only important if there's a crime that affects settled people.'

I keep driving. 'I have my orders, Delia. As soon as we're off duty and in ordinary clothes, then we'll take a drive over to Spiddal and see what we can see.'

'If it was your daughter someone had run off with, would you wait until you were off duty to go and look for her?'

The question hangs between us, and I know the answer as well as she does.

There's a left turn coming up, heading for the coast. I take it. To hell with Detective Inspector Brady.

* * *

WE FIND Natasha's phone in the field near Spiddal, and it's a horrible moment. The field is full of thistles and briars; no one would go in there intentionally. And the phone clearly didn't just drop out of a pocket; it's smashed against a rock, so it must have been thrown from the road. It's a miracle it's stayed working at all for Delia to locate it.

From here, we're searching for Natasha blind.

And yet not completely blind. I know this area well. I was a guard here for two years when I started, and as far as I remember, this little road we're on goes only to the coast. If they took her down here, maybe they had a boat? It's the only way out unless they come back up this road.

Darren is from around here as well. I call his phone and put him on speaker as I navigate the small narrow road at speed.

'Darren, I'm out towards Spiddal on the coast road. I'm looking for a landing place, something small, a hidden beach of some sort. I seem to remember –'

'Is Delia with you?' he asks anxiously.

'She is, and she's listening.'

'We're looking for Natasha,' calls Delia.

'Delia, leave this to me,' I say. 'Darren, wasn't there a small pier just below that pub, the something Pot...the Lobster Pot?'

'The Cray Pot,' he says. 'It's been closed for years now. The pier was to bring the barrels in in the old days. Look out for a red house on the bad corner –'

Suddenly the line goes dead. There's terrible mobile phone service out here. West Galway is a notorious black spot for coverage; it goes in and out all the time depending on the rain and the wind. But it's OK; I know where I'm going now.

I drive on as fast as I dare on the wet misty road and eventually reach the red house and the sharp bend. We're still quite high above sea level, and I can see the expanse of grey ocean before us. The pub is closed – it looks like it burned down – and so I take a left turn down an even narrower lane dropping down towards the sea. It's barely more than a farm track, with waist-high dry stone walls on either side. When I get closer to the coast, I pull into a gateway and get out of the van and climb up on the wall. And amazingly, still a long way below me, I can just make out the rear end of a black Mercedes, parked down by an old long-forgotten pier.

Delia gasps, close to my ear. 'It's them!'

I hiss, 'Get back to the van. The keys are in it. Park it across the lane to block the Mercedes, then get behind that stone wall and run towards the road until you find a signal and call Galway for armed backup. Keep low and don't let anyone see you.'

I take my baton from the holster I'm wearing.

I've had firearms training, but I've never actually carried a weapon or met a criminal with a gun. Uniformed Gardai in Ireland are unarmed. It's better that way, safer for us, I truly believe. Guns are in the country, of course – you get some drug gangs that get arrested with arsenals that would make small African dictatorships look like *Sesame Street* – but for the most part, the ODCs don't bother with them. Ordinary decent criminals. We have no guns, they have no guns, fewer people get shot.

Right now I wish I had a gun. I don't think these are ordinary decent criminals.

The rain is misty, the visibility poor. I drop down off the wall and make my way along the track. Below me, there's a yacht tied up beside a small weedy pier, and a short, stout man is standing on the deck. I can't swear to it, but it looks like Chunkie Keogh. He's wearing a long dark coat – well, it's long on him, probably it's a jacket on anyone else – and a baseball cap. What on earth is Chunkie doing here, far from Spain?

Standing on the pier looking down at Chunkie is a tall, thin man. I'm too far away to be sure it's the man from the graveyard, but I think it is. Another man gets out of the Mercedes, and he and his skinny colleague drag a limp body from the back seat. With Chunkie's help, they lower it off the pier onto the deck. All I can see is a head of blonde hair hanging down.

Natasha.

OK, Mags, stay calm. Think. There's a sheep track almost overgrown with brambles to my right, on the other side of the stone wall; maybe I can get down closer without being seen if I go that way. But then what? As per Gardai regulations, I always carry a light baton, pepper spray and handcuffs, but a baton and pepper spray aren't going to scare a man like Chunkie Keogh.

But – and maybe this is mad – Delia's words are ringing in my brain. What if it was Ellie down there, with a deadly unscrupulous man? What would I want my local guard to do? Wait for backup? Run and find someone else? Like hell I would. Natasha is only sixteen, and if she's left on that boat with Chunkie, there's a good chance she'll never be seen again. I squeeze through a tumbledown gap in the dry stone wall and creep a little way along the brambly sheep track, keeping my head down.

Below, the engine of the boat fires up and a ripple of white water spreads out around the propeller as it starts to manoeuvre. Oh God. This is it. They're going. Poor Natasha. Poor Delia. Poor Dacie McGovern, who might die knowing I didn't do all I could to save her granddaughter...

I can't just watch and do nothing.

Knowing this is probably the last thing I'll ever do, my heart alive with love for Kieran and the girls, I jump to my feet and run headlong down the footpath. My clothes are ripped apart by the brambles, but I don't care. Leaping down onto the small stony beach, I scream as loud as I can, 'Stop! Gardai! Drop your weapons. You are surrounded!'

Chunkie Keogh turns. He has a gun in his hand. He scans the landscape to check my absurd claim about having him surrounded and then he fires. I feel a searing pain and then nothing.

CHAPTER 24

I can't open my eyes. I want to, but it's like they're glued shut. I force myself, but the bright light sears my retinas and I shut them again.

Later. It might be minutes or hours – I've no idea. I hurt. I'm not sure where. Everywhere maybe. But I'm so tired.

I see Kieran and my girls. They're smiling and laughing in the... Where is that? It's a garden. They're having a barbeque, and it looks like great fun. Nora is there, wearing a Mickey Mouse apron, and there's a woman with Kieran. Blonde, with red lipstick.

I wake again. It's dark now and there's noise, but all I can think of is the thirst. I'm too tired to wake up, I can't, but my mouth is so dry... I try to open my lips and make a sound. I think I do, but maybe not. I try again. I need something to drink.

Then mercifully something wet meets my lips. It's not a drink, it's colder, a cloth or a sponge or something. Some liquid trickles into my mouth. I can't swallow. The liquid rests against my throat. I try to swallow but I can't. Panic. I'm drowning but I can't move. Voices then. And more noise. Someone lifts me, an arm around my shoulder, pain at the movement. I want to scream but I can't. Then darkness again.

A long time passes, or maybe not. It's bright again. And it still hurts to open my eyes. I hear voices but they sound so far away. Yet I recognise them, I think. A high voice, a child, and a deeper one. Then a woman. I can't make out what they're saying.

I wake again. Someone is pulling my eyelid up, a searing light. I make a sound. Then I hear him in the background.

'Mags, oh, Mags, love, please wake up, please…'

Then another voice, much nearer and less emotional. 'Mags, my name is Doctor Liam O'Reilly. I'm one of the doctors here in UHG. You've had a nasty injury, but you're all right now, and your husband is here, so don't worry about anything.'

UHG? What's that? Somewhere it makes sense. I do know what that is, but I can't quite remember. Then I picture a letter with UHG written on it. University Hospital Galway. An appointment for Ellie for an X-ray on her knee after she got a knock playing football.

The doctor is gone. What was his name again? I try to open my eyes; I manage it for a second. I see a flash of Kieran's face. He's holding my hand and crying. I'm dreaming, I think. Kieran doesn't cry. I fall asleep again.

The next time I can open my eyes a little more, despite the light. I need a drink. Someone is there by my bed. I open my mouth. 'Drink,' I manage.

That thing again, the sponge on a stick – I see what it is now. The person giving it to me is a young woman.

'Welcome back, Sergeant,' she says.

I recognise her voice and try to focus on her face. It isn't a nurse, it's…Delia. I'm so happy to see her alive, although I can't remember why I thought she was dead. 'What happened?' I croak.

She shakes her head at me. 'Maybe we'll leave it till you're better.'

'Tell me now.' My voice is faint but firm. I try to smile.

She smiles a little herself and rolls her eyes. 'Okay, Sergeant Munroe. Well, Chunkie Keogh fired twice at you. Your shoulder is broken and you have a fractured skull and you had a brain bleed, but everything is fine now. You just need to rest and recover.'

It is coming back to me, a vague outline of everything up until the shooting, like seeing shapes in the distance on a foggy day.

'What happened?' I ask again. Every word is hard to force out of my body.

'You mean afterwards?'

I nod and feel like a ton weight has just rolled from one side of my skull to the other.

'OK. Do you remember you phoned Darren about the pier?'

'Darren...' The name is definitely familiar. His face appears out of the fog.

'He lost you because the phone service out there is awful, but he's been so used to following me and Natasha around the last couple of weeks, he couldn't help himself. He made Michael drive straight there in the squad car.'

I croak, 'They couldn't have made it in time.'

'They didn't! Well, they kind of did in the end, but only because... You remember the "boys and their toys" thing you said?'

'What toys?' I'm confused.

'The transmitter thing I nearly sat on, the one you told me to put in the glove compartment. I ran up the road like you said, but I still couldn't get any reception on my phone, so I snuck back to the van and tried fiddling with that. A Polish man answered, and I told him everything, and I wasn't sure if he even understood me but he did. Apparently he phoned the guards in Spiddal and the coastguard and the ambulance, but before he did all that, he contacted all the other Polish roofers and Kieran, and they all leapt into the one truck and went there. They were first on the scene because they weren't even that far away.'

I'm horrified by the thought of Kieran confronting those dangerous criminals, unarmed. 'But Chunkie Keogh...'

'He saw what was happening, so he took off in the boat. I'd turned the van across the lane like you told me, so when the men in the Mercedes tried to escape back up the way we came, they found themselves blocked in. They jumped out and ran across the fields. They didn't even see me – I was hiding behind the stone wall like you told me to.' She is grinning, enjoying telling the story.

'And Kieran called me back on the transmitter thing. I told him

I'd heard gunshots, but I didn't know yet you were hurt. He told me to take the first aid kit from the back of the van, and I ran down to the beach and saw that you'd been shot in the shoulder and your head. You were losing so much blood. But even then when I told him it was you, Kieran talked to me all the way – he was so calm – about how to give you first aid, and I did everything he said about pressing really hard on the shoulder wound...' She stops and shivers.

'But then it got worse. You went all still and white and I couldn't feel your pulse, but Kieran still didn't panic. He was so patient. He told me how to do CPR, pushing on your chest. He told me to do it to the beat of some old song, "Stayin' Alive". I didn't think I knew it, but then he started singing it and I remembered it, and it gave me the rhythm to keep your heart beating...'

I whisper. 'I can't believe this... Delia, you saved my life.'

'Only because of Kieran. I found your pulse again, and he kept talking to me the whole time, and then suddenly he was there. He came racing down to the beach. They'd had to abandon the truck because the van was in the way, and the Polish lads were chasing after the two fellas in the Merc who were trying to escape – they ran across the fields, through ditches and briars and everything. The roofers were fitter and faster, and they managed to catch them and bring them down, keeping them trapped, face down in the mud, until the armed unit arrived.'

Now I'm staring at her with my mouth literally wide open. How much wilder is this story going to get?

She laughs at my expression. 'Then Kieran picked you up, still out of it but breathing at least, and ran with you from the beach, up the hill to the van, and then he laid you in the back and kept giving you CPR while I drove like the clappers to meet the ambulance. Oh, Mags – I mean, Sergeant Munroe – you're so lucky your husband knows all this stuff. You wouldn't be alive only for him.'

My eyes fill with tears. 'Where is he?' I'm intensely grateful to Delia for being so courageous and clever and following Kieran's instructions so calmly, and I'll make sure she knows how much when

I can express myself better. But for now, I realise I just want my husband. 'Where's Kieran?'

'Your mam and the doctors sent him home to get some sleep. He's been here day and night since they brought you in, but they finally convinced him to leave for a few hours. He'd only go if I stayed, in case you woke up. I'll go out in the corridor now and ring him and your mother as well. She's been minding the girls all this time.'

I remember someone else, with a thump of my heart. 'Natasha?'

Delia beams. 'She's grand, and so were the two other girls on board, kidnapped and drugged the same as Nat. When the coastguard found the boat, it was drifting onto rocks. Your man Keogh was gone, no sign of him – they must have sent another boat to pick him up when everything went pear-shaped. But the coastguard was able to get to them and save them. And the men from the Mercedes told the guards everything. The kidnappings were all to do with the Keoghs' latest racket, and it all went back to Blades.'

'So Blades *was* mixed up with drugs?' I croak.

'No, but it was Blades that started what happened... I mean, it wasn't his fault, but it began with him. Do you remember I said Blades had a picture of Natasha on his cell wall in Limerick? Well, we've found out now one of the settled guys got saying what a cracker she must be and how he was sure he remembered being with her one night and all that kind of thing. Blades had a big fight with him in the yard – that's why he had another week added to his sentence – saying she was his girl and he wasn't going to have any fellas talking like that about her.'

It feels like my brain is wrapped in cotton wool. I know the answer is obvious, but my thought processes aren't working like they should. 'But what's that to do with Keogh...'

She pulls a face of utter distaste. 'Trafficking. Girls like us, who don't go with men until we're married, well, there's more demand, it seems, and so Keogh thought he hit on an idea, and better again the guards wouldn't care as much if a Traveller girl disappeared, so all the safer.'

I remember then, Ronan talking about not wasting police time, and I feel a deep disappointment with my own profession. A single tear rolls out of my eye and down into my ear, where it lodges. I hate to admit it, but I can see why Chunkie thinks kidnapping Traveller girls might be an easy crime to get away with. I try to move my arm to take Delia's hand, but it hurts too much. I ask, 'And Blades?'

'He must have heard something about the Keoghs' plan in the jail, and so then when he got out, he saw the men following Natasha and suspected what was happening. He wasn't even supposed to be going with Nat – she was engaged to Joseph then – and so there was nobody he could tell except Michelle. He should have gone to you, of course, but, well, you know how it is, and he was trying to protect her.

'Anyway, the two in the Merc admitted that's why they had orders to shoot him, because he kept getting in the way and they were worried he was on to them.'

It's all too much. Blades should have been able to come to me, to tell me what was happening, but she's right – I do know how it is.

'Your nana must be relieved. Tell her I said...'

Delia's composure leaves her, and the girl's eyes fill.

'What?' I ask.

'Nana died, Sergeant, the stroke. They told us it was better. She would hate to have been left...the way she was.'

'Oh, Delia, I'm so sorry...' I really am. This is a huge loss to all who knew Dacie.

My brain hurts, trying to absorb it all, and suddenly I feel tired and vulnerable. I whisper, 'Can you call Kieran now?'

She nods and takes out her phone and leaves the room, and I use the break to rest. I feel weary and in pain, but so glad Natasha and the other girls are alive.

The door opens again, and I pray it's Kieran, though it seems very quick.

It's Ronan Brady.

He comes to stand over me, all solemn but also pleased. 'Ah, Mags, you're awake, thank God. Delia just told me. You've no idea how worried I've been for you.'

I try to speak, and he leans down to listen. 'Say again, Mags?'

I whisper, 'Sorry for not following orders.'

He grins, straightening up. 'It's me that should apologise, Mags. I'm so sorry for even giving you that order, and you were dead right to ignore it. You'll get the Scott Medal at this rate – I mean it. Such bravery to face down one of the most wanted criminals in Europe on your own.' He shakes his head, smiling. 'You're some cop, Mags Munroe. Your country owes you a great debt. I never realised what I had when I brought you onto the team.'

It's good to hear. I say, 'I couldn't have done it without Delia.'

He nods. 'I've apologised to her as well. We had a long chat actually, and the upshot of it is I'm going to see if they will consider an early application for her to the Garda College. I've asked her if she'd consider it, and she said she would. Her mother and father will have a canary, it seems, but the days of Miss Delia McGovern doing what she's told by Mam and Dad are well in the past, I'd say, after this escapade. I've got onto the recruitment section and told them she'll be an asset, not just because she's a Traveller but because she has the makings of a fine guard, no doubt about it.'

I must have drifted off to sleep again, because the door opening wakes me. It's the man I want to see more than anyone else in the world.

CHAPTER 25

'*Y*ou're sure you want to do this?' Kieran asks as we drive out the road towards the halting site.

'I do.'

I'm only out of hospital a few days. I'm still sore and get tired easily, but we've been invited to this ceremony, and for a Traveller family to let us in at such a precious time is a very big thing. The girls are with us too, in their best dresses. Delia passed on the invitation; she's been calling to see me every day. I know they've been putting this off until I was well enough to come; normally it would have been done sooner.

'OK, but if you get tired, just give me the nod, all right?'

I smile, putting my hand over his. He leans over and kisses me. And then tucks a strand of my hair behind my ear.

'I can't believe I almost lost you, Mags...' His voice cracks.

'But you didn't, thanks to you and Delia. If you hadn't been able to do the first aid...' I manage a smile.

'Ah, y'see? What am I always telling you? Everyone needs to know first aid.' He laughs and winks at our daughters in the rear-view mirror, and I have never loved him more.

Kate and Ellie have been wonderful, keeping me company all day and getting me cups of tea and chocolate biscuits. Kieran even told Poppy and Dean that we didn't really use the green vegetables now because I'm laid up and he can't cook, so we'll cancel the order for now and get back to them when we want more. Poppy, the lovely girl that she is, offered to give him a crash course on vegan cookery, but of course he managed to wriggle out of that too. The idea of Kieran Munroe learning how to cook chickpeas and lentils makes me laugh. He can just about manage sausages and spuds or a spaghetti bolognaise once he has a jar of tomato sauce to add to the meat and if you don't want anything else in it, but that is where his culinary skills begin and end.

Mam is doing most of the cooking anyway. The fridge is groaning with food, and Mam's freezer too. Bertie the butcher has sent word that she is to call and just take whatever she wants from the shop any time, and I have to smile at that. Getting back in my good books, I suppose, but I'll take it and let bygones be bygones.

Even Nora has dropped off some quiches. I joked with Mam that I might have to check them for broken glass in case it's a ploy to finally finish me off for once and for all. But she told me that when Nora called, Kieran sat her down to listen to how brave I am and how proud he is of me and how lucky the Gardai are to have me. It sounded a bit over the top, but it feels nice to have him so firmly on my side and not at all on hers, even though in my heart of hearts I've known that all along.

Sharon has been picking up and dropping the girls to school, and Kieran has started taking Ellie to youth theatre rehearsals in Galway. Her friends Trish and Catriona have joined too. Kieran told their mother that it was free to join and he'd be dropping and collecting Ellie anyway so it was no bother to bring the girls, so the three of them go off each week, delighted with themselves.

We drive into the site, and after Kieran has parked the car, he goes around and opens the passenger door, helping me out. I walk slowly now, but the doctors tell me that in a few weeks, I'll have physio and they'll get me moving properly again. He links my arm on one side, and Kate holds my other hand.

The entire McGovern clan are there waiting for us, as well as Father Doyle, standing silent and sombre, all Dacie's children and their spouses first, then grandchildren and great-grandchildren. They're all dressed in their finery. Natasha is wearing her black funeral dress and jacket and looks like a battered little bird; all the brash confidence has been knocked out of her, the poor kid. It is hard to imagine her as the same girl who called Duckie out on his terrible attitude.

Delia is beside her, holding her hand. I catch Delia's eye, and she gives me a smile. She told me last week that Natasha sat down with her parents and said she would marry in the coming years, but not now and not Joseph. It is unheard of really for a girl to refuse a match so long established, but Delia said they were just so grateful she was all right, they agreed. I'm relieved. Natasha is traumatised by all that happened to her; she needs time.

Dacie's caravan, which is decked out in ribbons and flowers, stands alone, much further away from the other vans now than was usual. Today is the day they will burn her home and all her possessions. It is the tradition of the Travellers, less often practised now, but Dacie was traditional and this is how she wanted things done.

To my astonishment, the whole extended family starts clapping as I walk towards them, and Dacie's eldest son, Delia's father, Jerome, approaches us. He is a big blustery man with dark hair cut in a fringe. He has gold rings on his fingers and tattoos on his hands. When he speaks, everyone is silent.

'Sergeant Munroe, Mr Munroe and Ellie and Kate, thanks for coming today. My mother had great time for you, and we wanted you here, to be with us today. Now, before Father Doyle says the prayers and we burn my mother's home, I just want to say something.'

He goes to stand in front of the decorated caravan. He speaks in the distinctive accent of the Travellers. 'Mammy, Nana, Dacie, whatever you called her, she was a decent woman. She lived a long time – we don't know how long exactly because she never told us her age and there's no record. She had a good strong marriage to my father, Paddy, God rest his soul, and she bore us all without complaint. Times were much harder for our people then, living under canvas winter and summer, but she only ever said good things about them days. And now she's gone to heaven and she's with my father, we hope. Today we'll burn her van and her things as is the tradition, and I'm glad to include Sergeant Munroe and her family in the day. Dacie died happy, thanks to Sergeant Munroe, who saved the life of our Natasha, and we'll always be very grateful to her for that. My mother was in the hospital only a few days, but we were able to tell her what you done for us, and so I know my mother is too. So if I or any member of this family can ever do anything for you, Sergeant, you just need to ask.'

I know that to an outsider, this might seem like just a nice, polite thing to say, but a Traveller's word given this way is their bond, so I know it's true.

Jerome nods, and a little girl I recognise as Julia, the child Kate invited to our house after the Communion, approaches us. In her arms is Dacie's patchwork quilt. The child has been schooled in her speech, and she delivers it loud and clear.

'Nana always said you admired this, so we want you to have it. It was very special to her, and she would want you to have it, Sergeant Munroe.'

I can't stop the tears now, no matter how hard I try. I take it and hold it tightly. I can't speak; the words won't come. They want me to say something, but I just can't. I cast a glance at Kieran, and he squeezes my hand.

'You can do it,' he murmurs. 'I'm right here.'

I swallow and do my best. 'On behalf of my husband and myself and our daughters, we are so sorry for the loss of Mrs McGovern.' My voice is raspy and cracking with emotion. 'Your mother and grand-mother and great-grandmother, she was so proud of you all. She took such interest in each of you, and she would fill me in whenever I visited, on the babies, the weddings, and she was so happy that you were all doing so well.' I pause, feeling all their eyes on me, these people who are so used to getting no consideration whatsoever from settled society. 'She was a brave-hearted woman who stood by her family through thick and thin. To add to that, she was my friend, and

I'll miss her. May her grandchildren and great-grandchildren follow in her footsteps. And may she rest in peace.'

Kieran puts his arms around me, and I rest against him, the effort of talking making me weak.

Father Doyle says some prayers, and then Jerome speaks again, this time in Gammon, the language of the Travellers. They all respond, and my girls are intrigued at hearing it.

Then Jerome and some of the other men take the five-gallon drums of petrol they have stored to the side and douse the caravan. Everyone stands well back before they throw a lighted taper at it. We feel the heat instantly, and I know Kieran is in the horrors at the danger of it all. He draws us even further back from the flames.

And everyone stands around watching in silence as Dacie McGovern's soul is set free.

The End

I SINCERELY HOPE you enjoyed this book. If you did I would really appreciate it if you would leave a review here:

https://geni.us/MagsMunroeAL

THE SECOND BOOK in the Mags Munroe series is called *Growing Wild in the Shade* and can be pre-ordered here:

https://geni.us/MagsMunroe

It will be published in the summer of 2022.

If you'd like to join my readers club, and get a free novel to download just pop over to my website, www.jeangrainger.com

ABOUT THE AUTHOR

Jean Grainger is a USA Today bestselling Irish author. She writes historical and contemporary Irish fiction and her work has very flatteringly been compared to the late, great Maeve Binchy.

She lives in a two hundred year old stone cottage in county Cork, Ireland with her husband Diarmuid and the youngest two of her four children. The older two have flown the nest, and are learning the harsh realities of buying their own toothpaste. There are a variety of animals there too, all led by two cute but clueless micro-dogs called Scrappy and Scoobi.

ALSO BY JEAN GRAINGER

To get a free novel and to join my readers club (100% free and always will be)

Go to www.jeangrainger.com

The Tour Series

The Tour

Safe at the Edge of the World

The Story of Grenville King

The Homecoming of Bubbles O'Leary

Finding Billie Romano

Kayla's Trick

The Carmel Sheehan Story

Letters of Freedom

The Future's Not Ours To See

What Will Be

The Robinswood Story

What Once Was True

Return To Robinswood

Trials and Tribulations

The Star and the Shamrock Series

The Star and the Shamrock

The Emerald Horizon

The Hard Way Home

The World Starts Anew

The Queenstown Series

Last Port of Call

The West's Awake

The Harp and the Rose

Roaring Liberty

Standalone Books

So Much Owed

Shadow of a Century

Under Heaven's Shining Stars

Catriona's War

Sisters of the Southern Cross

* * *

If you would like to read another of my series, here are the first few chapters of *The Star and the Shamrock*, a series set in Ireland during WW2 for you to enjoy.

The Star and the Shamrock

Belfast, 1938

The gloomy interior of the bar, with its dark wood booths and frosted glass, suited the meeting perfectly. Though there were a handful of other customers, it was impossible to see them clearly. Outside on Donegal Square, people went about their business, oblivious to the tall man who entered the pub just after lunchtime. Luckily, the barman was distracted with a drunk female customer and served him absentmindedly. He got a drink, sat at the back in a booth as arranged and waited. His contact was late. He checked his watch once more, deciding to give the person ten more minutes. After that, he'd have to assume something had gone wrong.

He had no idea who he was meeting; it was safer that way, everything on a need-to-know basis. He felt a frisson of excitement – it felt good to actually be doing something, and he was ideally placed to make this work. The idea was his and he was proud of it. That should make those in control sit up and take notice.

War was surely now inevitable, no matter what bit of paper old Chamberlain brought back from Munich. If the Brits believed that the peace in our time that he promised was on the cards, they'd believe anything. He smiled.

He tried to focus on the newspaper he'd carried in with him, but his mind wandered into the realm of conjecture once more, as it had ever since he'd gotten the call. If Germany could be given whatever assistance they needed to subjugate Great Britain – and his position meant they could offer that and more – then the Germans would have to make good on their promise. A United Ireland at last. It was all he wanted.

He checked his watch again. Five minutes more, that was all he would stay. It was too dangerous otherwise.

His eyes scanned the racing pages, unseeing. Then a ping as the pub door opened. Someone entered, got a drink and approached his seat. He didn't look up until he heard the agreed-upon code phrase. He raised his eyes, and their gazes met.

He did a double take. Whatever or whomever he was expecting, it wasn't this.

CHAPTER 1

Liverpool, England, 1939

Elizabeth put the envelope down and took off her glasses. The thin paper and the Irish stamps irritated her. Probably that estate agent wanting to sell her mother's house again. She'd told him twice she wasn't selling, though she had no idea why. It wasn't as if she were ever going back to Ireland, her father was long dead, her mother gone last year – she was probably up in heaven tormenting the poor saints with her extensive religious knowledge. The letter drew her back to the little Northern Irish village she'd called home…that big old lonely house…her mother.

Margaret Bannon was a pillar of the community back in Ballycregggan, County Down, a devout Catholic in a deeply divided place, but she had a heart of stone.

Elizabeth sighed. She tried not to think about her mother, as it only upset her. Not a word had passed between them in twenty-one years, and then Margaret died alone. She popped the letter behind the clock; she needed to get to school. She'd open it later, or next week...or never.

Rudi smiled down at her from the dresser. 'Don't get bitter, don't be like her.' She imagined she heard him admonish her, his boyish face frozen in an old sepia photograph, in his King's Regiment uniform, so proud, so full of excitement, so bloody young. What did he know of the horrors that awaited him out there in Flanders? What did any of them know?

She mentally shook herself. This line of thought wasn't helping. Rudi was dead, and she wasn't her mother. She was her own person. Hadn't she proved that by defying her mother and marrying Rudi? It all seemed so long ago now, but the intensity of the emotions lingered. She'd met, loved and married young Rudi Klein as a girl of eighteen. Margaret Bannon was horrified at the thought of her Catholic daughter marrying a Jew, but Elizabeth could still remember that heady feeling of being young and in love. Rudi could have been a Martian for all she cared. He was young and handsome and funny, and he made her feel loved.

She wondered, if he were to somehow come back from the dead and just walk up the street and into the kitchen of their little terraced house, would he recognise the woman who stood there? Her chestnut hair that used to fall over her shoulders was always now pulled back in a bun, and the girl who loved dresses was now a woman whose clothes were functional and modest. She was thirty-nine, but she knew she could pass for older. She had been pretty once, or at least not too horrifically ugly anyway. Rudi had said he loved her; he'd told her she was beautiful.

She snapped on the wireless, but the talk was of the goings-on in Europe again. She unplugged it; it was too hard to hear first thing in the morning. Surely they wouldn't let it all happen again, not after the last time?

All anyone talked about was the threat of war, what Hitler was going to do. Would there really be peace as Mr Chamberlain promised? It was going to get worse before it got better if the papers were to be believed.

Though she was almost late, she took the photo from the shelf. A smudge of soot obscured his smooth forehead, and she wiped it with the sleeve of her cardigan. She looked into his eyes.

'Goodbye, Rudi darling. See you later.' She kissed the glass, as she did every day.

How different her life could have been...a husband, a family. Instead, she had received a generic telegram just like so many others in that war that was supposed to end all wars. She carried in her heart for twenty years that feeling of despair. She'd taken the telegram from the boy who refused to meet her eyes. He was only a few years younger than she. She opened it there, on the doorstep of that very house, the words expressing regret swimming before her eyes. She remembered the lurch in her abdomen, the baby's reaction mirroring her own. 'My daddy is dead.'

She must have been led inside, comforted – the neighbours were good that way. They knew when the telegram lad turned his bike down their street that someone would need holding up. That day it was her…tomorrow, someone else. She remembered the blood, the sense of dragging downwards, that ended up in a miscarriage at five months. All these years later, the pain had dulled to an ever-present ache.

She placed the photo lovingly on the shelf once more. It was the only one she had. In lots of ways, it wasn't really representative of Rudi; he was not that sleek and well presented. 'The British Army smartened me up,' he used to say. But out of uniform is how she remembered him. Her most powerful memory was of them sitting in that very kitchen the day they got the key. His uncle Saul had lent them the money to buy the house, and they were going to pay him back.

They'd gotten married in the registry office in the summer of 1918, when he was home on brief leave because of a broken arm. She could almost hear her mother's wails all the way across the Irish Sea, but she didn't care. It didn't matter that her mother was horrified at her marrying a *Jewman*, as she insisted on calling him, or that she was cut off from all she ever knew – none of it mattered. She loved Rudi and he loved her. That was all there was to it.

She'd worn her only good dress and cardigan – the miniscule pay of a teaching assistant didn't allow for new clothes, but she didn't care. Rudi had picked a bunch of flowers on the way to the registry office, and his cousin Benjamin and Benjamin's wife, Nina, were the witnesses. Ben was killed at the Somme, and Nina went to London, back to her family. They'd lost touch.

Elizabeth swallowed. The lump of grief never left her throat. It was a part of her now. A lump of loss and pain and anger. The grief had given way to fury, if she were honest. Rudi was killed on the morning of the 11th of November, 1918, in Belgium. The armistice had been signed, but the order to end hostilities would not come into effect until eleven p.m. The eleventh hour of the eleventh month. She imagined the generals saw some glorious symmetry in that. But there wasn't. Just more people left in mourning than there had to be. She lost him, her Rudi, because someone wanted the culmination of four long years of slaughter to look nice on a piece of paper.

She shivered. It was cold these mornings, though spring was supposed to be in the air. The children in her class were constantly sniffling and coughing. She remembered the big old fireplace in the national school in Ballycreggan, where each child was expected to bring a sod of turf or a block of timber as fuel for the fire. Master O'Reilly's wife would put the big jug of milk beside the hearth in the mornings so the children could have a warm drink by lunchtime. Elizabeth would have loved to have a fire in her classroom, but the British education system would never countenance such luxuries.

She glanced at the clock. Seven thirty. She should go. Fetching her coat and hat, and her heavy bag of exercise books that she'd marked last night, she let herself out.

The street was quiet. Apart from the postman, doing deliveries on the other side of the street, she was the only person out. She liked it, the sense of solitude, the calm before the storm.

The mile-long walk to Bridge End Primary was her exercise and thinking time. Usually, she mulled over what she would teach that day or how to deal with a problem child – or more frequently, a problem parent. She had been a primary schoolteacher for so long, there was little she had not seen. Coming over to England as a bright sixteen-year-old to a position as a teacher's assistant in a Catholic school was the beginning of a trajectory that had taken her far from Ballycreggan, from her mother, from everything she knew.

She had very little recollection of the studies that transformed her from a lowly teaching assistant to a fully qualified teacher. After Rudi was killed and she'd lost the baby, a kind nun at her school suggested she do the exams to become a teacher, not just an assistant, and because it gave her something to do with her troubled mind, she agreed. She got top marks, so she must have thrown herself into her studies, but she couldn't remember much about those years. They were shrouded in a fog of grief and pain.

CHAPTER 2

Berlin, Germany, 1939

Ariella Bannon waited behind the door, her heart thumping. She'd covered her hair with a headscarf and wore her only remaining coat, a grey one that had been smart once. Though she didn't look at all Jewish with her green eyes and curly red hair – and being married to Peter Bannon, a Catholic, meant she was in a slightly more privileged position than other Jews – people knew what she was. She took her children to temple, kept a kosher house. She never in her wildest nightmares imagined that the quiet following of her faith would have led to this.

One of the postmen, Herr Krupp, had joined the Brownshirts. She didn't trust him to deliver the post properly, so she had to hope it was Frau Braun that day. She wasn't friendly exactly, but at least she gave you your letters. She was surprised at Krupp; he'd been nice before, but since Kristallnacht, it seemed that everyone was different. She even remembered Peter talking to him a few times about the weather or fishing or something. It was hard to believe that underneath all that, there was such hatred. Neighbours, people on the street, children even, seemed to have turned against all Jews. Liesl and Erich were scared all the time. Liesl tried to put a brave face on it – she was such a wonderful child – but she was only ten. Erich looked up to her so much. At seven, he thought his big sister could fix everything.

It was her daughter's birthday next month but there was no way to celebrate. Ariella thought back to birthdays of the past, cakes and friends and presents, but that was all gone. Everything was gone.

She tried to swallow the by-now-familiar lump of panic. Peter had been picked up because he and his colleague, a Christian, tried to defend an old Jewish lady the Nazi thugs were abusing in the street. Ariella had been told that the uniformed guards beat up the two men and threw them in a truck. That was five months ago. She hoped every day her husband would turn up, but so far, nothing. She considered going to visit his colleague's wife to see if she had heard anything, but nowadays, it was not a good idea for a Jew to approach an Aryan for any reason.

At least she'd spoken to the children in English since they were born. At least that. She did it because she could; she'd had an English governess as a child, a terrifying woman called Mrs Beech who insisted Ariella speak not only German but English, French and Italian as well. Peter smiled to hear his children jabbering away in other languages, and he always said they got that flair for languages from her. He spoke German only, even though his father was Irish. She remembered fondly her father-in-law, Paddy. He'd died when Erich was a baby. Though he spoke fluent German, it was always with a lovely lilting accent. He would tell her tales of growing up in Ireland. He came to Germany to study when he was a young man, and saw and fell instantly in love with Christiana Berger, a beauty from Bavaria. And so in Germany he remained. Peter was their only child because Christiana was killed in a horse-riding accident when Peter was only five years old. How simple those days were, seven short years ago, when she had her daughter toddling about, her newborn son in her arms, a loving husband and a doting father-in-law. Now, she felt so alone.

Relief. It was Frau Braun. But she walked past the building.

Ariella fought the wave of despair. She should have gotten the letter Ariella had posted by now, surely. It was sent three weeks ago. Ariella tried not to dwell on the many possibilities. What if she wasn't at the address? Maybe the family had moved on. Peter had no contact with his only first cousin as far as she knew.

Nathaniel, Peter's best friend, told her he might be able to get Liesl and Erich on the Kindertransport out of Berlin – he had some connections apparently – but she couldn't bear the idea of them going to strangers. If only Elizabeth would say yes. It was the only way she could put her babies on that train. And even then… She dismissed that thought and refused to let her mind go there. She had to get them away until all this madness died down.

She'd tried everything to get them all out. But there was no way. She'd contacted every single embassy – the United States, Venezuela, Paraguay, places she'd barely heard of – but there was no hope. The lines outside the embassies grew longer every day, and without someone to vouch for you, it was impossible. Ireland was her only chance. Peter's father, the children's grandfather, was an Irish citizen. If she could only get Elizabeth Bannon to agree to take the children, then at least they would be safe.

Sometimes she woke in the night, thinking this must all be a nightmare. Surely this wasn't happening in Germany, a country known for learning and literature, music and art? And yet it was.

Peter and Ariella would have said they were German, their children were German, just the same as everyone else, but not so. Because of her, her darling children were considered *Untermensch*, subhuman, because of the Jewish blood in their veins.

To continue this novel click this link

https://geni.us/TheStarandtheShamrocAL

Printed in the USA
CPSIA information can be obtained
at www.ICGtesting.com
LVHW040021060524
779409LV00001B/38

9 781915 790019